By Chloe Neill for Gollancz:

Heirs of Chicagoland series
Wild Hunger
Wicked Hour
Shadowed Steel

Chicagoland Vampires series
Some Girls Bite
Friday Night Bites
Twice Bitten
Hard Bitten
Drink Deep
Biting Cold
House Rules
Biting Bad
Wild Things
Blood Games
Dark Debt
Midnight Marked
Blade Bound
Howling for You (eBook novella)
Lucky Break (eBook novella)
Phantom Kiss (eBook only novella)
Slaying It (eBook only novella)

Dark Elite series
Firespell
Hexbound
Charmfall

Devil's Isle series
The Veil
The Sight
The Hunt

AN HEIRS OF CHICAGOLAND NOVEL

DEVOURING DARKNESS

CHLOE NEILL

First published in Great Britain in 2022 by Gollancz
an imprint of the Orion Publishing Group Ltd
Carmelite House, 50 Victoria Embankment
London EC4Y 0DZ

An Hachette UK Company

1 3 5 7 9 10 8 6 4 2

A CIP catalogue record for this book is
available from the British Library.

ISBN (Mass Market Paperback) 978 1 473 23062 0
ISBN (eBook) 978 1 473 23063 7

Printed in Great Britain by Clays Ltd, Elcograf S.p.A.

www.chloeneill.com
www.gollancz.co.uk

Since all is well, keep it so:
wake not a sleeping wolf.

—WILLAM SHAKESPEARE, *HENRY IV*

DEVOURING
DARKNESS

ONE

Immortality required expecting the unexpected. And occasionally, heels.

Sometimes the unexpected was a mercenary fairy with a very sharp sword, or a shapeshifting monster, or a detachment of angry vampires at the door. And sometimes it was a pizza box taped to an art gallery wall . . . with a five-thousand-dollar price tag.

"*Reflections on Post-Consumerism*," the woman beside me said, reading aloud the tag beside the box. "A very interesting choice of media, don't you think?"

Lulu Bell, nonpracticing sorcerer and my best friend since childhood, her chin-length dark hair falling across her face, was doing her best to look serious and Very Intellectual. She was an artist, and I was here to support her and offer up some much-needed bestie time, which had been hard to come by lately.

I was Elisa Sullivan—vampire and newest staff member of Chicago's supernatural Ombudsman's office. Chicago had always been a hot spot for supernatural surprises, and that was especially true lately, with the detachment of vampires and mercenary fairies. The increase in activity hadn't been conducive to quality time with friends. So we were in this small white-walled gallery on a Saturday night, mingling with a crowd that was mostly human, who'd come to appreciate the art and sample tiny cheese cubes and listen to music that was part ocean wave, part jazz.

"I think pizza is best mid-consumption," I said, with as much gravity as I could muster.

The woman gave me a withering look before stalking off, apparently unimpressed by my critique.

Lulu snorted. "The pizza box is nonsense, but some of the other pieces are pretty good."

She wasn't wrong. There was a portrait of a former president rendered in neon lights. Rainbow streamers of plastic letters hung from the ceiling and made different words depending on your position. A hyperrealistic panorama of a Chicago traffic jam—uncomfortable content but remarkably detailed execution.

"The wine is excellent," I said, holding up the plastic cup of silver-gold liquid. "And the people watching is even better."

The opening of an independent gallery in a neighborhood of warehouses and up-and-coming shops attracted all kinds. They ran the gamut from matrons with designer heels and pink-tipped hair to probable artists who were younger than us and had the hunger in their eyes. They wanted their own openings and SOLD stickers, and the validation that came with both.

I wasn't an artist—not by a long shot—but I had tried to look appropriately cool. I paired a flowy green top with black leggings and my favorite black boots. The green was a shade darker than my eyes, and I'd left my long, wavy blond hair down. I'd left my sheathed katana, a vampire's favorite weapon, in the vehicle I'd borrowed for the night. And while I didn't think there was much threat from this crowd, I still felt vulnerable without it.

"I like this," I decided, and glanced at Lulu. "Thanks for inviting me."

Her smile was warm. "You're welcome, Lis. Thanks for coming with me." She knocked her cup against mine. "To girls' nights."

I'd toast anything that put that kind of light in her eyes. A light I hadn't seen in a while.

A human approached us—dark skin and dapper suit, trimly fit around a strong body. He smiled tentatively at me, then Lulu. "Lulu Bell?"

"That's me," Lulu said. "Hi."

"I'm Clint Howard," the man said, offering her a hand.

"Oh my god, sure!" Lulu said brightly, shaking and then gesturing to me. "Elisa, this is Clint. He owns the gallery."

"Nice to meet you," I said. "You've got a lovely space here. And . . . an eclectic collection."

His grin was wide and a little sly. "We're a space for emerging artists. And speaking of which, I saw your piece on Halsted. I'd love to talk to you about an installation."

Lulu's eyes went wide. She was a muralist and specialized in outdoor projects; her brightly colored creations covered at least a dozen brick walls in Chicago. We were here, in part, because she wanted to improve her connection to Chicago's art community. Mission accomplished.

"I'd love to. I love the installation you organized at Garfield Park."

Clint's smile was wide and bright. "Thank you. That was nearly a year in the planning. Bureaucrats," he added with an eye roll.

"Sups have them, too," Lulu said. "Anyway, it's gorgeous."

He nodded. "We're looking next at a spot in Hyde Park. Not far from Cadogan House, actually," he said, offering me a smile.

Hyde Park, a Chicago neighborhood on the city's South Side, was home to Cadogan House, one of the city's four vampire houses. My dad, Ethan Sullivan, was the House's Master, and my mother, Merit, was its Sentinel. I'd been born and raised there, although I rarely spent time at the House now.

Someone across the room called Clint's name. He lifted a hand. "Right there," he said, then smiled at Lulu. "I'll call you," he said, then nodded at me and moved across the room.

"Merry Christmas," I said, grinning back at Lulu. "You got your present early."

"Oh my freaking god," she said, the words a single roller coaster of sound. "That was Clint freaking Howard."

"So I heard. You're amazing, and he recognized it." I gave her a poke. "You're going places, kid."

"I'd like to go to that spot in Hyde Park," she said, then narrowed her gaze at me. "You don't think your mom had anything to do with this, do you?"

"Arranging murals? No. She loves you like her own kid, but that's not really her style."

But my father? Entirely possible. Vampires loved making deals, although I had no idea what an art gallery owner would want from the Master of a House of vampires. And besides, "You have the talent. You don't need anyone making calls for you."

"Thank you," she said, and before I could respond, she'd wrapped her arms around me. "Thank you," she repeated.

"You're welcome."

Two more hours of chatting, of deciphering paintings, of reading artist statements . . . and I was done and ready to be somewhere else. This wasn't my scene.

But because Lulu deserved my support, I put on a smile when she came toward me, the light in her eyes still as bright as it had been when we'd walked through the door. It was the happiest I'd seen her since I'd returned to Chicago a few months ago. Maybe she'd finally found her place—a place where she belonged. That possibility lifted a weight I hadn't known I'd been carrying.

"Hey," she said, and gestured to a group of people behind her. "So Clint asked if I want to go get drinks with him and a few of the others." There was hope in her eyes. "I don't want to bail on you, but . . ."

"Go," I said. "Absolutely go."

"You're sure you don't mind?"

"Not at all. But take an Auto home."

"Oh, of course." She leaned in. "He wants us to talk about art and installations and—oh my god, Lis. What if this is my moment?"

I squeezed her into a hug. "There will be a million moments, Lulu. But yeah, this could be one of them." I let her go and grinned as she blew out a breath and tried not to look too eager. Then she joined the others, leaving me alone beneath a pinpoint light.

My screen beeped, and I pulled the slender and signaling rectangle of glass from my pocket and checked the display. It was a call from Roger Yuen, Chicago's supernatural Ombudsman and my boss. I was an associate Ombud, and new to the team, so I answered it quickly.

"Hey, Elisa," he said. "I know it's your night off, and I'm really sorry for the interruption, but we have an emergency."

"Just a minute," I told him. "Let me get somewhere quiet." I walked outside as Lulu's group began discussing where to find the city's best craft cocktails.

When I reached a small grassy area a dozen feet away, where metal sculptures made from old tractor parts hulked in the grass, I lifted up the screen.

"Okay," I said. "What's going on?"

"I need you to rescue someone."

TWO

A drenaline, prompted by those words, was like a comfy sweater. "Who needs rescuing?"

"One of my informants. She's in trouble. I'm going to keep it brief because we need to hurry. And I'll apologize for dumping this on you and Theo; I'm on childcare duty tonight and don't have time to arrange for a sitter."

"I understand. No worries. You've talked to Theo?"

"The timing there is . . . sensitive," he said. "But I sent him a message. He should be on his way to you. Shit—I assume you're still at the gallery with Lulu, right?"

I had no idea what "sensitive timing" involved my partner tonight, but I'd find out soon enough. "Yeah, I'm outside. Give me the basics."

"I'll send you some docs," he said, "but her name's Rose Doerman. She's a sympath. She can manipulate others' emotions. It's like vampire glamour but dialed in, and usually less powerful. She lives in Edentown, Illinois."

Edentown was southeast of Chicago, a town perched at the edge of the Illinois-Indiana border. It was a 1960s development built for commuters to Chicago who wanted plenty of space between themselves and their day jobs.

"She's been feeding me information here and there for the last three years. Usually small-time stuff: Sups grifting humans. Human gangsters dipping into magic and spellselling, that kind of thing. Someone figured out she's been helping us. They cornered her outside her place, jumped her. She managed to get away, but not without injuries."

"Where is she now?"

"I only know she made her way to a spot she considers safe. She's going to give it a little time, make sure she wasn't followed. When she's sure she's clear, she'll go to a bus stop in the old downtown—corner of Main and Third," he said. "It's usually empty at night. White female, five foot six, medium build, thirty years old. Blond hair and blue eyes. Although it probably won't be hard to miss her given the injuries."

"Where are we taking her?"

"The safe house in Back of the Yards."

That was a neighborhood on Chicago's South Side. I hadn't seen the house, but I knew its location.

"We'll make it work," I promised him. "We'll get her back."

Ten minutes later, a sleek black convertible pulled to the curb in front of the gallery. Theo climbed out, stylish in a gray-checked button-down, dark slacks, and black Oxford-style shoes. His skin was dark brown and his hair was black and short. His somber eyes were wide beneath a strong brow.

At the moment, those eyes looked flat. Presumably, I guessed, because of the woman at the wheel. Detective Gwen Robinson was the Chicago Police Department's supernatural liaison and generally worked with Ombuds on matters that required more firepower. She was out of uniform tonight, looking gorgeous in an ivory pantsuit that gleamed against her medium brown skin. Tonight her hair was shoulder-length and curly, and pulled back at the sides with small rose-gold clips.

It was pretty obvious they'd been on a date. And since I'd

heard nothing about it, probably a first date. Which explained the "sensitive timing."

"Detective Robinson," I said, giving her a nod. "Great night for a drive."

"It was," she said with a thin smile, then lifted her dark eyes to Theo. "Although it turned out to be a very short drive."

"I'll make it up to you," Theo promised. "After we rescue Rose."

Concern shadowed her face. "You sure you don't want backup?"

"I think we need to keep this low key," he said, and glanced at me.

I nodded. "If there's any chance to save her cover, we need a small team, quick-moving. But we'll call the locals if it gets to that."

We looked at each other awkwardly for a minute, until I realized they were waiting for me to give them a private moment. So I turned back, took a sudden interest in the posters and flyers that nearly covered one wall. Lot of missing cats in this neighborhood.

"Good night, Elisa," I heard Gwen say.

Figuring it was safe, I turned back to see the car speed away again.

"You've got the Pack's SUV?" Theo asked.

I'd borrowed the vehicle from my boyfriend, the son of North American Central Pack's Apex.

"I do. It's parked down there," I said, and pointed down the block. "I had wine, so you're driving."

"We didn't get to wine," he said grouchily as I offered him the key fob.

"What did you get to?" I asked as we climbed into the car.

"Very little. We were planning on Italian food and some very good Merlot. Instead, I'm driving to Edentown. Which nobody wants to do."

"Other than the people who live there," I said. "Since when are you two an item?"

"Would have been forty minutes, although we spent most of it in the car. This was our first date. And it took a month to get her to agree." He gave me a sour look.

"Blame the assholes in Edentown," I said.

I'd have loved a coffee, but there was no time. So while Theo drove, I reviewed the dossier Roger had provided.

"Do you know this woman?" I asked, scanning through the materials on my screen.

"No. I mean, I know Roger had informants who only wanted to report to him, but he doesn't share them. Anything interesting in the background?" Theo asked.

"Nothing that stands out," I said, again scanning the materials on my screen. "Parents dead. Looks like there was some drug activity there. She came into her magic at thirteen. She figured out she could use her magic for the grift and fell in with the human crowd her parents ran with—mostly bangers, miscreants, and assholes. Larceny and forgery are also favorites. Nothing violent, which is probably why Roger agreed to work with her."

"But she could use the juju on us?"

"From what Roger said, her power isn't strong enough to manipulate the unwilling. And she doesn't have much incentive since we're the ones trying to help her. But I'll let you know if I feel anything unusual."

Theo laid on the horn when a taxi nearly sideswiped us, then glared at the driver as we passed him. "And what happened tonight?"

"Someone in her crew figured out she's been feeding us information and beat the crap out of her. Roger said she managed to get away, but I don't think he had many details. I'm hoping she's at the rendezvous spot, alone, and we can get her to the safe house without incident."

Theo snorted. "You haven't been on this job nearly long enough."

"Long enough to get a shiny badge," I said. "But I know that's a long shot. Because Chicago."

"Because Chicago," Theo agreed, with not a little affection. "She may be the Second City, but she's first in our hearts."

Chicago's South Gate loomed on the road ahead of us, a large structure of pale stone that arched over the roadway, with a smaller arch on each side. Each was topped by a black mansard-style roof, with mini turrets beside the central arch. It was a relic of the city's past, the only remaining structure from a building destroyed during the 1871 fire that engulfed the city. It was moved south of the city in the years after the fire; Chicago had expanded so much in the meantime that the gate was nearly back within the city limits. It was wide enough to cover the four-lane road, so we drove right through it. And when we'd made it to the other side, I looked at Theo.

"Did you hold your breath?" That was the rule when driving under the gate or past a graveyard or over a bridge in Chicago. Ignore it at your own risk.

"Of course. I don't need a curse hanging around my shoulders."

"Hard same." Especially given our current assignment.

Theo turned the vehicle onto a narrower road that led into Edentown proper. Angled toward the road, a billboard promised a "new paradise" and happy children playing baseball, but the neon light that bore the town's name was out, and only the first "n" and "o" worked.

"Well," Theo said. "That's ominous."

"Not welcoming," I agreed. "But if people are running a criminal enterprise here, they probably prefer not to advertise."

The city's center, such as it was, hadn't fared much better. The downtown was a block of tall brick buildings, most boarded up. A few still had doors with hand-lettered gold signs advertising whatever businesses had once been inside. They were empty and dark now, much like the streets.

We drove toward the bus stop, found a woman waiting alone beneath the plastic awning. She had pale skin, no makeup, and dark blond hair pulled into a ponytail. Her eyes were blue, and the left was swollen and bruising. Her nose was long and rounder at the bottom. Her lips were generous, but the bottom one was swollen and split. A backpack was slung over one shoulder.

"They definitely got her," Theo said.

"Yeah," I said, and was instantly furious.

Theo pulled to the curb.

"Keep an eye out," I told Theo.

He nodded, and we climbed out and closed the doors.

Something felt just slightly off, like a painting hung just off center. It took me a moment to figure out why. Lights were on in a few of the buildings, but there were no voices, no sounds from screens showing late-night shows. There were no vehicles, no barking dogs, no traffic noise. Only dead silence.

"It's too fucking quiet," Theo murmured.

"There's magic in the air. And not the Disney kind."

He looked at me. "Can you tell the source?"

I shook my head. I'd never met a sympath and didn't know what their inherent magic felt like. "I don't think it's manipulation, though."

I turned my attention back to the woman. There was no mistaking the real and deep-set misery in her eyes, or the shadows beneath them, but the unease increased as we walked toward her.

"Rose?" Theo asked.

"Yeah." She looked at each of us nervously. "You're Theo and Elisa?"

"We are." He pulled out his badge, offered it.

She nodded. "Roger said you'd be coming." A car revved its engine somewhere behind us. "We need to get going. They're probably driving around and looking for me." But her voice didn't waver. She sounded like a woman who'd faced hardship before. Possibly while grifting the vulnerable, I reminded myself.

I opened the back passenger door. "Their vehicle?" I asked.

"Red sport sedan," she said, climbing in. "It's fast. They stole it from a parking lot in the city."

I gave the dark street one more look before closing her door and climbing into the front passenger seat.

Theo started the car, locked the doors, and we took off.

First thing, I sent a message to Roger, letting him know we'd picked up Rose and were headed back to Chicago, and there hadn't been any issues. And apparently jinxed us, as an engine roared behind us less than a minute later.

I checked the side mirror. The vehicle wasn't red, but it was a sport sedan. Bright purple with running board lights in the same color. Flashy for criminals.

Theo steadily accelerated, testing them. They kept pace and, in their glowing car, moved closer.

"Rose," Theo said. "Do you recognize the car behind us?"

She turned back, the movement nervous and jerky, and swore. "That's Pratt's car." She swore again, turned back. "I didn't think they'd followed me to the bus stop."

"They didn't," Theo said, gaze flicking between the rearview mirror and back window. "They pulled out after that last intersection. They'd been waiting."

"Someone signaled them?"

"That would be my guess. This is probably the second team." His voice was careful, controlled, but his hands tightened on the wheel.

Rose turned around again, looked at us imploringly. "Whatever happens, don't stop. If you stop, they'll kill all of us."

"I don't plan on stopping," Theo said. "They won't put another mark on you."

While he drove and comforted, I leaned the screen out the window to get a photo of the vehicle and its plate, and sent a message to Roger: VEHICLE IN PURSUIT.

His answer was nearly instantaneous. SENDING TO CPD. KEEP ME POSTED.

"You got the info?" Theo asked.

"Yeah. And told Roger."

"Then let's lose these assholes."

If I was being honest, I wasn't sure he could do it. The Pack's SUV was a solid ride, but people didn't usually add running board lights to vehicles they hadn't already souped up.

But I clearly hadn't managed my expectations of my partner effectively—that had been the lesson on my first day of my official Ombud training—as I nearly squealed when he whipped the vehicle down a side road with the skill of a racer.

The purple car accelerated, and rubber squealed in the darkness as they took the turn behind us. With smooth aplomb, Theo accelerated again, made another turn, and swerved around a minivan that was taking a much more leisurely route to its destination. The purple car moved in again, and Theo skimmed through a light just before it turned. The car followed despite the red light through a barrage of horns.

"Assholes," Theo muttered, "disrespecting the law like that," and turned hard enough to have me grabbing the door. He drove to the next light, turned again, and then we were racing toward South Gate.

That's when I felt the shudder, the vibration that seemed to rise up from the ground but rippled through the air.

"What is that?" Rose asked.

"Earthquake?" said Theo.

"I don't know," I said, and kept my eyes on the road, scanning for danger. But the car, while closing the gap, was still nearly a hundred yards behind us.

The air went heavy and cold, and the SUV slogged, the engine revving as it tried to push its way through the semisolid slurry the air had become. There was magic here, and not of the pleasant variety.

That slurry became nearly solid, and the SUV rocked like a giant had taken a swing at it. The vehicle swung hard to the left, tires skidding as inertia battled magic. Theo grunted as he worked to keep the wheel straight, but I felt the tires leave the road and prayed we wouldn't flip—or hurt the woman we'd been trying to save.

We made a complete circle and came to a grinding halt, the vehicle hitting asphalt again with a resounding *thud*.

"What the hell was that?" Theo asked.

"Magic," I said.

"What are you doing?" Rose demanded. The tears were pouring now, her eyes wheeling with fear. "You have to keep going! We can't fight them. We don't have the power."

"Whatever it is, it stopped our car," Theo said, trying to turn the engine over. It made no sound.

Adrenaline started pumping again.

Rose cursed, turned again to watch the road, as if monsters would emerge behind us. "Shit. They're going to kill me."

"They aren't," I said. "Theo and I aren't going to let anything happen to you."

She wasn't convinced. "You said you'd help me get out. Does this look like help to you?" Her voice was nearing hysteria.

Fortunately, vampires had a wide range of skills.

"They won't get to you," I said again, pushing as much glamour as I could into the words.

I don't know if that worked—could sympaths even be glamoured?—but her heaving breaths slowed a little.

I reached for the door handle. I hadn't had much wine at the event, but I was utterly sober now. "Stay with her."

"You aren't going alone. I'm your partner." Theo's voice was lower now, more intense.

"And she's the mission, so you're going to protect her with your body and soul. Call 911 and get this road blocked off. We don't need more cars getting stuck because they tried to drive into—whatever this is. And tell Roger. Because maybe he'll know what it is."

"Be careful. I don't want the wolf's claws in my back."

That wolf was Connor Keene, my boyfriend.

I opened the door and climbed out, then unsheathed my katana, sending metal pinging amid the wind's howls and whistles. The hair on the back of my neck lifted.

And that wasn't my only reaction. By some quirk of biology or magic, I wasn't alone in this body. There was another consciousness, a supernatural presence, which shared the space. I called it "monster" because it was usually eager for a fight. It had no interest in whatever was going on here, but I'd earned enough of its trust that it didn't disappear completely. I could feel it watching, hovering, in case it needed to add its strength to mine.

Appreciate it, I thought, and closed the door as quietly as I could, not sure if that would help or not; something clearly knew we were here.

I crept forward through the soup of fog that now glowed faintly green and thought of a horror story I'd read as a child about the things that lived in the mist. Monster was notably unenthused that we were moving toward the danger.

I waved an arm through the fog as if that would clear it up and give me some visibility. It didn't, but the green glowed brighter as I approached the gate—or the place I thought the gate had been. There was no sign of any other vehicle, including the one that had been chasing us. There was no sound of traffic or the squeal of tires as other cars were caught in the magic.

The air grew heavy and cold, and swirled around my feet like ocean waves. Voices began to emerge from the direction of the

gate. A multitude of them—sobs and growls and groans that coalesced and grew into banshee-like screams. The volume made my
ears ring.

Then the howls began. Not human but animal. Canine. Yips
and howls that put goose bumps on my arms and had me wishing
I'd stayed in the car with Theo.

And then fingers, frigid fingers that tingled with magic, grazed
the back of my neck. "Hilarious, Theo," I murmured, even though
I knew, rationally, that he wasn't there. He was still in the car,
now hidden by the fog, protecting Rose.

I made myself look back . . . and screamed.

There was a face behind me, or what might have been a face. It
was pale and gauzy and mostly transparent, its mouth and eyes
stretched into horrifying angles.

"*Noooo*," it yelled out, like a whistle through hollow bones,
and tightened its grip on my shoulder.

We were under attack.

By ghosts.

I wasn't sure how I knew that. I didn't doubt the existence of
ghosts—not when a childhood friend had been a necromancer and
I had a degree in supernatural sociology. I'd just never seen one
IRL. But the evidence was too strong to ignore. The cold, heavy
magic. The voices on the wind. The goddamn horror of the thing
that was staring back at me and digging bone-claws into my
shoulder.

I didn't think ghosts were supposed to manifest *physically*;
they weren't supposed to have substance. They were supposed to
be ethereal. Whispers and fog and, yeah, sudden cold tempera-
tures and electrical spikes. Not fingers squeezing with enough
force to bruise—or magic that felt physically repellant.

"*Nooooo*," it hissed again, with creepily perfect timing.

Was it saying no to me? To Rose? Some kind of refusal to let
her leave the gang she'd run with?

Since I was the one in the middle of it now, I had to push through the fear and horror, and remind myself who and what I was—and what I was holding. I raised my sword, swiping it around my body and through the creature. Its torso was less dense than its fingers, but it was still like slicing through that same magical slurry.

Its scream pierced the air, as sharp as my blade. And then it oozed.

It was my turn to say, "No," but it was more of a plea as the specter fell into a pool of pale green sludge that smelled like sour milk and luminesced in the darkness. And coated my blade with enough magic to have it vibrating.

"Freaking ghosts," I said, and flicked the handle to send the ooze swinging through the air and splattering onto the road.

That just made them angrier, prompting more screaming, with voices resonant as bass drums and screechy as nails on a chalkboard. Every nerve in my body was on alert, waiting for the onslaught.

They came forward by the dozen. Some whistled past me, turning the air to ice, while others grabbed at my hair, my shirt, my ankles. I wielded my katana like it was both sword and shield, slicing through them, trying to fight my way through this waking nightmare.

"Noooo," they screamed again, a chorus of hatred. The howling began again, and I felt movement around my legs, heard the snapping of jaws, the pounding of feet, as ghostly hounds brushed past my legs.

Because this nightmare needed a little sprinkle of extra terror.

Then there was another hand on my shoulder, and I whipped the blade and turned, and found myself with my blade pointed at Theo's chest.

"Damn it, Theo! Give a girl a damn warning." My heart was a battle drum.

"I was trying to be quiet," he said, and pushed the blade down with a fingertip. His service weapon, a handgun, was in his other hand. "And noble. I heard screaming and decided keeping you alive was now priority one."

"Rose?"

"Vehicle. Locked in." Theo's gaze darted wildly as clawed hands and faces coalesced and disappeared around us, looking for an opportunity to attack. "Are we . . . are these ghosts?"

"Yep."

"Ghosts aren't supposed to be real."

"Your partner is a vampire."

"Vampires aren't dead."

I was glad he'd remembered that. All rumors to the contrary were the basest insults.

"I definitely don't like ghosts. And is it me, or do they . . . smell?"

"Sour milk," I said, and he nodded.

"Old and musty and sour milky," he agreed. "In addition to the general horror show. I'm never going to sleep again."

"Certainly not without someone standing guard," I agreed.

Something howled behind us, and we turned to face it with gun and blade lifted and ready. More faces emerged from the fog, stretched and horrible, eye sockets dark and empty, mouths gaping. "*Go back,*" they hissed, and swiped before we could dodge, pushing both of us backward. Ghosts from other directions joined in, shoving us with hands cold enough to suck the air from my lungs. They were maneuvering us south, I realized. Away from the gate and back toward Edentown.

"We aren't going back there!" Theo shouted. "So do your worst!"

They took him at his word.

The ground began to shake again, throwing us into each other. The sound of falling bricks followed, and we turned back to see chunks of the gate falling away, hitting asphalt, shattering. The asphalt under our feet began to crack, and the wind grew fiercer, sending a hurricane of rock and grit swirling in the air.

I hit my knees and nearly fell into a growing ravine in the road—and would have if Theo hadn't grabbed me. Hand around the belt of my katana, he hauled me back onto semisolid ground.

"I think you pissed them off," I said as he offered me a hand and helped me to my feet, knees singing with pain from the impact.

"My bad," he said. "Who the hell did she piss off?"

"Or what?" I said. "Something that doesn't want her leaving."

Another rumble, and the ghosts amped up their assault. Stones began flying off the gate's façade like they'd been propelled from a volcano.

"Car!" Theo yelled, his hand still on mine, and we ran for it, or at least in the direction we thought it should be. The fog was still thick, green, and nearly impermeable. And when the firmness of asphalt gave way to grass, we knew we were in trouble.

"Wrong way!" I called out over the screams and howls, and we turned around and were nearly crushed by a stone, half as tall as I was, that struck the ground in front of us like an arrow and with enough force to push its shorter end nearly a foot into the dirt.

"Keep your eyes open," I said, and put a hand on Theo to keep him at my side. Then I closed my eyes and listened for more whistling of projectiles so I could determine our location relative to the gate.

"There!" I said, opening them again and pulling Theo toward the asphalt, straight ahead and then veering toward the right, where I hoped I'd correctly judged the SUV to be. If we missed it, maybe we could make our way to the edge of the fog and circle back without getting nailed by—this was Chicago, after all—future architectural salvage. I felt a moment of guilt that we'd left Rose in the car on her own, but it seemed safer for her in there than it was out here.

We shuffled through the mire, arms outstretched, until I heard the whistle on my left.

"Watch out!" I screamed and pulled Theo forward and out of the impact line—but I still heard the awful thud, the vicious crack, the sharp intake of breath.

I hadn't gotten him fully clear, and fear was a band around my lungs.

"Fuck," Theo said, and stumbled. I caught him, grateful for increased vampiric strength. And, being vampire, could smell the metallic scent of blood.

"Where?" I asked.

"Arm," he said, and it took him two tries to get out the word. I couldn't see it, not through the haze. But Theo was a former cop, and this wasn't his first injury in the line. Anything that put that thick slur of pain in his voice had to be bad.

"We're going to the car," I said. With his uninjured arm across my shoulders, we limped forward again, ignoring the crash of stones to our left and right. I was listening for the sound of stone on metal, hoping they wouldn't hit the car, for both Rose's sake and ours. Five seconds later, my foot kicked tire, and even monster was relieved.

And then the world went silent.

As quickly as it had begun, the wind stopped, and along with it the howls and roars of ghosts. The greenish fog began to clear, the air to warm again.

"I think it's over," I said, but still scanned the area for any lingering attackers. I had no better idea about why it had ended than I had for why it had started in the first place.

"I think I need a doc," he said, and I looked down at the hand that gripped his left arm. Blood that swirled green with magic—ghost essence?—seeped through his fingers.

A lot of blood.

"Shit," I said, as I pulled away his fingers. Blood and bone were sickeningly intermingled. I breathed out hard through pursed lips. "You made a mess of yourself, Theo."

The blood triggered my automatic vampiric craving, but I ignored it. This wasn't the time or the place or the person . . .

"Don't bite me," he said, through his own clenched teeth.

"Oh, and that's just so tempting, let me tell you." I sheathed my katana. My blouse had a drapey tie at the neck. I ripped it away, fashioned it into a kind of sling, and tied it around his neck. It would at least keep the arm still until we could get help. And I realized I used parts of my clothes often enough to deal with wounds that I was seriously in need of a tailor.

"Only a few steps more," I told Theo, opened the door, and helped him inside.

And found the back seat empty.

I stood on the running board to give myself a little height . . . and saw no one.

Rose was gone.

"What?" Even injured, Theo half turned in his seat to look at the empty second row. "Son of a . . . where did she go? I locked the door—did she let someone in?"

"The magic could have messed with the electronics," I said.

"They grabbed her," Theo said, voice quiet. "This was some kind of distraction."

"We don't know that for sure," I said. But I didn't like the heavy guilt that settled in my stomach. Roger had asked us to rescue a woman who was plainly being hunted by something big and powerful. And we'd failed.

Chicago and Illinois law enforcement vehicles squealed to a halt on both sides of the gate, or what remained of it. Gwen ran toward us, one hand holding her badge aloft, her other hand steadying the holstered weapon at her hip.

"What the hell happened?" she asked, and looked with fear toward Theo, who sat with eyes closed in the front seat.

"The people gunning for the woman we were sent to rescue made a last stand at the gate." I gave her a description of their vehicle. "And they used a ghost army." It sounded more ridiculous aloud, but the truth often did. "Theo's arm is pretty messed up. Where's the closest ER?"

"Chicago South," she said, and walked to the open passenger door, stared down at him. "You better heal up fast, Martin, because you still owe me a date." Her voice was steady, but there was fear in her eyes.

"Got it," he said. "No interruptions."

"No interruptions," she agreed and closed the door. "Don't wait for an ambulance. I'll get you a police escort."

I nodded and hoped the SUV would start now that the attack was over.

Gwen must have seen the concern in my face. "What else is wrong?"

"Rose is gone—the woman we were supposed to keep safe."

Her brows lifted. "Gone?"

"She was in the backseat and the doors were locked. Theo and I were fighting the ghosts, and when we came back, the car was empty."

"Well, damn," she said, and frowned while she considered. "You get Theo to the ER. I'll handle things here, and I'll look over the area personally for any signs of struggle, or an indication of her direction."

"Thank you," I said.

"It's my job," she said, as an officer approached us. "Officer Garibaldi, there's an injured Ombudsman in this vehicle. Escort the car to Chicago South ER, and let them know you're on the way."

"Ma'am," he said in agreement, then looked at me. "My vehicle's parked just behind you. I'll pull in front, lead the way."

"Thank you again," I said to both of them, then looked at Gwen. "Can you ask Roger to meet us at the hospital? I'll explain what happened when we're there." And I wasn't looking forward to that.

"I will. Go," she said, giving Theo a meaningful look before moving aside for the cruiser. "Keep your eyes on the road—and him."

"He's my number one priority."

THREE

It's not as bad as being shot with an arrow," Theo said, as the escort and I drove at very illegal speeds toward the nearest emergency room.

The arrow had been the fault of the city's mercenary fairies. Theo winced, jaw tight, as we hit a pothole. That was the fault of the city.

The officer who led the way was a solid driver and wasn't afraid to use lights or sirens. We made it to Chicago South in record time, and the SUV's passenger door was open before the wheels had stopped spinning. A nurse looked in. She had brown skin, gray hair, and a steady expression. She gave Theo an up and down, and her eyes didn't so much as widen at the glowing break in Theo's arm.

"Well, we'll probably just have to cut that arm off," she said with a smile that told me sarcasm was her favorite language. I liked her immediately.

"Be gentle," Theo said, and she helped him out of the vehicle and into a waiting wheelchair.

"You're friends are just inside," the woman said, then wheeled Theo in.

I moved the SUV out of the loading zone and jogged back inside. By the time I made it back in, Theo had already been wheeled into some secret part of the building. But in the small waiting room at the edge of the lobby, I found Roger Yuen and Petra Jassim, our other associate Ombud.

Like Connor, Roger liked running even when no one was chasing him. Unlike Connor, he was human. He was tall with a runner's lean build and had medium brown skin, short dark hair, and dark eyes. He dressed casually unless there was a meeting with the mayor or her consultants on the agenda, and wore jeans and a polo-style shirt today in a somber black.

Petra was an aeromancer and tech genius. Her long dark hair was up in a tail today, showcasing her dark eyes and rounded cheekbones. Her skin was light brown, and she'd paired dark leggings with high-top sneakers and a long-sleeved shirt with GEEK across the front.

"Theo?" I asked.

"Already taken back," Roger said. "And is being treated by one of Petra's cousins, apparently."

"It's not her, is it?" I asked Petra quietly. "The one with the eighteen bridesmaids?" The one whose wedding Petra had apparently cut short with a bit of her aeromancy and some strategic lightning. "The one you pissed off?" I asked, my voice a little firmer now.

"Yes," she said grimly. "Yes, it is. But she won't hold it against you or Theo. Just me. Do you want to pretend we're dating? She's very marriage-focused, and she'll report to my parents."

"Is lying to her really the best course of action here?"

"Probably not," she said.

"Have you heard from Rose?" I asked Roger.

He shook his head. "There's a BOLO for the purple car, but they haven't located it yet."

Not entirely surprising, I thought. "It's probably secure in a garage right now, waiting for new plates."

Roger moved a bit closer, lowered his voice. "Gwen said you were attacked by ghosts? Is that who took Rose?"

"I'm not sure. After we lost the pursuers, everything was fine until we got to South Gate. The vehicle died, the temperature dropped, and we were suddenly the only cars on the road. Then ghosts emerged from the gate—or so it seemed—and attacked us. Ghosts with enough power to vocalize, physically stop our vehicle, fight both of us, and tear chunks of stone out of the gate. Theo got out of the car to help me. Then he got hurt, and when I got him back to the SUV, it was empty."

"They vocalized?" Petra asked.

I nodded. "They kept saying 'no,' and at one point said to 'go back.'"

She frowned. "What does that mean?"

"They didn't want Rose leaving them," Roger guessed.

"That was my thought."

"No sign of other vehicles?" he asked.

"None. There was a magical fog, so I couldn't see anything. But I didn't hear any fighting, and she seems like the type who would have fought back."

"I agree."

"Did she work with necromancers?"

"Not that I'm aware of. And if she had friends—or enemies—with the kind of power you're describing, she didn't tell me about it."

"I'm sorry, Roger," I said, and the guilt flooded again. "I'm sorry we couldn't get her to the safe house."

"Nonsense," he said quickly, and gestured to the waiting room. "You risked your lives to do your job. I don't know if I underestimated how powerful her enemies were or if she wasn't candid enough."

"I think the ghosts would have killed us if they could have," I said. "They were intent on—I don't know—stopping her? Taking her back?"

Roger squeezed my hand. "I'm glad they didn't. It's not impossible that she got away on her own. If you were under attack because of her, she might have thought the best course was getting out and away, getting you in the clear. Hopefully, she'll call once she's somewhere safe."

Petra whistled, tilted her screen to us to show a photo of the scene that had been shared online. Spotlights had been set up casting garish shadows on the gutted gate. "Who has this kind of power?" Petra asked.

"I don't know," Roger said. "But we'll find out."

And hopefully before they hurt anyone else.

I was tired and desperate, so I opted for waiting room coffee. It was not good. I added enough sugar and creamer to make it almost drinkable, then settled in to let the caffeine do its work.

By the time I turned around again, he was just . . . there.

Connor Keene, prince of the North American Central Pack. And very much mine.

He was tall and broad-shouldered, with dark wavy hair and brilliantly blue eyes. A lock of hair curled superheroically over his forehead, and even the teenage girl in me—who thought the teenage Connor was an irritating punk—sighed a little.

Part of that was just his intense sexiness; he was powerfully handsome. Part of it was love. I hadn't planned on falling for a guy who'd driven me crazy when we were younger. But feelings were unpredictable that way.

He strode toward me, ignoring the stares of the nurses who watched him like he was a very expensive meal they were extremely ready to devour. He had that effect on people, and it probably didn't hurt that he was wearing workout gear: black sneakers, black shorts, and a sleeveless black technical shirt that showed off plenty of muscle.

Lulu came in behind him, still wearing her ensemble from the art show.

"I hope you don't mind," Roger said, "but I made a call."

"Not at all," I said.

Connor reached me, put his hands on my face, concern darkening his blue eyes. I heard the nurses across the room sighing.

"You're all right?" he asked.

"I'm fine," I said. "Theo's still being treated."

Lulu was next in line for a hug.

"Did you ditch your party?" I asked.

"It was winding down," she said with a smile, "so I took an Auto. This is more important."

Given how much she loathed supernatural drama, it meant that much more that she'd come. "Thank you," I said.

"So, what the hell happened?" she asked.

"Long story short, ghosts and a missing informant."

"Ghosts?" Connor asked.

"Yeah, of the human and canine varieties. So if you have any sway with your ghostly brethren, tell them I'm pissed."

"Did you get bitten?"

"No. It was the human ghosts that did the damage. They could pack a punch. And we think they took Rose."

Connor squeezed my hand. "We'll get her back."

A woman emerged from a treatment area. She wore a white jacket over brilliantly purple scrubs and came toward us with a businesslike stride. She looked enough like Petra that they might have been sisters. This must be the doctor-cousin.

She reached us, gave us an evaluating look. "I'm Dr. Anderson. I'm helping Mr. Martin."

"Roger Yuen, Connor Keene, Lulu Bell, and Elisa Sullivan," Petra said, introducing us. "This is my cousin, Dr. Anderson."

The doctor nodded, brisk but polite, then turned her gaze to Petra, held out a small vial. "Mr. Martin agreed I could provide this to you."

Petra took it, held it up to the light, where it glowed faintly green.

"He's okay?" Lulu asked.

"Are you immediate family?" she asked.

"No," Lulu drew out the word, as if that might stretch it a bit closer to yes.

"In that case, I'm sorry, but the law prohibits me from sharing his health information." She sniffed the air, looked at me, and moved closer. Then she turned me around, stopped when she faced my back. "You were struck as well," Anderson said, gentle fingers probing near my shoulder.

"It's fine," I said. "Vampires heal quickly."

"I'm aware of supernatural propensities," she said. "Supernatural anatomy is a required course at most American medical colleges." And with that professional aplomb, she pushed aside my shirt to inspect it further, fingers gentle but unhesitant. "Quick healing depends on the nature of the injury. And this looks very . . . green. Puncture wounds, four of them."

"Ghost claw," I said sheepishly, as everyone else leaned in. "Come on," I muttered. "Would a treatment room be too much trouble?" I wasn't especially shy, and these were my friends and colleagues, but being medically inspected in front of them was different.

"Every room is occupied," she said. "Wait here. You've got ooze in it, and I want to clean that out." She clipped efficiently into the back.

"Ooze," Roger said with a wrinkled nose. "I don't care for that word."

"Roger has a weak stomach," Petra said, pulling a contraption—a chunky piece and some sort of wand—from her leather messenger bag and futzing with the dials.

"Not weak," Roger said. "Just . . . particular."

"What is that?" I asked, gesturing to the contraption.

"It looks like a toothbrush made love to a toy car," Connor said.

"It was a dental drill," Petra said, lips pursed as she frowned at the screen, tapped some buttons. "I call it a 'spectrascope.' And the patent on this bad boy is going to keep the office in doughnuts and coffee for . . . Well, a fortnight at least."

"A fortnight's worth of coffee," I said. "You really know how to woo a girl, Petra."

"I do," she said with a gleam in her dark eyes. "Anyway, when I heard there were ghosts, I brought this along. It's in the testing phases and doesn't provide nearly as much information as I'm hoping it will someday, but it should at least give us some basics."

Petra pressed a button on the machine. If it was supposed to have done something . . . it didn't. The machine remained silent and still. Frowning, she pressed it again, got nothing. So she whacked it against the back of a visitor's chair.

Two of the nurses' heads popped up, both frowning.

"Sorry," Roger said with a smile and a light wave. "We're just having equipment problems."

Anderson came back with a small tray, put it on a side table. "Sit," she said, and pointed to a chair.

"I'm really fine."

"Or you'll turn into a ghoul because you've been infected with something."

"That's a joke, right?"

Her stare was steady and level. "Do you want to test the theory?"

I obviously didn't, so I waited while she cleaned the punctures with something that stung, then something that cooled. Then she put a light bandage on it, put my shirt back into place.

"Keep that clean," Dr. Anderson said, putting the implements back on the tray, including gauze that glittered green.

I felt my gorge rise again, had to look away. Maybe Roger wasn't the only one with the weak stomach. At least where ooze was concerned.

Petra's spectrascope started humming, finally operational. She held the wand over the bit of gauze, and it chirped merrily. "Hmm," she said. She repeated the procedure twice, then dismissed her cousin with a flick of the hand. "You can take that back. We're done with it."

Dr. Anderson rolled her eyes, but left us.

"Hold this," Petra told Connor, and thrust the vial at him. He held it out at arm's length as she ran the wand over it. More frowning, and she took the vial back, put it in a pocket of her bag, presumably for some kind of later testing. Or squicking us out at the office.

"One more sample," she said, then looked at me. Petra held it up, ruffled my hair with the wand.

"Much too close," I said. "Back the spectra up, please."

More chirping, then a sustained beep that I surmised meant the device had come to some conclusion.

"What does it say?" I asked.

Petra frowned, blinked at it. "I think it's giving me a year." She turned the screen around to show us the display and looked confounded. Which wasn't an expression I saw on Petra very often.

"Eighteen seventy-two," Roger read aloud. "What does that mean? The ghosts were from 1872? Died in 1872?"

"I'm not entirely sure," Petra said. "Could be the date of the magic."

"The attack happened tonight," I said. "How could that be the date of the magic?"

"Maybe the gang Rose ran with bought a really old spell and haven't used it until now," I said. "Maybe they'd been saving it for something big."

"Maybe," Petra said.

"Does 1872 ring a bell for anyone?" Roger asked.

"Not for me," I said. "But something the year before does: 1871. That's the year Chicago burned."

* * *

They called it the Great Chicago Fire because it burned through three square miles of the city, racing northeast from a spot south of downtown Chicago. Hundreds of residents were killed; tens of thousands were left homeless.

Humans told various stories about the fire's cause, including a lantern knocked over by a cow owned by woman named Mrs. O'Leary. But I'd learned the truth from my parents—and my (honorary) uncle Malik. It hadn't been humans who'd started the fire, but a rogue sorceress. The Order, the organization of sorcerers, had been banned from Chicago for the actions of its member.

"What the hell?" Roger murmured, his gaze pinched in worry. He ran a hand through his hair. "We've got an informant who worked with low-level criminals, an attack by ghosts, and some century-old magic. I don't know how to reconcile those things." He looked around at us. "Do we know any Sups who were here when the Great Fire happened?" His gaze settled on me, apparently expecting vampires—with their immortality—were the best bet. And he was correct, at least as far as I was aware.

"Cadogan House didn't move here until 1883," I said. "But Uncle Malik was here before that. I'll give him a call."

"We're getting close to dawn," Connor reminded me. "And you're injured."

Because he was correct on both points, I didn't argue. "I'll reach out and ask if we can talk tomorrow," I said, offering the compromise.

"Don't you know a necromancer, too?" Petra asked.

I did. Ariel Shaw was an old acquaintance, and she didn't have especially warm feelings toward me. She and Lulu had been close when Ariel had been deep in the throes of a magical rebellion. I'd been a rule follower and probably a little bratty as a teenager, and I hadn't approved. I'd also loved Lulu and hadn't wanted to lose her to someone who seemed to excel in getting into trouble. More recently, I'd helped Ariel untangle herself from a coven of witches with a doomsday plan.

"I can reach out to her, too. Maybe she can give us some insight about the ghosts."

Detective Robinson walked into the lobby, arrowed straight for us. "Any news?"

"Not yet," I said. "Any sign of Rose?" I found myself leaning toward Gwen, hoping she could relieve the guilt.

But she shook her head. "There's no obvious sign of struggle at the scene, although it's hard to tell given the damage. There are some tracks through the grass, and I've got uniformed officers canvassing the area."

"Thank you," I said.

She nodded, glanced at Roger. "The mayor has been filled in by our chief but wants an update on the supernatural end. We took photographs of the scene, and I'll send them to you."

I hadn't even thought to take photographs or to ask her about them. I said as much.

"You were hurt," Roger said kindly, as if reading the regret in my voice. "You had an injured partner, and your first thought was getting him to safety. Things like this are why we partner with the CPD"—he shifted his gaze to Gwen—"and greatly appreciate their help."

"All in a night's work," she said philosophically.

Ten minutes later, Theo was rolled out of the treatment area with a very goofy smile.

"I feel really, really good," he said as he was wheeled outside to the hospital's front portico.

"You probably got the good drugs," Petra said.

"Maybe," he said, drawing out the word coquettishly, then turned that goofy smile on Gwen. "Should have gone on that date. Probably wouldn't have gotten busted up."

For a moment, her eyes softened, and the cop-like edge disappeared. "Probably. But there will be a next time."

"Damn right. With good food and wine"—he slid his gaze to me, and the smile went pouty—"and fewer broken bones."

"I didn't break them," I murmured. "And I told you to stay in the car."

"You need a ride home?" Roger asked.

"He has a school bus," Petra explained.

"A school bus?" Connor asked, glancing across the dark parking lot.

"I do not," Roger said. "But I have four children, a wife, and two hundred-pound dogs. My vehicle fits them all." He pressed a button on his screen, and after a few seconds of waiting, an enormous—well, school bus was the best description, really—rolled silently toward us, sleek and white as the literary whale, the gleaming exterior broken only by the long lines of tinted windows.

"Fully auto drive," he said, beaming as doors opened and steps descended.

"It's something," Connor agreed, nodding in the way of People Who Liked Cars.

"Let's get you in, buddy," Petra said, and we helped Theo into the backseat.

"We'll touch base at sunset," Roger said.

We waved them off, leaving me, Lulu, and Connor alone in the lot. I glanced at Lulu. "You need a ride?"

"Auto will be here in less than a minute," she said. "But thanks. You really going to call Ariel?"

"Do you think she'll give me grief if I ask her for a consult?"

"Of course she will," Lulu said. "But that's just her personality. She's not so bad."

"She got you into trouble. A lot."

Lulu's stare was flat. "Lis. Have I ever done anything I didn't absolutely one hundred percent want to do?"

*   *   *

We waited until Lulu was safely tucked into the Auto. It was inching toward dawn as Connor drove the SUV back to his town house. I messaged my parents on the way home, told them what we'd seen, asked for any information they could provide. I sent a similar message to Uncle Malik. They proposed we meet at Cadogan House just after dusk, and I accepted.

That left only Ariel. I went three for three, sending her a message, too, and asking for whatever help she could provide. Giving her the chance to read and respond seemed less aggressive than just calling her up.

We made it to Connor's neighborhood, Humboldt Park, with minutes to spare, hurried inside the tall brick town house, with its interesting mix of masculine and Art Deco furnishings. Being a shifter, or at least a shifter whose parents owned a business and invested wisely, apparently paid well.

"Food?"

"*Blurg,*" was the approximate sound I managed. I was tired and sore, and my shoulder itched with a ferocity that made me wish I could borrow Eleanor of Aquitaine's scratching post. But since I was across town and didn't care to steal from Lulu's very bossy cat, no luck there.

The curtains were already drawn against sunlight, but I could feel it rising, lurking on the edge of the horizon, the vampire's greatest enemy. Even a few seconds would burn my skin through, leaving a scar if I managed to escape, or my remains if I didn't.

"Up we go," Connor said, and before I could object, he hoisted me over his shoulder and headed for the stairs.

I didn't have the energy to object.

"I don't like cutting it close," he said.

"I don't like being toast."

"I don't like the idea of you being toast."

When we reached his luscious master bedroom, with its gleaming fireplace and enormous bed, he dropped me onto the bed's silk coverlet. I flopped out, arms and legs extended.

"Blood?" he asked and pulled off one of my boots, then the other.

"Not tonight, honey," I said, waving a hand.

"Shame," he said. "I've heard the bite can be . . . interesting."

That had me looking up. I hadn't bitten him yet—that was at least one relationship level beyond where we were now. But I wouldn't say it hadn't crossed my mind. I was a vampire, after all, and he was gorgeous and strong. And shifter blood was literally full of magic.

But I hadn't been sure if a shifter—the prince of the NAC Pack—would be willing to be bitten.

"I'm feeling more energetic now," I offered.

"Thought that would do it." There was a small marble bar in one corner with a wine fridge. He'd added bottles of my favorite bottled blood products—no nonconsensual human-swilling for ethical vampires, thanks very much—and pulled one out.

"Coriander mint?"

"No. I don't want salad."

Glass clinked as he shifted bottles. "Plain?"

I made a grabby hand. He brought the bottle back, and I all but pounced on it. The top was off and the bottle was empty in seconds.

"Sorry," I said. "And thank you. I think I needed that."

"It's the spectral ooze," he said, putting the bottle on the night-stand and stretching out beside me. I curled into him.

"I don't want to hear those words ever again."

"I don't know if we'll have a choice." His voice had gone seri-ous, which wasn't usual for him. He was worried.

"Yeah," I said, and patted his chest as dawn approached. "We may not have a choice. But we'll deal with it together. We protect each other."

We always did.

FOUR

I dreamed of grasping hands and shrieking ghouls and woke with a hard shudder, my heart pounding. The screeching was my screen, beeping an incoming call.

My body was still heavy, and I knew we were only seconds past dusk. So it didn't surprise me to see Roger's name on the screen.

"Roger," I said, sitting up and, in the process, dislodging Connor, still drowsy. He grunted, pulled a pillow over his head and sleep-tousled hair.

"Any word from Rose?" I asked.

"Nothing yet," Roger said.

"Damn," I murmured, and Connor put a hand on my arm, just enough to remind me he was there.

"CPD found nothing on the trail confirming whether Rose had made it or, if she did, where she'd gone. Fortunately, there was no more trouble at the gate overnight. They've started shoring up the structure to repair it, with the hope of getting the roads open again in a couple of months."

Traffic in Chicago was already bad, and a complete shutdown was going to be a nightmare. "I'd like to go back out there tonight, take a look at the scene."

"I was going to suggest it," Roger said. "I think Theo probably needs a little time."

"I'll go, and I'll bring a shifter with me." I lifted my brows in question, and Connor lowered the pillow, nodded.

That had Connor tossing away the pillow, scrubbing hands over his face. "I'll get a shower," he said, and climbed out of bed.

"Good plan," Roger said. "Keep me posted."

Destiny was payment for a debt owed, and she was beautiful. She was the gleaming Italian espresso machine Connor bought as penance for his moving into the town house—and out of his family home—without even telling me.

I was standing at the kitchen island, drinking espresso from a wee cup to prepare for the night, when Connor strolled in, hair still tousled and damp from the shower.

"You're interrupting my date with Destiny."

He grunted, pulled an enormous protein drink from the fridge. It looked like a slurry of backyard grass and dirt. "That joke grows staler by the night. And I still can't believe you named a coffee machine."

"She's an *espresso* machine, and she gives me great pleasure. The least she deserves is a name." Vampires might be creatures of the night, but we're also creatures who appreciate caffeine. Destiny satisfied that need. Mostly.

Connor took a drink, then glanced at the size of my cup. "You might as well use a thimble."

"I'm already jumpy about Rose. This is more than enough. And I don't own a thimble." I tilted my head at him. "Do they still even make thimbles? Those are for sewing, right?"

"No idea," he said.

Since I'd had plenty of blood the night before and wasn't feeling the need for more right now, I'd toasted an everything bagel. I tore a chunk from the edge, chewed. "Workout wear. Protein drinks. You're going to ruin your reputation."

His grin was wild. "Lis, my reputation was ruined a very long time ago in many enjoyable ways."

He wasn't wrong. Connor had been the belle of the supernatural ball since he'd been a teenager. There were few eyes—human or Sup—that hadn't shown their appreciation, and he'd rarely been without a gorgeous girl on his arm.

He took another drink. "How's the shoulder?"

I rolled it experimentally. "Good. And I didn't turn rabid or luminescent during the day."

"That you know of," he said with amusement. "You could have been a vampiric night-light."

"I feel like you'd have opened with that if it had happened."

"And taken pictures and video, and made some very nice royalties."

"Shifters are always about that hustle."

He snorted, because hustle was typically not a shifter characteristic. Except where finely smoked meats were concerned. He took my bagel, bit in, then offered it back.

"I'm heading to Cadogan House after Edentown and then to talk to Ariel, if she gets back to me. I can drop you off beforehand if you want."

"I'll go with you. I'm curious about dead people, and I like talking to your parents."

That had me pausing with the bagel halfway to my mouth. "What?" I lowered it. "You used to hate parental interaction."

"That's because I was usually dragged over there to apologize for something."

"There's a reason we called you 'puppy.'"

He grinned at me. "And there's a reason we called you 'brat,' brat."

He clinked his plastic jug against my tiny cup. "To a drama-free night," he said, and we drank.

"Does that taste as bad as it looks?"

He swallowed. "No. It's actually worse." He flexed his biceps. "But worth it."

Having seen those muscles—and the muscular rest of him—I couldn't disagree.

"I can respect the hustle," I said, and pressed a kiss to his lips. "Let's go back to Edentown."

At my request, Connor drove the SUV—after looking it over for any damage from last night. He found a few dings, probably from the gate stones being hurled about, but nothing major, so we hit the road.

The road was blocked on the north side by CPD cars and police tape, and traffic was being detoured to an exit. Connor drove up to the vehicles, and I leaned over and pulled out my badge, still shiny.

"Ombuds' office. We need to look at the scene."

The cop used his radio to check in with someone, then waved us through.

Connor drove slowly the quarter mile to the gate. From this side, the structure looked relatively unscathed. But then he drove onto the shoulder, circled around to the south side. It did not look unscathed from that angle. Beneath the hard bright lights the CPD had set up, gaps and holes pocked the gate's surface. The asphalt was still broken by chunks of stone nestled in the craters they'd made. And while there was no green fog, there was still a tinge of magic in the air.

"Damn," Connor said, as we climbed out of the SUV. "I believed you, but seeing it in person is—harrowing."

"It was harrowing last night."

Before I could object—there were cops and construction workers everywhere—he'd pulled me against him until our bodies were aligned. And then he gave me a kiss so hot my knees went wobbly.

"What . . . was that for?" I asked when I could breathe again. And ignored the whistles around us.

"Gratitude," he said, dropping his forehead to mine. "That you're still alive."

"I'm fine," I said. "You can be my consultant and help me look. You take the structure, or as close to it as you can." Scaffolding had been erected on this side of the gate, and workers were attaching wooden struts and supports to keep it upright. "I want to check out the path she took."

Connor pulled a small flashlight from his pocket, offered it.

"Good consulting already," I complimented, and headed toward the grass and the flags left by the CPD.

There wasn't much to see near the road—just the faint indentations made by someone who'd moved through the shin-high grass. They led down to a ditch, then up again to a grassy field marked ominously by the white-silver skeleton of a tree long-since dead.

The world was quieter without the rush of traffic, and I walked, scanning the ground for footprints or broken undergrowth. The trail wasn't consistent, but it was straight. I followed it until I could hear only the songs of frogs and katydids, probably the last before winter's fall.

"Come on, Rose," I murmured. "Show me that you made these tracks. Show me where you are. Show me you're alive."

Because that was the hope. That she'd made it through despite our failure to protect her.

But the trail petered out at a dirt road that divided the meadow from a field of yellowing corn. I shifted the flashlight's beam back and forth, but found nothing useful. The road was poorly maintained and rutted into concrete hardness, so it was impossible to read the tracks, or at least for a beginner like me.

I closed my eyes, tried to tune out distractions and get a sense of the magic of the place, but I didn't detect any unusual buzz.

Just the faint background vibration that seemed to be Chicago generally.

I blew out a breath, opened my eyes again, and caught a glint of something in the flashlight's beam. But when I kneeled down, found nothing but rock and grit from the road.

Deflated, I walked back to the scene.

I found Connor crouched on the asphalt studying one of the divots in the road. He traced a finger across the broken edge, and I could see the concern in his eyes. The fear that I'd faced down magic strong enough to make that mark. I knew he was proud of what I did, but also that it cost him not to object to the danger.

He rose as I walked toward him. "Anything?"

I shook my head. "There's a trail about a quarter mile to a dirt road. But nothing on it. Anything here?"

"There's no sign of her."

Guilt crept in again, even though I knew it wouldn't be useful. But that didn't make it any less potent.

My screen beeped the moment Connor turned on the vehicle.

I answered it. "Hello, Ariel."

"So, what exactly happened with the ghosts?" she asked. She didn't sound irritated, but eager, so I laid it out for her.

"So something tried to grab your girl, and you have unspecified ghost emissions."

"Emissions," I decided, was worse than "ooze." But basically, she was right. "Yes. Petra dated it, or the magic or whatever, to 1872. So there's something very old in it. But we don't know what. Or who."

The line was quiet for a moment, but I heard gentle scratching in the background. Nail file, I bet. I was getting very good at detecting.

"I'll try to raise one ghost, but that's it. I have other things to do tonight."

"I'm not trying to raise an army," I said. "Just find a girl and identify a poltergeist."

"Not a poltergeist," she said. "Not based on your description. Regardless, I have a client."

That had my attention. "A client?" The last time I'd seen Ariel, she'd been working in a bar for a woman who turned out to be a murderous coven leader.

"It's community service," she said. "Part of my agreement . . . after the coven."

The barkeep/coven leader had been convinced the murders she perpetrated would help prevent a coming apocalypse. Ariel, who'd nearly been a victim herself, had gotten probation for failing to report the leader; she and the other coven members had been under the leader's magical thrall. I hadn't seen Ariel since we'd rescued her, and I hadn't known she'd gotten community service, but was glad to hear it. Ariel had always been self-involved. Maybe doing the public some good would do her some good, too.

"You're doing free séances for your community service?"

"Yep. They gave me the official training and everything. *Mortui vivos docent.*"

My brain finally clued in. "You've joined the MVD," I realized. The phrase she'd said meant, roughly, "the dead teach the living." It was the motto and namesake of the MVD Association, which was the professional group for necromancers—those who spoke to the dead. There were regional MVD groups across the world.

"Is it a good gig?" I asked.

"It'll be better when I'm getting paid, but it was the right thing to do. Especially since Maddy and Marley don't have the touch." They were her older sisters, who apparently hadn't inherited the necromantic gift. "Anyway, I've got an opening later," she said, and gave me a time and an address. "Be punctual."

I sent a message to the team, advised them Ariel had agreed to the séance as part of her community service. Petra and Theo—who demanded to be included—would meet us at the location, which I realized after searching was an apartment complex in Schaumburg. Ariel's new apartment, I guessed.

"You still want to tag along for that, too?" I asked Connor.

"I do."

"Then don't fluster Ariel. I think she still has a crush on you, and she'll need to concentrate."

"I have no interest in flustering anyone but you."

I humphed, found a rather ecstatic message from Roger: ROSE SENT MESSAGE USING OUR CODE. SHE FEARED CAPTURE AT GATE SO MADE RUN FOR IT. LAYING LOW UNTIL SHE FIGURES OUT HER NEXT MOVE.

"Well, that's good news," Connor said.

"Yeah," I said.

Connor looked at me. "Why do you sound suspicious? She used the code word."

"I'm not entirely sure," I said. "Occam's razor, right? The simplest answer is usually the correct one. We didn't hear any other vehicles at the gate, and Gwen found a path through the grass. So I can buy she walked out on her own. She didn't know us and took a chance when she could. But that's it? After everything that went down, she waits nearly a day to tell Roger, and then doesn't explain what happened? And there's no apology for getting us mixed up in it?"

"I'm not a cop, but I don't think criminal informants are known for their empathy. And she's laying low. Maybe she didn't have time for details."

"It's a text message," I pointed out. "She can send a text while hunkered down. It's not like she has to traipse over to the telegraph office."

"Would one traipse to a telegraph office?"

I smiled against my better judgment. "I don't know." I sighed and tried to shake off the suspicion. "I should be grateful—Rose is safe, so we didn't fuck up our mission last night."

"You didn't fuck it up either way," Connor said. "But her being alive also means her gangland friends didn't get her—and they're going to keep looking. They may have more ghosts in store."

"Yeah," I said. "I thought of that."

He leaned over, kissed my forehead. "We'll get you a coffee. Then we'll go talk to vampires and dead people."

Because—and I can't stress that enough—those were two very different things.

Since I was feeling less guilty, we grabbed coffee from a Leo's drive-through. It was my favorite coffee place, and I was well and thoroughly addicted. It had also been one of my best ideas—and greatest victories—to request an all-you-can-drink card from Leo's as a "signing bonus" when I'd joined the Ombuds.

Cadogan House was, I guess, my ancestral home. It was a white stone mansion in Chicago's Hyde Park neighborhood, situated near the front of a rolling lawn of manicured gardens and lush greenery, and bordered by an imposing wall and gate.

I paused as we walked through it, having been waved inside by the guards who'd known me for years. My second important gate of the week, and this time one I passed through easily.

The door was opened by a clutch of vampires on their way out. I didn't recognize any of them.

I guessed they were Initiates. Vampires who'd become Novitiates—full members of Cadogan House—following their Commendation. It wasn't a step I'd taken, and I had no regrets about that decision. I loved my parents but didn't want to be beholden to a Master vampire. That wasn't the life for me.

They smiled at us, and I heard the whispers as we walked into the House, which smelled tonight of gardenias and cinnamon.

"That's their daughter," they murmured. "And the prince."

A totally innocuous comment, but one that made me wish I had a title, too. I could be Princess Elisa. Oh, yes. Just pass me a crown. I'd rock that and a scepter, too.

The house was bright and cheerful, with gorgeous art and crown molding, and enormous flowers on a pedestal table just behind the antique security desk. "They're waiting in the Master's office," said the vampire at the desk, and we walked over gleaming hardwoods down the hallway to the House's administrative offices.

Although my father had updated the furnishings—design styles apparently weren't immortal—the office's layout hadn't changed over the years. There was a desk, a sitting area, a long conference table, and a long bank of windows that looked over the lawn. The storage boxes on one end were new, though. That would need some interrogating.

My parents stood together with Uncle Malik when we walked in, my dad's hand on Uncle Malik's shoulder as they laughed about something together. Uncle Malik wasn't my biological uncle, but he was family in every way that mattered. He'd been my dad's second in command before becoming a Master in his own right and starting Washington House, so he'd been in Cadogan—and a crucial part of the running of it—as I'd grown up.

My father, tall, fair-skinned, and blond, wore his typical black suit, even in his own home. His eyes were the same green as mine. My mother's fair skin was a contrast to her long dark hair and pale blue eyes. She wore jeans and a crimson blouse with a V-neck.

"Hi," I said, glad to see them both, but wishing it were under different circumstances. I could feel monster hovering, a bit suspicious of my mother, who I suspected knew something was different about me—even if she didn't know what.

It didn't help that monster was energized by the presence of her sword only a floor below us, locked in the House's armory since it held the spirit of the Egregore, the supernatural creature that had ravaged Chicago. The magic used to trap the Egregore had allowed me to be born and had somehow created monster.

Monster wanted that sword. Badly.

Dad kissed my forehead. "Good evening." Then reached out to shake Connor's hand. "Connor."

"Mr. Sullivan. Ms. Merit," he said.

My mother said hello to Connor and came across to hug me. She felt the same as she always had, looked the same as she always had. I suspected if I hadn't grown up with immortal and unchanging parents, I'd have found it weird. But that immutability had been a comfort as I'd grown up, as I'd changed, matured, and tried to find my own place in the world.

"What's all this?" I asked, gesturing to the boxes when she let me go again.

"We were cleaning out the basement storage area," my mother said. "And that reminds me . . ." She rustled through an open box, then pulled out something very pink.

"Oh, no," I muttered. "No. You can just put that back."

It was a floppy-armed doll with a bright pink dress and a bare plastic head. My mother held it out by its arms and made it do a little dance.

My parents were vampires. Political, powerful, wealthy vampires. But they were still (save me) parents.

"I thought you might want your favorite doll," my mother said, and offered it to me.

"Why doesn't it have hair?" Connor asked, regarding it with mild horror as I snatched it away from her.

"She chewed it out," my parents said simultaneously.

"Wow," Connor said, brows lifted in mock horror.

"I was three," I said, walking back to the box and stuffing it (gently) back inside.

"There's some OK Kiddo merchandise in there, too," my mother said.

Connor's eyes went wide as he turned to look at me. "OK Kiddo? The boy band?"

"We don't need to see that," I said, putting the lid back on the box. Securely. This wasn't as scary as fighting an army of ghosts, but it was exponentially more mortifying.

"We're good," I said, turning back to them. "That's more than enough nostalgia for one night."

"I think it's very sweet," my mother said. "I'll just put the box in your room."

"That would be best."

"We'll be discussing this at length later," Connor whispered.

"Oh, we're never discussing this again. Unless you want to discuss the Super Mullet."

Connor was an undeniably handsome man, and he'd never been not handsome. But there'd been a few months of awkward when he'd let a girlfriend cut his hair. He'd gone from shoulder-length waves to what Lulu and I deemed the Super Mullet. For very good reason.

"I do not," he whispered.

"Does anyone want a drink?" my dad asked.

"I'm fine," I said. Two double shots were still echoing in my bloodstream. It was the sweetest echo.

"Connor?"

He held up a hand. "No, thanks."

My father nodded. "We should probably get to business. Let's sit," he added, and we moved to the seating area.

"Why don't you tell us what happened?" Uncle Malik said, and I repeated the tale, and apparently with enough detail that Connor's grip on my hand tightened with concern.

"Any chance you'd like to become a stay-at-home vampire?" Mom asked, her fingers linked tightly with Dad's.

"It had a certain appeal last night," I admitted. "Much less ghost ooze."

My mother looked as horrified as I probably had. "I don't care for that word."

"The substance is worse," I promised. "Rose messaged Roger today and said she was fine. So our focus, at least for now, is the ghosts."

"You think it had something to do with the Great Fire?" Uncle Malik asked.

"Maybe only coincidentally? Petra had this device, and it measured the—apologies in advance—ooze from the ghost attack. The magic in it originated in 1872. Did anything happen around that time?"

"You know the Great Fire wasn't really started by Mrs. O'Leary's cow?"

I nodded. "It was a sorceress."

"Yes," Uncle Malik said. "A sorceress trying to make a familiar."

Familiars were usually animals who'd been magicked by a sorcerer to act as servants or helpers. Lulu's mom, my (honorary) aunt Mallory, had tried to use familiar magic to bring my dad back to life after he'd been killed in a fight with another vampire. Mallory managed to bring him to life again, albeit via magic that had nearly destroyed Chicago.

Dad looked at mom, covered her hand with his, squeezed, the love and appreciation obvious between them. Whatever else my parents may have taught me, they'd taught me the value of partnership. Of loving, trusting, and appreciating a partner who always had your back.

Partly because that made me think of Connor—and partly because I didn't need to watch my parents making lovey eyes at each other—I glanced at him, found his gaze on me. He nodded his understanding.

"As you might imagine," Uncle Malik said, "the experiment didn't go well for either party. Making a familiar is old magic, evil magic—intended to take control of another living being."

"The Great Fire," I said. "That was one of the repercussions. And after the fire, the Order was kicked out of Chicago."

Uncle Malik nodded. "The sorceress—and the Order by extension—shouldered the blame for the destruction. While humans began rebuilding the city, the sorceress was placed on trial. She was executed, the Order banned."

"Who did the banning and the executing?" I asked. "I mean, did they remove the Order or the individuals?"

"Supernaturals were still assimilated then, mostly trying to act human. So information was harder to get, and there were no screens, television, radio. There was only word of mouth, and the truth tended to change as each person passed it on. That said, I'm not sure how reliable this is, but I'd heard both the Order and the sorcerers were forced out. And my understanding was the evictions were carried out by Order members from other states. They were horrified at what the sorceress had done and afraid of what humans might do if they discovered sorcerers living among them."

"So theoretically there were no sorcerers in Chicago in 1872," I muttered, frowning as I tried to think this through. "Who could have done this magic?"

"Sorcerers who weren't known to the Order," Connor offered.

"Or," Dad added, "other supernaturals who can do magic but aren't considered sorcerers—they don't have that range of magic. Necromancers, for example."

"That would explain the ghosts." I looked at Uncle Malik. "I don't suppose you knew any necromancers back then?"

"I didn't, nor of any big magic they were working. There was still magic in Chicago; you could feel it, just as you can now. But I don't recall feeling anything of the scale you're describing." He frowned, looked up and away, and his gaze became unfocused, as if watching memories replay.

"The mood in Chicago after the fire was . . . grim," he said after a moment. "So many lost in the blaze. So many homeless, businesses destroyed. I remember sadness. I remember the hard work of rebuilding. I remember the chaos of that time." He looked at my dad, gaze focusing again. "And I remember when a vampire brought his people to Chicago and asked me to join them."

"One of the best decisions I've ever made," Dad said with a smile.

"Perhaps second to your Sentinel," Uncle Malik said, then looked at me. "I'm not sure if this helps you."

"It helps," I assured him. "We've ruled out sorcery, which narrows the playing field."

We just had to figure out what remained.

FIVE

We declined several more offers of food and drink, made apologies, and left to pursue the ghost angle. Mom agreed to call Mallory and see if she or Lulu's father, Catcher, had heard anything about post-fire magical shenanigans, and my father headed to the House library to get the Librarian and his wife, Paige (a sorceress in her own right and former Order archivist), on the research as well.

"A lot of people on the hunt," Connor said.

"We need all the help we can get." I gestured back to the House. "So, based on that conversation, whatever magic was worked in 1872 probably wasn't worked by a sorceress. It had to be someone else. A specialist, like a necromancer. But we don't have any idea why. Maybe Ariel can help with that."

He stopped when we reached the SUV. "I'm not sure what to call him."

"Who?"

"Your dad."

I looked at Connor and was shocked to see uncertainty on his face. Shifters were rarely uncertain, and that was especially true for the prince. I narrowed my gaze at him. "Tell me what you talked about when you two had that little chat a few weeks ago."

"No," he said with a crooked smile. "That was none of your business."

"Then what you call him is none of mine," I said with a grin. "What did you call him when you were a teenage punk? Ice Man, right?"

"Not to his face."

"Good decision," I said as we climbed into the vehicle. "Follow that instinct."

We drove to Schaumburg, a suburb on the city's West Side, where Ariel's apartment complex was located. It was along the expressway in an area mostly populated by hotels, business parks, and restaurants for the lunching and traveling business crowd. Along the way, I sent a quick summary to the team of what we'd learned at Cadogan House.

We met Theo and Petra in the parking lot. They'd driven the Ombuds' van, the office name stenciled in tall black letters along the side. Someone had stuck a bumper sticker of the same design along the length of Theo's cast.

"Are we paying for that advertising?" I asked with a smile.

"He *really* enjoyed the drugs," Petra said.

"And now it won't come off," Theo grumbled, before sticking a finger inside the edge of his cast.

"Quit messing with it," I said.

"It itches."

"It can't possibly itch yet. You've had the cast on for one day."

"So it's psychosomatic," he said. "That doesn't make it itch less."

I gave him the haggard sigh of the long-suffering work spouse. "Were you able to get some sleep?"

"Yes. Petra was right about the drugs," he said with a smile. "So no sorcerers in Chicago in 1872? That's the Cadogan House conclusion?"

"At least not that were known to the Order," I said. "They've got Paige and the Librarian looking into it. You'll know what I know as soon as I know it."

We headed for the stand-alone brick building with fluted columns and a gym and a party room sign on glass-fronted double doors.

Petra went in first, and I noticed Theo waited until she and Connor were inside before pausing at the threshold. It occurred to me that I hadn't been a very good work spouse, which needed rectifying.

"Are you up for this?" I shifted my gaze to his arm and then back again. "And I'm sorry I didn't ask before now. Petra and I can handle if you aren't."

"I'm a little freaked out," he said quietly, something he'd admit to a partner, but not in front of the rest of them. He lifted his casted arm. "It's not this. It's the ghosts and the damn howling and that breeze. Every time something touches me, I think I'm being haunted."

"I know the feeling. Ariel will be in control during the séance, at least." I frowned. "Although maybe that doesn't help much."

"I'll step out if I need to," he assured me, and I was pretty sure he was trying to make me feel better.

"I appreciate a man who can set boundaries," I said, and opened the door.

"Is he okay?" Connor whispered when we joined him inside the party room, which had been decorated to look like someone's den: fireplace, couches, side tables. Counters lined one side, and a swinging door led to a small kitchen.

"He'll hold," I said.

"Of course he will," Connor said. "He's a fighter, just like his partner."

Ariel stood in the middle of the room, hands on her hips as she surveyed it. She was long and lean, with light brown skin and dark curly hair that was pulled back into a poof away from her gorgeous face. Her eyes were wide and the color of amber, her lips generous and colored today a somber tint in an eggplant shade. She wore a T-shirt of the same shade with the MVD's logo in an orangey yellow, boots in that same bright color, and fitted jeans. Credit where credit was due: the woman had style.

She looked back as we tromped in, nodded. And a flush rose on her cheeks when she caught sight of Connor.

"You know me, Connor, and Theo," I said. "This is Petra Jassim. Petra, Ariel Shaw."

"Hi," Ariel said.

"Hi," Petra said. "I'd offer a handshake, but . . ." She held up a gloved hand.

Ariel just looked at it blankly. "But . . . you have an infection?"

"She's an aeromancer," I said. "She'll shock you. Literally."

Ariel's eyebrows lifted in interest. "No shit."

"Zero. Necromancer, eh?"

"Yeah."

"Cool."

"Cool."

I had a feeling we were witnessing the blooming of a very weird friendship.

"I reserved the party room for two hours," Ariel said. "I have a roommate, and she doesn't like ghosts in the apartment."

Who could blame her?

"So what am I working from?"

Petra pulled out the vial from yesterday. "Will this be enough?"

Ariel grimaced as she took it, held it up to the light. "It's very green."

"Is that unusual?" I asked.

"No clue." She lowered the vial again, looked at us. "We usually have stuff that belonged to the deceased. A watch. A hat. That kind of thing. Not their . . . fluids."

"There were no watches or hats at the gate," I said. "We're working with what we've got."

"Which is 1872?"

"Pretty much," I said. "If it helps, the magic probably wasn't done by a sorcerer."

"Well, obviously," Ariel said, as if that were the most obvious thing in the world. "It's ghosts. I mean, at most a sorcerer might help kindle the magic, but this is necromancer territory."

That confirmed Uncle Malik's take.

"How does this work, exactly?" Theo asked. "The necromancing?"

"With eye of newt and graveyard dust," Ariel said.

His gaze remained level. "I'm pretty sure you're kidding, but as I've never been at a séance before, I'm not entirely sure."

"I'll do my prep, try to make contact. I'm powerful enough to share the ghost's image, or at least as much of it as I can produce on short notice. Go get a drink if you want, then find a spot and stay there. We want as little movement as possible while we're communicating. It's distracting."

Theo took a coffee stirrer and was shoving it into his cast. He closed his eyes, and I was half-surprised his back leg didn't wiggle like a dog's as he scratched with obvious enjoyment.

"This is going to be a long recovery," I murmured, taking a seat on the end of the couch.

"Good Ombuds itch their partners," Theo said, sitting beside me.

"That's not even remotely true, and you just got to second base with that coffee stirrer. She's your partner now."

Connor snorted, leaned against the arm of the sofa near me as Petra sat on the floor, legs crossed.

Ariel pulled ceremonial objects from a black leather backpack: a candle, a silver bell, a piece of indigo silk. She placed the silk on the coffee table—around which hundreds of bridal shower guests had probably gathered—and put the candle, the bell, and the vial we had given her atop it.

She sat cross-legged in front of the table, rolled her shoulders, then looked at each of us. "Quiet and still," she said. "I cannot stress that enough."

"No distracted ghosts," Petra said. "Got it."

With a mild smirk, Ariel looked back at the assemblage on the table. Then, with careful, intentional movements, she lit the candle, uncapped the vial, and rang the bell. The candle's scent was light and floral, and the bell's sound was clear and harmonic, and echoed nicely around the room. But it still creeped me out; our interaction with the coven had ruined me for bells, even though I understood the good intentions of this magic.

"My name is Ariel Shaw," she said, eyes closed and voice clear. "I seek an audience with any of those whose essence is contained within the vial presented here."

Magic began to gather in the room. This was her power, calling out to the place where spirits resided, facilitating their appearance in our plane. We all waited for a response, watching the space above the coffee table for a sign of life.

And then the air began to grow cold, heavy. The vial shook on the tabletop, the ooze now faintly luminescent. Instinctively, I looked down at Theo's cast, was relieved to find it wasn't pulsating with green light.

"Come forward," Ariel said. "Come forward and claim your audience and be heard."

Another wash of magic from her end, and the temperature dropped more, enough to have our breath fogging the room. The old magic was stronger now, although I wasn't sure if that was a remnant of the magic from the gate or a ghost that was eager to have its say.

Light began coalescing above the coffee table, pale and green and shimmery as good nail polish.

Theo grabbed my arm with his noninjured hand, fingers digging in. The former cop who'd faced down all manner of monsters was definitely over ghosts.

"Ow," I murmured.

"Sorry," he said, but didn't let go or loosen his grip. Granted, his last encounter with a ghost had him in the emergency room, so I could understand the apprehension.

"Claim your audience," Ariel said again, and the floating light became more distinct, swirled, and pulsed until a figure appeared.

She was a woman with pale skin, a slightly uptilted nose, and lips that were currently pursed into displeasure. Her hair was curly and arranged in a complicated updo, with a small hairpiece of lace and flowers—I think it would be called a "fascinator"—cocked at an angle atop the pile of it. Her dress was high-necked, big-shouldered, and narrow-waisted, and definitely from another era.

Victorian, I thought, from the late 1800s; 1872-ish, probably.

I was a little surprised the ghost appeared female and was so nattily dressed. I'd had the sense the human ghosts at the gate had been male, and they certainly hadn't worn fancy clothes. If she hadn't been at the gate, maybe she'd been the one to work the magic?

"Well," Petra whispered, "I did not have ghost-in-a-fascinator on my bingo card this year."

"Right?" I whispered.

"What's a fascinator?" Connor asked quietly.

"The little hat," Theo said, gesturing, and earning a sharp look from Ariel.

When we were still and quiet again, she looked back at the ghost. "State your name, spirit."

The ghost's mouth moved, but no sound emerged. Ariel swore quietly, rolled her shoulders, and stared more intently at the woman. Whatever magic she'd passed along in that instant did the trick.

"I am Patience Minerva Gillicutty," the ghost said. The words still had a tinny quality, but given she was speaking to us From The Beyond, or whatever, it sounded pretty decent. Vinyl quality, at least.

"Date of birth?" Ariel asked.

"I was born in the year of our lord, 1848, in the city of Chicago, Illinois. Why have you summoned me?"

But before we could answer, Patience's nostrils flared. She swung her head back and forth as if sniffing the air. Then she let loose a stream of curses that would have made a sailor's eyes water. The air grew colder yet, so our breath became vapor, and the woman's visage rose nearly to the ceiling, her eyes bulging with apparent fury.

I felt Connor shift beside me. Theo's eyes went wide as moons. Petra looked absolutely enamored.

The ghost glared at us. "I can smell the abomination on you! Who did it? Who let the demon back in?"

SIX

For a good ten seconds, the room went absolutely silent. "Demon?" I asked. "What demon?"

"A demon?" Petra asked. "Are you sure?"

The ghost looked at her. "Of course I'm sure. I'm the Chronicler." Her nostrils flared again. "And can you not smell the sulfur? The brimstone? Foul and rank and already polluting our world."

I had to work not to sniff myself.

Her gaze narrowed, and a frigid breeze blew through the room. "The very same stink that marked our city when she spilled chaos around it. Who let it in?"

Every word was an accusation.

"Nobody let it in," I ventured. "We don't even know what it is."

Slowly, Patience's gaze shifted to the two of us. If I could have turned myself invisible, I would have, just to escape that accusatory stare. "*It* is a chaos demon."

"A chaos demon," Petra said.

I remember the chaos of that time. That's what Uncle Malik had said, and my blood chilled.

"Eglantine," Patience said. "That's its name."

"There were ghosts," I said. "Human and canine, but nothing else. I don't know what a chaos demon looks like, but we didn't see one."

"Hold up," Petra said. "Let's start at the beginning." She was writing notes on her screen as Patience talked. "There was a demon in Chicago whose name was Eglantine. Variety," she said as she tapped, "chaos demon."

"A creature which was drawn to Chicago after the Great Fire," Patience said, "and fed on the city's pain and grief and fury. And tried its best to destroy what remained of it."

"When did it come to Chicago?"

"In 1872," she said. "What year is it now?" Theo told her, and her eyes widened. "So long since, and the magic did as it ought. It beckoned me to tell the story, as is my duty among the Guardians to do so."

"We tested the magic," Petra said. "And it showed a date of 1872."

Patience nodded. "Eglantine was exiled the same year by the collective efforts of Chicago's remaining supernaturals. The Guardians," she added proudly. "Those who swore an eternal oath to drive out the demon and protect the city from its return. I am the Chronicler. It was my role to tell the story of the demon Eglantine and its efforts to destroy Chicago."

"How did it attempt to do that?" Petra asked.

"It is a chaos demon," Patience said again. "It's singular purpose—and the source of its power—is creation of chaos. That's the reason for its existence, its fuel, its desire. It is a hording demon; we believed it scouted the city to attract others of its ilk. To create more chaos, to feed more fully. To nest in Chicago and turn it into something rotten, wicked, spoilt."

Her gaze narrowed. "Why do I smell it again? You must have allowed it in or facilitated its entrance. The Guardians' wards cannot simply break."

"What wards?" Theo asked.

"The wards built to keep Eglantine from returning and to keep the others out. You don't think we'd leave the city without protection, do you?"

I had no idea what I was supposed to believe. I was no less confused than I'd been last night. But we were on a different kind of deadline now: Ariel wasn't going to be able to hold open this connection forever, so we needed information, and we needed it quickly.

"What are the wards?" I asked. "I mean, I understand the concept—they're barrier or protection spells. But what wards do you mean?"

Patience's gaze went a little unfocused, and she seemed confused by the question. Which was weird. "I . . . don't remember precisely," she said, and seemed discomfited by that.

Petra watched her for a moment, gaze narrowed, then looked at me. "Tell her what happened, Elisa."

"We were . . . proceeding toward Chicago in our . . . carriage," I said, recalling a Victorian ghost wasn't going to be up to speed (sorry not sorry) on modern roads and Autos, "when magic erupted from Chicago's South Gate. It's a large arcing structure," I said, demonstrating its shape with my hands. "Ghosts came out and attacked us. They stopped our carriage and injured me and my partner. They kept saying 'no' and 'go back.'"

She looked at each of us in turn. "You are not demons."

"No, we are not. We were with a sympath, who was being pursued by her enemies."

"Which must have included a demon," Patience said, and seemed relieved that particular piece of the puzzle had fallen into place.

"But they weren't trying to get into Chicago," Theo said. "They were trying to keep our victim with them."

"They were chasing you into Chicago," Connor pointed out. "Maybe that would have been enough."

We all looked at Patience, who nodded. "The wards were triggered by the demon's proximity."

"How many are there?" Petra asked.

"There are—" But she broke off as if the thought had been wiped from her mind. She cleared her throat. "I am sorry. I do not know."

"They didn't tell the Chronicler how many wards there were?" Theo murmured.

"Where are they?" Petra asked.

Patience looked distressed, rubbed her forehead. "I'm sorry. I do not know."

"Is there a written record?" I asked. "Maps or physical plans?"

"I do not know," Patience said again. And this time, I felt the faintest pulse of magic. I believed her—and I thought there was a reason she didn't have any more information.

"Who are the other Guardians?" Petra asked. "Can we speak with them?"

We all knew the answer before she said it. "I do not know."

"How are we talking to you?" Theo asked.

"I built a connection into the farthest ward so I could explain . . . what I could remember."

And what she could remember—or what she was able to say—was limited. By old magic or new?

Patience frowned, looked away. "It should not have been able to break through. Each ward ought have been strong enough to stop the demon."

"It didn't stop me," I pointed out. "Or Theo. The ghosts injured us but did not stop us."

"You are not chaos demons," Patience said. "It was not meant to stop you."

"Maybe the wards have gotten weaker," Ariel said.

We all looked at Ariel. "What?" Patience asked first.

"Well, it's been more than a hundred years since the magic was put into place. And there's been big magic in Chicago lately. I mean, the fairies tried to pull the green land here. That's portal magic—big magic."

We'd stopped Ruadan, the fairy who'd turned chunks of Chicago into rolling hills of misty green, and turned him over to the queen of the fairies, Claudia.

"The green land?" Patience asked.

"Long story short," Petra said, "there's been a lot of magical upheaval in Chicago in the last few months."

"Claudia said something about Ruadan tearing open the world. Messing up place and time." I looked at Patience. "Maybe that weakened the wards enough to give the demon a chance?"

"I do not know," Patience said. "The demon was very canny. Perhaps it was watching and waiting for an opportunity to attempt reentry. We must have failed to consider that." And the dismay was clear in her voice.

"You didn't fail," I said. I wouldn't say I liked Patience, but I knew supernatural guilt when I heard it—and sympathized. "You protected the city for more than a century. Now it's our turn."

"Why would the demon come back to Chicago?" Connor asked. "It could go anywhere. Why wait for its chance to return?"

"Chicago was its home," Ariel said simply. "I don't want to be crass, but if chaos demons feed on pain and suffering, Chicago has plenty to offer. Maybe it liked the flavor."

"What's the worst-case scenario?" Theo asked. "If we don't get the demon out fast enough?"

Patience stared at us for a full minute. "You do not understand. This *is* the worst-case scenario. It will create chaos, call to the others of its kind, and they will flock to the city and do more of the same. It will become a haven."

It hadn't done anything yet, or at least not that we'd heard. Unfortunately, I wasn't sure if that was because the demon had been successfully repelled at the gate, or because it had gotten into Chicago but hadn't had time enough to inflict damage.

"Do other cities have wards and gates?" I asked.

"Not all cities are Chicago," was her cryptic reply.

"Will the wards continue to work once they've been triggered?" Petra asked, ignoring her tone.

"It depends on the ward."

"Can the ward be reset?"

"It would depend on the ward." Her words were slow, intentional, and I had the sense Patience was trying to work around whatever magic seemed to be inhibiting her from answering the question.

"What about the dogs?" Theo asked, scratching absently at his arm. "Some of the ghosts howled like dogs."

Patience blinked. She seemed surprised by the inclusion of canines. "I suppose because demons hate dogs." Her tone was matter-of-fact, as if the animosity were obvious and common knowledge.

"Huh," Petra said. "I'd have thought they hated cats."

"Dogs are loyal and protective," Patience said, and I had to fight not to give Connor a look he wouldn't have appreciated. "That's antithetical to demons."

"And cats are basically tiny demons," Petra said, nodding.

Eleanor of Aquitaine was proof enough of that.

"How do we stop the demon from causing chaos? From calling to the horde?" I asked.

"You must seal it."

"Seal it," Theo repeated. "What does that mean?"

"Putting it in a cage," Ariel said.

"A metaphysical cage," Patience corrected. "It requires a careful and powerful spell crafted specifically for her."

"Like a binding?" I asked, thinking of the creature Mallory had bound into my mother's sword. And in doing so, bound me to my mother's womb. Monster twitched again.

"No," Patience said. "A binding is physical—a physical creature is joined with another or subsumed into another physical object. Demons are not creatures of the human world, and they are not merely physical. A seal is metaphysical. Sealing returns a demon to its proper plane of existence. Sealing locks the door."

"Why didn't you seal this one?" Theo asked.

Patience blushed a little. "Because we didn't have its name."

"You said its name was Eglantine," Theo said.

"That is a false name, a name it has adopted for use in the human world. The demon's real name is a sigil—an ancient symbol. Each demon has one."

"Like Prince," Theo said. "Used a symbol instead of a name."

"Which prince?" Patience asked.

Theo waved that away. "Never mind."

"So every demon has a sigil," Petra said. "But you don't know what hers is."

Patience nodded and seemed shamed by the admission.

"And how do we find it?" Theo asked. "Is there a sigil catalog or calling card or—"

"Only she can provide it."

"Oh, good," I muttered, breaking the silence that fell after that little apple. "More good news."

Patience looked down her nose at me. "Sarcasm is the tool of the weak-minded."

"Agree to disagree," I said. Sarcastically. "So if this demon made it into Chicago, in order to stop her, we have to figure out her sigil, which only she knows. We have to find her, and we have to use metaphysical magic in order to lock her down again."

"Correct."

I blew out a breath. The world had just gotten very, very complicated.

"Demons," Petra said after Ariel let Patience go again and the rest of us had gone outside for fresh air. "I did not expect that."

"I work for the Ombuds," Theo said. "But even by that standard, that"—he gestured back to the room—"was very woo-woo."

"Seconded," Connor said.

"Super woo-woo," Petra agreed.

"Was Rose working for demons?" I asked. "I feel like Roger would have mentioned it if she'd admitted that to him."

"Maybe she didn't tell him," Petra said.

"Or maybe she didn't know," Theo said. "People work this hard to exorcise a demon; maybe the demon's wise enough to keep their identity secret."

"I think you're missing an obvious candidate for the chaos demon," Connor said.

"Who?"

"Rose."

We all stared at him.

"She's a sympath," Petra said, "not a demon, and she's been Roger's informant for years. She's given him data, information that's helped bring down other criminals."

"And she was trying to get into Chicago," Connor added.

"She was being chased out of Edentown," I countered. "That's not the same thing." But I didn't like the unease that was beginning to gather in my chest.

"I have a *lot* of research to do," Petra said. "On sigils, on sealing spells, and we still don't know where the other wards are. Or what inadvertent damage they might do."

"We'll break up the work," I said. "You take the demon. What does she want? Why is she here? Can we find that first and capture her that way? And keep your eye out for the sigil. I'll update Cadogan and request they focus on the Cadogan library—any demon treatises, historical documents—anything that might bear on this."

"Can you have the Librarian or Paige call me?" Petra asked. "That might be easiest."

"I will."

Theo scratched his chin. "You're thinking other Sups were interested, wrote some things down?"

"It's possible," I said. "Just because the Guardians didn't keep records doesn't mean someone else didn't."

"And what are we going to do?" Theo asked.

"We're going to try and keep the city safe in the meantime. And when you need breaks, you can work with Petra."

He rolled his eyes at that.

Petra cleared her throat. "We also need to update Roger."

"Not it," Theo and I said simultaneously.

"Well, I'm not talking to him alone. We're all Ombuds. We'll be Ombudding together."

I updated my parents and Uncle Malik, advised them we were facing a very specific enemy, and gave them their assignment and Petra's contact information. Then we Ombudded together and called Roger at the office. He looked and sounded as baffled as we were.

"A demon," Roger said. He kept repeating that word over and over, as if the repetition would cause it to make sense. "Surely we'd have known if she were working with demons. If she'd been in league with someone that powerful—who posed such a danger to her—she'd have told us."

Connor cleared his throat. Petra, Theo, and I looked at each other. And they both said, "Not it," first. I mouthed a silent curse, and steeled my courage.

"Roger," I said, "the only people who got close to the gate were me, Theo, and Rose."

"Right."

"And Theo and I aren't demons. So it is possible . . ."

I trailed off because his face went wan. And then bright with anger. "No. It's not possible. I've known her for several years. I checked my records—the information she's given us has led to multiple arrests. That's not demonic."

But maybe she's a chaos demon, I thought, who might enjoy throwing her competitors behind bars.

"She deserves more than our suspicion," Roger said. "It's only right. The Cadogan House library—"

"They're on it," I assured him. "I'll let you know if they find anything. We're all working to figure out what we can as soon as we can."

And hopefully we'd be fast enough.

"I'll tell you one thing," Theo said, when we'd ended the call. "I'm not interested in people being secretive about their big plans to protect the city. For god's sake, *write that mess down*. People die. They forget. Years pass, and demons tell sob stories and end up walking back into the damned city, and we have no idea how to work the security system."

"I think Patience was spelled," Petra said.

"Spelled?" he asked.

"Some kind of memory spell, which would make her forget everything she knew about the demon, the wards, the magic."

"Except for the information specific to her job," I guessed. "She's the Chronicler, so she's supposed to tell people—in very general terms—the story of the demon's ouster."

Petra nodded. "Yep. That's probably why she's the one Ariel was able to contact. It was probably built into the spell as a security measure. No single Guardian knows the entire system, so a demon can't dismantle it by manipulating a single human."

"So no one Guardian has too much power or knowledge," Connor said.

Theo nodded. "I get it. Still think they should have left a handbook."

"Could someone undo the memory spell?" I glanced at Petra. "Would that be possible?"

"I don't know. They worked pretty hard to keep things quiet here, and Patience is a ghost. I'm not sure how you'd even go about unspelling a ghost."

"And that still doesn't get us the sigil," I murmured. "Damn it."

Theo's expression went grim. "Didn't Lucy Dalton say something about 'darkness coming' when we were in the grain elevator?" She was the coven leader and murderess who had gotten Ariel and others involved in cultlike magic.

"Yeah," I said grimly. "She said she was killing people to prevent an apocalypse."

Theo's eyes darkened, probably remembering the sight of Ariel unconscious in a circle of salt on the stained concrete floor. "She said we'd drown in its power."

Sups were prone to hyperbole, but I had to wonder if she'd been telling the exact truth. "Maybe she knew something we didn't."

Connor was sending a message to his dad about what we'd learned. And the reply had what looked like bafflement on his face.

"What's wrong?" I asked.

He blinked, looked up at me, and seemed to shake it off. "I need to go to Pack HQ."

"Is everything okay?"

"I'm not sure. Something about some pissed off Pack members trying to start a fight."

"Do you need backup?" I asked.

Connor put his screen away, looked at me. "Actually, a vampire might come in handy. Might shift things up a bit."

"I see what you did there," Petra said, although she was looking at her screen.

I glanced at Theo. "Any objection if I deal with this other Sup nonsense?"

"You're an Ombud. Go Ombudding." He glanced at Connor. "Do you need me, too?"

"I think the vampire will be dramatic enough."

Theo looked a little forlorn. "Is this because I'm in a cast?" he asked, and as if that had reminded him of the problem, he began scratching again.

"Of course not," Connor said, and gently knocked a knuckle against the cast, the hard *thunk* of sound proving its solidity. "That thing would be very handy in a fight."

En route to Ukrainian Village, the neighborhood where the NAC Pack had made their Chicago den, I sent Lulu a message. She didn't want supernatural drama, but she needed to know there was a demon in town and the danger it posed. And she needed to warn her parents.

I found a message from Jonathan Black, who was half sorcerer and half elf. He'd briefly dated Ariel during her coven involvement and had tried (or so he'd said) to get her away from it. He'd also "accidentally" attacked me, could use his magic to hide who he was, and had anonymous "clients" for whom he provided unknown services. Brokering information seemed to be one of them. Which I suppose made him my informant.

NEED TO TALK was the entirety of the message. I didn't have time for him now, so I put the screen away.

The NAC Pack's ancestral home was in Memphis, Tennessee, home of ribs and blues and a very big river. Here, they'd constructed a sleek building of steel, glass, and brick. What had started as a seedy bar that sold five-star barbeque had become an entrepreneurial dream—a full commercial kitchen for their catering company, a clubhouse for the Keene family, and a garage for motorcycle wrenching. And also a seedy bar. Because shifters would be shifting.

There were no obvious signs of warfare when we pulled up to

the curb, no sounds of battle when we climbed out and into the welcoming arms of Delicious Meat Smells. We walked in through one of the open garage doors, where shifters worked on cars and bikes and weight racks had been installed so Pack members could work out when the weather was warm enough. Which, for them, was most of the time.

There were only a couple of shifters in there now, which was unusual. Connor nodded at them, and they watched warily as I followed him through the maze of vehicles and rolling stools and car parts (a transmission, maybe?) and into the building proper.

We heard noise coming from the sticky-floored bar, but not the usual thump of grinding rock. This sounded more like an argument.

A good, old-fashioned shifter fight? Yes, please. Vast improvement over ghostly hands.

"Ready?" Connor asked.

"Right behind you," I said, and brushed my fingertips against his.

He pushed open the door and paused in the doorway until all heads had turned to him and the music was turned down.

There were a lot of heads—forty or fifty shifters, including some of Connor's uncles and his dad, Gabriel Keene, the Apex of the North American Central Pack. He was tall and broad-shouldered, with dark blond hair, tan skin, and golden eyes. And the magic that dripped from him was undeniably unfriendly.

Fortunately, I found two allies in the crowd.

Alexei Breckenridge was Connor's best friend and a generally quiet shifter with a giant crush on Lulu. He was tall and broad-shouldered, with pale skin, hazel eyes, and dark blond hair that was short and carefully styled. "Stoic" seemed to fit him best, except when it came to food and his apparently never-ending hunger.

Beside him stood Daniel Liu, a Packmate and notorious flirt.

He met my gaze, gave me a wink, then pushed his straight, dark shoulder-length hair behind his ears. He'd acted as my security while vampires had been stalking me and wasn't easily perturbed. He had light brown skin, dark eyes, and cheekbones models would weep for.

There was at least one obvious enemy—a shifter named Miranda with a giant grudge against vampires and particular hatred of me. We'd arranged a temporary truce, or so I believed, since I had some dirt she didn't want revealed. Her expression was grim but not, I thought, directed at me.

Monster waited quietly by, taking in the magic and the tension.

"Connor," his dad said, and the crowd parted to let us walk through. I felt Alexei and Dan move through the crowd to take positions at our backs and appreciated the sentiment.

The focus of attention was a trio who stood in the middle of the room. The man in front had suntanned skin, cropped dark hair, and a face that was ruggedly handsome. The "rugged" coming from a scar on his square jaw and a previously broken nose. He wore jeans over scarred cowboy boots, a gray T-shirt with a darker graphic, and a well-worn leather jacket.

"I guess we can finally get started," he said flatly. "I'm Cade Drummond," he said, then gestured to a woman and man standing behind him. "This is Breonna; this is Joe."

Breonna was little shorter than me, with suntanned skin and dark hair pulled into a ponytail. She wore leggings and a cropped tank, showing off her trim and muscled figure. Joe was tall and thin, with a sharp, narrow face, pale skin, and shaggy blond hair.

"We're here from Memphis," Cade said, and I heard the slight Southern twang in his voice. "And we're sick of the Keene family fucking up the North American Central Pack."

SEVEN

The bar wasn't huge, and tightly packed as it was, the peppery shifter magic nearly filled up the remainder of the room, as if pushing out the air. I had to remind myself to breathe through it.

Gabriel crossed his arms, and his expression portrayed boredom. "Do we really need the drama? You have issues with Pack decisions, you know how to reach me."

"And what good would it do?" Cade asked, casting his gaze over the crowd. It was easy enough to guess he hadn't come here for a dialogue.

"We've become too involved in the human world, the vampire world, the fairy world," he continued. "All the worlds except ours. Where's the focus on Aurora? On strengthening the Pack? On building our ranks?"

Aurora, Alaska, was the spiritual home of North American shifters. This wasn't the first time Pack members had raised concerns about the shifters' involvement in the world—either too much of it or not enough. But I hadn't previously witnessed someone actually saying it to Gabriel's face.

Cade's eyes searched, settled on me. "Hell, there's a vampire in the room right now."

"There is," I said. "Would you like to see my fangs?"

There were amused snickers in the crowd. Maybe I'd managed

over the last few months to actually make a few more shifter friends.

Cade rolled his eyes, turned his gaze back to the crowd. I'd been dismissed.

"Aw," I said quietly, knowing my audience. "That hurts my feelings."

But the low chuckles made me feel better.

"You think the other Packs would stand for his? Would put up with it? Not just *mixing* with vampires"—there was enough disgust in his voice to make clear he meant something more physical than mere "mixing"—"but bowing to them. Who the hell do they think they are?"

"Well, they think they're immortals," Gabriel said. "So I guess that gives them one up on us."

It wasn't often that shifters complimented vampires in situations like this, and his gaze narrowed as he waited for Cade's reaction. Testing, I thought. Wondering how deeply the hatred ran. Or whether it was a show for the crowd.

"Tainted," Cade said, throwing a look of loathing in my direction.

I gave him a wink.

"You want us to return to the woods?" Gabriel asked. "To pretend the world around us doesn't exist? The Pack made its decision to stay at ConPack more than twenty years ago. You're refusing to honor?"

"The world has tainted us," Cade said. He must have enjoyed the taste of that word given how much he used it.

Gabriel tilted his head at the interlopers, such a canine movement, and raised questioning brows. "You think life in the human world is so bad, why didn't you return to Aurora with the others? Hell, you could still join them."

"You're missing the point," Cade said. "You're behind the times."

"You're bitching about 'mixing' with vampires, and I'm behind the times?" Gabriel stalked toward him now, and power filled the room as if he'd swept a mantle off his shoulders. "Since you don't live in Chicago, and don't know the people you complain about, I'm going to give you the benefit of the doubt, and instead of beating your ass the way it needs beating, I'll offer a warning."

Another step forward, magic spilling heavily into the room now, collecting at our feet. Connor's father would leave no doubt of his strength.

"I'm the Apex of this Pack," he said. "My family has held the position for generations. Not because we ignore the world around us but because we respond to it as a Pack based on what the Pack needs. You think you could do a better job?"

Another step, and now the toes of their boots touched. Gabriel stared into Cade's eyes. Cade, in his first good decision, didn't say a word. So Gabriel said the word that mattered.

"You're welcome to challenge me."

There were no beatings, but the Pack didn't give the interlopers much love when Gabriel pushed Cade aside and strode back into the inner rooms where Pack decisions were made. They were all but shoved out of the bar with grumbles about insulting the Apex.

But I heard mumblings, too. There were a few shifters who didn't disagree that the Pack was traveling a dangerous course.

Connor made no comment as we followed his father into the back. His face was set in stern lines, his body tense and ready for a fight.

Daniel Liu appeared at my side. "Elisa. You look ravishing, as always." Dan enjoyed playing with fire, but he was as loyal to Connor as they came.

"Mr. Liu, handsome as always. What's the story with the three stooges?"

"You'll be shocked to learn," he said quietly, "that they've never participated in Pack decision-making before now."

"They suddenly got bored?"

"Or they're testing the waters," Daniel said.

For becoming the Pack's future Apex, he meant. As Gabriel's son, Connor was next in line for the throne. But even he could be challenged by a member of the Pack, and the Keene family seemed to assume that someone would take a chance.

That was one part of the Apex process I wasn't looking forward to. It was a physical battle of strength, each opponent showing their qualifications to stand as the Pack's single leader, warrior, spokesman. I didn't doubt Connor's strength or his skills. But the fight would be brutal, and whether he won or lost, he would bear the scars of it.

We walked into the lounge, where a handful of shifters, including three of Connor's uncles—Eli, Derek, and Ben—waited. A bottle of whiskey was passed.

"The fuck is wrong with these people," Ben said, his simmering gaze on the doorway that led back to the bar. "Passive-aggressive bullshit." He was the youngest of Connor's uncles.

"This isn't the first time someone has brought complaints to the Apex's door," Gabriel said philosophically, "and it won't be the last. We'll deal with it as we always have."

"First time someone's done it when a demon is also threatening Chicago," Connor muttered.

His dad nodded.

"And if they want a challenge?" Eli asked. He was the oldest of Connor's uncles, behind only Connor's aunt Fallon in the family order. (Yes, they'd been named in reverse alphabetical order.)

"They'll get one," Connor said. The tone was matter-of-fact and without hesitation.

"Watch it, puppy," Eli said with a smile. "You wouldn't be doing the fighting." He gestured toward Connor's father. "Not until this one's done with the throne."

Gabriel grunted. "Which isn't today. The ones who complain

are never the ones who help, who put in the time and the labor. They sit around and stew in their self-righteousness, decide they could do things better. They throw around words and gin up their courage—literally. And that's usually the most they do."

"And if they decide they want something more?" I asked.

All eyes turned to me. I hadn't meant to speak; this meeting wasn't for me. But as an Ombudsman, as Connor's girlfriend, as a person who had friends in the Pack, I needed to know what might come next. It was my nature.

"Vampires," Derek said good-naturedly. "Always like to plan."

"She is her parents' child," Gabriel said with a smile. He took a seat at the worn table, kicked up his feet, crossed his booted ankles. "It may be, Elisa, that these fools return to Memphis and learn to make better use of their time. Maybe they'll rile up the Pack, and if the Pack wants changes, we'll do what needs to be done."

He shifted his gaze to Connor, and his magic shifted along with it. No longer merely the magic of the Pack's Apex predator, but of a father. "It's my intention to pass the coronet to the next generation. And I don't intend to let them interrupt that process."

The coronet was the Pack's crown; it had been placed on Connor's head as an infant when he'd been initiated into the Pack.

"To the prince," Eli said, and raised a glass.

"To the prince," came the echoing response, and with it a warm curl of magic that wound around the room, gathering us in. Goose bumps lifted on my arms as each shifter joined their magic to the group, to the whole.

This was Pack. Not just the name or the building or the individual components, but the members unified together in common purpose: holding the Pack.

A hand took mine. I looked over, found Connor's gaze on me, as if gauging my reaction to the moment and the power. Did he think I'd be overwhelmed by the magic? Smothered by it?

I nodded at him, squeezed his hand, knowing this was our future.

The neon sign above the door of the entirely unimpressive and low-slung building made no sense: It was a hot dog jumping out of a taco. It was a strange sign for a restaurant called Taco Hole. But it was a supernatural sanctuary, and it had some of the best food I'd ever tasted. And some of the hottest, to boot.

I walked inside the slightly dingy space, where all manner of supernaturals sipped margaritas or enjoyed enchiladas, including the nonpracticing sorceress at a scarred four-top. Lulu had already ordered, and the table bore her drink, two bowls of chips, and several bottles of Taco Hole's famous hot sauce.

"Thanks for waiting for me," I said dryly, taking a seat.

"I sent that text half an hour ago."

"I was half an hour away and knee deep in shifter nonsense."

"Are they still at Pack HQ?"

"They" were Connor and Alexei, whom she'd also invited to dinner. "They are. And they'll probably be a while."

She hadn't talked to me about what she and Alexei were to each other—not that I wanted the sordid details—and I wasn't sure she knew. I just wanted her happy, and I was pretty sure he did, too.

The waitress came over, her skin faintly green and iridescent. She looked down at me. "Yeah?"

"Special," I said, not even bothering to see what that might have been. "Burn me up."

"Drink?"

Vampires didn't usually frequent the Taco Hole, so I doubted they had bottled blood. Lulu was drinking something that looked like a sunset—brilliant layers of red and orange and pale pink—so I gestured toward it. "One of those."

The waitress nodded and walked away again.

I snagged a chip, munched. "Pass the extra hot, please." She did, and I poured it onto the chip, bit in. I felt the burn immediately. And reveled in it.

"I'm surprised you invited Alexei," I said.

She swirled her drink with a straw. "Like I'd have a choice. Connor would bring him anyway."

I made a noncommittal sound. "Are we here for a particular reason, or just dinner?"

"Just dinner. Food. Drinks. No magic."

"No Pack interlopers?"

She looked up. "Is that what happened?"

The waitress, who hadn't been gone more than five minutes, came back with drinks and food. Like Lulu's, my drink was ombré from top to bottom, from brilliant orange to deep crimson. I sipped and pursed my lips from the puckering sourness.

"Tart, right?" Lulu asked with a grin.

"I think my skeleton contracted." But I sipped again. There was sweetness, too, and they were fighting a powerful war. "What happened," I continued, "was a trio of muscular shifters shouting about how the Pack's gone wrong."

"So it's a day that ends in 'y,'" she said blandly. "That shit happens all the time."

"Yeah," I agreed. "But this feels different." I glanced back at the door, ensuring our shifters weren't on their way into the bar. "And I think they know it, too. They're . . . rallying."

Lulu snorted. "They've always rallied. That's why Connor got away with everything when we were younger despite being a little punk. Hot, but a little punk. And it always seems like the food was bigger when we were kids." She held up a tortilla chip. "Don't they seem smaller now?"

I looked down at my own chip. "Right? Sometimes I wonder if portions have shrunk or my hands have gotten huge."

"Both. You have those big-ass, sword-holding vampire hands."

I held them up, thrilled at her smile, even if sardonic. Or mostly sardonic. "I do not. They look like perfectly normal hands."

"For a vampire."

If she was joking, she was okay. So I could lay the rest of it on her.

"The séance," I began.

"Shit," she said. "I totally forgot to ask. You learned there was a demon?"

"Ariel was mostly pleasant, and we talked to a Victorian ghost named Patience, who told us the misery after the Great Fire lured a demon to Chicago. Said the demon did some damage, and because there were no more sorcerers in town, a band of Sups gathered together to kick the demon out and create defenses so she couldn't get back in."

Lulu had gone still, including the hand holding the chip. Then she put the chip down again. "So, the gate was some kind of defense?"

"That's what we think. And maybe the demon was chasing Rose." Or maybe it wasn't.

I gave her the usual warnings about being careful and the apology for dropping supernatural drama at her door. That was the unfortunate risk of being a supernatural in Chicago—the drama tended to find us. But news of a potential demon in Chicago didn't seem to scare her. She looked thoughtful and mildly curious, and I decided not to overthink what that might portend.

I was on my second drink—and loving every minute of it—when Connor and Alexei arrived. The waitress brought them beers immediately, and nods from both were apparently sufficient detail for their orders.

"Anything new?" I wondered. "River nymphs attempting to take over the Pack? Or river trolls?"

"Surprisingly not," Connor said, rolling his neck as he sat, then taking a long pull from the beer. Then he blew out a breath, turned to me, smiled. "Thanks for the assist."

"I only had to stand there and smile, mostly. I assume they left in peace?"

"They'll be back," Alexei said. "They had the look."

"Yeah," Connor said, grimly. "They will. That type usually doesn't know when to quit."

"Do they worry you?" I asked.

"The Pack worries me because it's my job to worry for the Pack. Or will be," he added with a grin of unerring confidence.

Will be in the future, I thought, and that set my brain spinning again. As Miranda loved to remind me, and as Gabriel had noted earlier, I was immortal. He was not. Shifters lived longer than humans, sure; the same was true of most Sups. But he wouldn't live forever, which made for a very bleak outlook for a happily ever after between vamp and shifter.

"What?" he asked.

"Just—a lot," I decided on. We both had enough to worry about; there was no point in jumping to the end. Life should be savored *now*.

The waitress brought their food, passing out the assortment of plates, along with a small squeeze bottle of brilliantly red liquid that she set in front of Alexei.

Alexei unwrapped the tamales on his plate, then squeezed out a river of bright red sauce on top of them.

"I didn't know sauces could emit light," I said.

"What is that?" Lulu asked.

"Miguel's special sauce," he said. "He's one of the owners. I talked to him last week and wondered if they had anything hotter. They do."

Lulu held out her hand.

Alexei stopped squeezing, glanced at her. "You won't like it."

"I'd like to decide that for myself."

He watched her in silence, then righted the bottle and handed it over.

She unscrewed the top, sniffed. And only barely managed to thrust it back at him before she began coughing. "Holy Batman Jesus. Is that battery acid?"

"Fermented peppers. Miguel's own hybrid. He calls them 'Filthy Susans.'"

Alexei resumed squeezing until the bottle was nearly empty, so it made gassy sounds as he worked to squeeze out the last of its contents, then pounded the bottle with a fist in case any drops remained. Then the top was off, and he was using a knife to fish out another dribble.

We'd all stopped eating to watch him and, for my part, to wonder at his patience and determination.

When he was satisfied he'd gotten the last drop, he screwed the top on again, set the bottle aside, and picked up his knife and fork.

"That was . . . intense," I said.

Alexei merely shrugged, chewed. "No point in waste. No point in hurrying." And then he slid that steady gaze to Lulu. "Some things take patience."

"With sauce that hot, are you worried you might accidentally taste your food?" I wondered.

"No. I had practice. Military school," he added.

"You went to military school?" Lulu repeated. "They made you eat hot sauce?"

"Yes and no."

I thought back. My family had ties with the Brecks, but my mother hadn't cared for socializing with Chicago's financial "elites," and they hadn't been fans of vampires. So we hadn't been close, and I'd only seen Alexei a few times before returning to Chicago a few months ago. I didn't know much about his background.

"My parents sent me when I was nine. The first time. I left, got caught. Left, got caught. Left, got caught. Five times total."

"Why military school?" Lulu asked.

He chewed, swallowed. "I didn't care about money. I was grateful for it, as much as a kid can be. But I didn't want to be the Breckenridge heir. And the family didn't appreciate that, thought they could push ambition and drive into me.

"The area was beautiful," he continued. "Upstate New York. Hills. Rivers. Trees. I wanted to be out there, not in macroeconomics. So I'd sneak out. Live wild in the woods as long as I could. Met some of the Consolidated Atlantic Pack. Good people. Wicked loud," he said with a grin. "But they always dragged me back.

"The school was . . . hard. They wanted to create soldiers. Most of the Conks—that's what they called us—were human. Few of us shifters. One kid's dad was friends with mine, so that's probably where mine got the idea. They preached being a unit. Being the same. As long as you were rich enough to pay the tuition, of course, and would keep to your own—support your own—when you got out."

Alexei talked so rarely—and never for this long—that Lulu and I had gone silent and still to watch and listen. Connor, who'd apparently heard the story before, continued to eat.

"The upperclassmen still picked their allies, their enemies. They didn't like me, but they respected my money. So the hazing was relatively minor. Locking us in rooms during dining hall hours, so we ate whatever cheap crap we could find. Hot sauce made it better."

And that, I thought, explained a lot about Alexei.

"A couple of them beat the shit out of a maintenance guy for getting a scratch on someone's car. He'd been taking down an old tree, and the car was parked illegally. School fired the worker, who probably needed the job, because why else put up with us assholes?"

"What about the ones who hurt him?" I asked.

Alexei met my gaze and his eyes were hard. Alexei often seemed stoic, but I wasn't sure I'd seen him this coldly furious. "They paid off the damage to the car, apologized for the trouble."

"Take care of your own," Connor said grimly, and Alexei nodded.

"None of them needed caring for. Not with the privilege they had. But yeah. That was the attitude."

"Is that when you left?" Lulu asked.

"It was the last time," he said. "I was gone nearly two weeks before they found me. I'm still not sure how, but wouldn't be surprised if a Conk ratted me out. I happened to pass by the maintenance worker's house when they hauled me back. He was outside playing with his kids. Didn't look defeated. Still bruised, even two weeks later, but carrying on." He shrugged. "I figured he was as good a model as any. So I decided that's what I'd do.

"I got through school. Did a little damage to the assholes on the way up when I could, of course. I knew the name, the degree, would serve me in the long run, even if I hated it then. So I learned to stick it out. Take the lessons I could." His cold smile went absolutely feral. "I saw to it that the local district attorney—he was friends with the maintenance worker—got a whiff whenever one of the assholes pulled something. They all left with criminal records their parents couldn't expunge."

"You learned to handle yourself," I said. "And to takes steps when you could."

He looked up at me, nodded. "I learned about loyalty. And hot sauce."

Silently, Lulu got up, went to the bar, and spoke to the waitress. When she came back, she was bearing another small bottle of red sauce.

"Eat up," she said, and took her seat again.

It wasn't exactly a proclamation of love, but it sure sounded like a beginning.

We all went back to the town house. Lulu stayed over sometimes if Alexei was there, and Alexei stayed over sometimes if Lulu was there.

We still had old magic to understand and Pack interlopers to manage, but Rose was safe, or so she said, and I hadn't been clawed by ghouls, so I considered the night a raging success. I wasn't going to think any more about demons until tomorrow.

Connor started a fire. He and Alexei reclined on the sofa. Lulu and I sat on the floor watching the flames roil, and let the heat soak into our bones.

When the fire began to burn down, Lulu yawned with both arms over her head, then rose. "I'm going upstairs."

She walked up the stairs, where the town house's guest rooms were located.

Alexei cleared his throat. "I'll go check on her," he said, and followed quietly.

"'Check on' covers a lot of ground," Connor said with a smile when the guest room door had closed on them both.

"I don't want to think about what ground they're covering, thanks. I want to enjoy this fire and the absence of ghost ooze in this room." And since I was feeling warm and relaxed, I smiled at him. "And possibly a prince."

He stretched his arms on the back of the sofa, and his grin was as wicked as they came. "Any particular prince?"

I rose and walked toward him, his gaze on mine growing hungrier with each step. I stopped just outside arm's reach. "Do you have a look book?" I mimed flipping pages. "That way, I can choose the one I want."

"A dangerous game," he said, a growl beneath the words, and stood up.

I grabbed his shirt, tugged him forward until our bodies were aligned. A wicked grin slowly lifted his lips.

"I'll take this one," I said, and nipped his bottom lip. Not hard enough to draw blood, but enough to remind him who and what we were.

He kissed me then, tangling his fingers in my hair. The kiss heated, evolved, until desire rose and we were both nearly panting from want.

And remembering we weren't the only ones alone in the house, I grabbed his hand, and pulled him toward the stairs. The master bedroom was on the third floor, and we hustled like we were being chased.

I beat him to the bedroom, turned around, and grinned. "I win."

He stepped forward, all arrogance and swagger, and looked down at me. "We'll see about that." It was a prediction . . . and a dare.

I wet my lips, and then we were on each other.

I pulled the shirt over Connor's head, ran my hands up his strong body, felt the shiver of skin beneath my hands, the rumble of the growl in his throat. He pulled me against him, hard and ready, and melded his mouth to mine, teeth and lips and tongue enticing, inspiring, and biting with just enough force to have me whimpering.

"Mine," he said, then tugged my hair just enough to have me arching back, kissed my neck. Shoes were toed off, and then his hands traveled up, reached my breasts, and ignited a new kind of fire. Then his hands were at my waist and pushing clothing lower until I stood naked before him.

He went to his knees and looked up at me like I was a queen. And I felt like royalty, bathed in love and magic and the awe in his eyes.

I'd fought for him, for his people. And while that wasn't the only reason we were in this room—or in this position—he would offer his gratitude.

His mouth found my center, and the world seemed to wobble. He chuckled with male pride and set to his work. He cherished me, worshipped me, until the fire he'd created subsumed me and left me boneless.

Then his jeans were down, his hand inside, pumping.

Arousal fired again. "Connor," I said, and my voice was hoarse.

"You do this to me," he said. "The desire. The wanting. Like no one else."

I moved back from him and toward his bed, beckoned him forward with a fingertip. He growled his approval, came to the edge of the bed, and hovered over me, those strong arms corded as he held up his weight. His grin had gone wicked again as I ran hands down his body and up again, savoring taut skin flushed with desire, muscles that were hard as granite. And the length of him, strong and eager and ready.

"On your knees," he said, and I turned over. I heard the slide of clothes, and then his body was against mine, hard and hot and aroused.

"Now," I said, and pushed back against him.

He plunged with a groan that nearly sent me over the edge, began moving with strength and finesse that made my knees wobble, and began to build that heat all over again. His teeth found my neck, and he nipped, a hand moving to my breasts, to my core, until we were moving together, minds and hearts and bodies aligned, and pleasure swamped us both.

Stars fell and the world felt right again.

EIGHT

A hot shower, a hot boyfriend, and no demon activity during the day made for a wonderful wake-up. And then I found Lulu in the town house's otherwise empty kitchen sitting morosely on a stool.

"What's wrong?"

"My parents are flying back tomorrow," Lulu said.

I stopped short. "They're coming here now? With all this"—I gestured vaguely to the city outside—"demon possibility?"

"I know, right?" She put down the screen she'd been perusing, walked to the fridge, pulled out a carton of orange juice. She took it to the island, sat down on a stool. But didn't open it. Didn't drink. I didn't presume to fully understand the complexities of their relationship, but I knew a battle when I saw one.

"And how do you feel about them coming out here?" I asked.

"I'll be glad to see them."

The tone of her voice wasn't a ringing endorsement. "How long has it been?" I'd only been back in Chicago for a few months now, and they hadn't been back since I'd been here.

"Nearly a year."

"Parents are a tricky thing," I said after a moment.

"You mean because a demon is maybe preparing to rampage through Chicago and spread god knows what kind of dark magic around here? Yeah. I feel uncomfortable about a demon being in

Chicago. I feel downright concerned about my mother being in Chicago while a demon is here. Especially with her . . . sensitivities."

To dark magic, she meant.

She trailed off, rubbed her temples. "I clearly still have some conflicting feelings where my mother is concerned."

"Why is she coming now? I mean, assume my mother told her what was going on, but why fly out?"

"She thinks she can help with those texts Paige was working on."

That had my attention. "What texts?"

"Have you not checked your screen?"

I looked around, realized I'd left it downstairs last night in our . . . haste. I grabbed it, found a message from my mother: THE LIBRARIAN FOUND A PORTFOLIO OF OLD DOCS DATED AFTER GREAT FIRE. STRANGE LANGUAGE, AND POSSIBLY SPELLS. PAIGE WORKING TO TRANSLATE.

I looked up at Lulu. "Your mom thinks she can help?"

"She's going to try. Paige sent her some images, but Mom thinks they don't make sense as written, and they probably need some kind of magical overlay. Paige hasn't done that before, so Mom offered to come out and work with her."

Lulu looked at me for a moment, seemed almost to say something. And instead opened the juice and drank from the carton. She was still holding something back. Something heavy that she seemed to want to confess but couldn't.

Monster nudged me a bit, just enough to remind me of its presence and the similarity between me and Lulu. That didn't make me feel better. It just made me feel dishonest.

But Lulu shook it off. "She's volunteered Cadogan House as a meeting spot. We can have dinner and whatever."

"That sounds great," I said, making it a statement, and assertion, and not open for negotiation. I wasn't thrilled at the idea of walking back into the House with Mallory there—not when monster was so interested in the sword, and she could probably see more of the magic than my parents. But doing tough things for the people we loved was part of that love. If she had any suspicions, I could play them off. I was getting better at that.

Still in my hand, my screen buzzed, and I nearly jumped. And found a message from an unexpected sender: SERIOUSLY NEED TO TALK ABOUT THE MAGIC, read the short text from Jonathan Black.

I only then realized I'd totally forgotten to respond to his message from yesterday. Informants weren't much use if you didn't let them inform.

Connor and Alexei came downstairs. "Why is your brow all furrowed?"

I looked up at Connor. "What?"

"Furrowed," he said again, and kissed the spot between my eyebrows. "Why?"

"Jonathan Black wants to talk," I said. "He messaged yesterday and I forgot to respond. So I should probably talk to him."

"I don't like him."

"I don't think I like him, either. But he has supernatural connections, and we need supernatural information." I sent Black a response, agreeing to meet him, then put my screen away. "Pack?" I asked him.

"All quiet," he said. "But the night is young."

Jonathan Black's mansion was on Chicago's Prairie Avenue, where Gilded Age entrepreneurs had made their homes. It was just south of downtown, not far from the lake. In terms of atmosphere, its old and elegant wealth was about as far away from the Pack's HQ as one could get. I'd taken an Auto, which pulled up in front of his stone house half an hour after his message.

Jonathan answered the door in a dark button-down and slacks. He was fit, with sun-kissed skin, blond hair, and ears that pointed slightly at the top. He wasn't hiding his magic today, and it prickled in the air like dust motes through a beam of light.

"Thanks for getting here so quickly."

"I was in the neighborhood," I lied. But he wasn't lying in wait for me in the dark, so that was at least some improvement.

He didn't look like he believed me but gestured grandly. "Come in."

I walked into his beautiful historic home, with its crown molding, tall ceilings, and fireplaces in every room.

"I need to know what happened two nights ago." There was confidence and demand in his voice. As if he refused to consider the possibility that I'd refuse to answer. No magic in it, at least. But I wasn't that easy.

"What happened two nights ago?" I asked, all innocence.

"There was a lot of magic. I figured the Ombuds might have been called."

I cocked my head at him. "How did you know there was a lot of magic?"

His look was bland. "Am I being interrogated?"

"Am I?"

That had his lips twitching. "Touché. I could feel the magic but didn't think much of it. It's Chicago. And then one of my clients called. They felt it and didn't care for it."

Referring to his unnamed "clients" was generally his way of refusing to share his sources or the details of his knowledge. "Who are your clients?"

"Entitled to their privacy," he said with a smile.

"What kind of Sups are they?"

"The kind who are entitled to their privacy," he said again.

"You want information, you give information," I said. "That's the deal. It's always the deal."

He snorted. "What am I, a supernatural informant?"

"You called me," I reminded him, and that had the smile falling. "You said you felt magic. What kind of magic?"

He closed his eyes as if replaying the memory. "I felt . . . a tremor. Like a muscle twitch but more. A kind of wave that passed through me."

The gate was miles from Black's house. Cadogan House was closer, and no one had mentioned feeling magic. Was it an indication of his power? Or sensitivity to it?

"What do you know about demons?"

That drained the rest of the color from his face. "That's not what I expected you to ask."

"Then how about this: In 1872, a demon was kicked out of Chicago, and magical protections were supposedly erected to keep it out."

He went very still.

"You've heard this story before," I surmised.

He ran a hand through this hair. "I want a drink," he said, voice now irritable. "You want a drink?"

"No." But I followed him into the kitchen, which gleamed with marble and glass and cabinets that stretched to the ceiling. A round iron bistro table with a glass top and two Parisian-style rattan chairs sat against the opposite wall. I took a seat, had a nearly tangible memory of time spent at French cafés. But those nights were behind me.

"You cook," I said, noting the professional-quality gas stove as he pulled an ornate bottle and glass from a cabinet, poured a finger of something dark green.

"I find it relaxing." Jonathan downed the liquid, poured another one.

"Is that absinthe?"

"It is," he said. He held out the glass. "Want?" he asked again.

"No. Tell me what you know about demons and wards. And

don't bullshit me," I added when I could all but read a "my clients" excuse in his eyes.

He put the empty glass on the countertop, and crystal rang against stone. Then he moved to a cabinet, opened a container of thin sesame breadsticks, offered one. I took it, crunched off the end.

He took one himself, sat at the table across from me. "I don't know much. I've heard rumors the city has a certain defense system against supernaturals. But that's all I know."

He watched me carefully for a moment, trying to gauge if that presumption was correct. But I was Ethan Sullivan's daughter. I'd long ago perfected the vampire poker face.

"And?" I prompted.

"And that's it. You're saying it was a demon."

"I'm saying a demon supposedly tried to get into Chicago. The magic you felt was an attempt to keep it out."

He frowned. "Is this about what happened by South Gate? The *Tribune* said the damage was due to a fight between supernaturals."

I hadn't read the story but wasn't surprised to learn the details released by the mayor's office had been vague. That would be much easier for the public to swallow than ANTIQUE MAGICAL FENCE FAILS; DEMON LOOSE IN CITY.

"It's related," I said. "Who told you the protections existed?"

His smile was thin. "You know what I'm going to say. My clients."

"What services do you provide to your clients?"

"Confidential ones."

"Were any of your clients in Chicago when the protections were put into place?" I was asking questions quickly, trying to keep him off balance. Theo had taught me that one.

"Not that I'm aware of."

Time to test our very uncomfortable theory. "How long have you known Rose Doerman?"

He blinked. "Who's Rose Doerman?"

The bafflement on his face looked genuine and might have been the first honest response he'd given since I walked through the door.

"A person of interest," I said. "Do you know any demons?"

"I don't cavort with demons."

"That's not what I asked."

He crunched into his breadstick. "Maybe I should have beaten you senseless."

Second honest thing, I thought, and remembered that he often chose violence. "You could try again," I said, and smiled—with fangs. "But it didn't work out so well for you the first time. I don't think you'd fare any better the second."

Black grunted, crossed his arms, slouched in his seat. I just watched him, one bite of breadstick at a time. He watched me back, gaze as narrowed and petulant as his posture. And I knew better than to trust a Sup whose moods changed so quickly, and for whom "petulant" seemed to be the default.

"I don't cavort with demons," he said again.

"Do you know any demon sigils? Have books of demon sigils?" Unlikely but worth the ask.

"No. My clients contacted me," he added after a moment, "because they felt a pull on the ley lines."

Ley lines were the lines of power that ran across the world. Three ran across Chicago, making it unusually magically active, as any Sup could tell you. And fairies, especially, as they'd tried to harness the added power of the two spots in the city where the ley lines crossed each other—including beneath Chicago's Grant Park.

"What about them?" I asked.

"The protections would have to be constantly powered in order to stay in alert mode—watching for the demon, I mean. And they've been in alert mode for more than century. The ley lines are the only magical power source consistent and powerful enough for that."

And a source the Guardians didn't think would run out or change too much in the interim. At least until the fairies started messing with things . . .

"So they're probably powering the defense system. And your clients felt more power being drawn from the ley lines the night South Gate was triggered?"

He nodded. "The ley lines hold enormous power. Yes, they're strong enough to power a defense system, as you called it. But that also means they could be used with weapons."

"Especially if there's a built-in link to the ley lines," I finished. "Something that's already been built to tap into it. And a demon might be just the type of creature interested in using the ley lines for its own purposes."

He nodded.

"Well, that's terrifying." Appetite gone, I put down the rest of my breadstick.

A concussive *boom* suddenly shook the house and everything in it, and light poured through the open windows. His drink was abandoned as we ran through the house and outside . . . and stared at the pillar of light that had burst into the sky a few blocks west, apparently from something on the ground.

"What the hell?" Jonathan murmured. Surprised, he sent his own shower of magic into the air.

This wasn't the same as the gate, at least not that I could see or hear from several blocks away. No green, no ghosts, no howling. But it was another bout of big magic. Was it a ward? Had the demon made its way into the city and triggered another defense?

"Call the CPD," I told him, "and stay here."

"Where are you going? You can't run toward that. It's dangerous."

"Yeah, that's my job and the point."

I took off at top speed. After a moment's delay, I could hear him pounding behind me, despite my orders that he stay at the house. I had no idea if he could take care of himself in a situation like this, but at least he was calling 911 as he ran.

I started a terse message to Theo: MAGICAL EVENT WEST OF PRAIRIE AVE HIST DIST. DEMON? WARD? I'M MOVING CLOSER.

And then I stopped short when lightning burst from the pillar of light, forking as it reached toward the sky, illuminating clouds and buildings.

If this was a demon ward, it had moved far beyond stone-throwing ghosts. Far, far beyond. Fear clawed at me but didn't seem to bother monster this time.

Safe inside you, it told me, apparently thinking I was a strong enough shell to keep it safe.

I die, you die. I guessed, but had no idea if that was true, mostly because I had no idea—or not a certain one—what monster was. But the sentiment had it coming to attention, and I could feel it stretch inside me like a protective layer, offering me what strength it could.

Much nicer, I complimented as the earth shuddered with magical thunder that rolled across the neighborhood, bringing humans to front porches and lights to windows.

I realized when Black reached me that I'd stopped running to stare at the sky and looked down at the unsent message on my screen.

LOOK FOR LIGHTNING, I added, sent it, and started running again.

Prairie Avenue Historic District was only a few blocks long and wide; west of the neighborhood was an artsy community of small shops, artisan coffeehouses, and dive bars. And on a night like tonight—with the Sox playing only a couple of miles away and the weather perfect—the area was full of patrons, many of whom now thronged sidewalks and stopped traffic to stare at the seemingly infinite beam of light and the lightning it had spawned.

I pushed through the humans, Black behind me, to get closer.

The beam had sprung from an old brick warehouse, one of the few buildings in the area that hadn't yet been renovated. Its banks of windows had been shattered, presumably when the light had burst from its belly like an alien. Something roared machinelike in the building's innards. It was presumably the source of the light and the film of old magic.

The light was nearly blinding. Since I'd never been human, I'd never lived in sunlight. I'd never seen the world so well illuminated and found I didn't like the sharp shadows it created. The way it highlighted the pale cheeks of humans in shock, the gum and dirt on the sidewalk. The way it made glittering jewels of the deadly glass that littered the ground. Darkness helped to hide ugly things; light helped to reveal them.

The building hadn't been the only thing damaged. At least a dozen people were down on the sidewalk, screaming or unconscious due to injuries caused by the glass and metal and brick that had exploded from the building. The scent of human blood was strong but held no appeal. Not when it had been gathered in fear and pain.

At least there was no chill in the air this time. No green fog and—thank god—no wispy hands reaching, slithering, but the sensation of old magic was undeniable.

What the hell was this? Other than terrifyingly dangerous.

"We have to move them away from here," I said, and pointed Black to a small parking lot in front of the shops beside the warehouse. "There," I told him, unsure if he'd actually help but having no one else to order around. "Let's corral them over there."

Without waiting for a response, I ran to the first human, began assessing. Two men with blood smeared across pale faces nicked by glass helped a hysterical woman on the sidewalk to her feet.

There was a cut on her leg, and one had thought to use the woman's scarf to stanch the bleeding.

I pulled out my badge. "Get her to the parking lot," I said, shielding my eyes as I faced the light, "and away from this. There might be more explosions."

I was grateful they didn't argue but moved the woman along. I moved to the next group of humans, nearly punched a cop who put a hand on my shoulders—I was still ghost-punchy—and showed him my badge, told him about the parking lot, the need to clear the area. The risk of more damage and injuries.

"Other units are stuck in the damn traffic," he said. "It's stopped two solid miles out. CPD is working on a perimeter."

"Work faster," I said when the roaring inside the building grew louder. I could feel the charge in the air, and I knew what was coming.

"Take cover!" I screamed, and human shrieks filled the air as lightning forked from the beam of light again.

Patience had said the wards were triggered by the demon's proximity. If this was some kind of ward, it appeared to have lost track of the demon, because the lightning stretched across the neighborhood in every direction like claws scratching a path toward their prey.

The world grew brighter as the forks descended, as if they were devouring the darkness itself. And then hell erupted. The strikes made contact with earth, sending *boom*s across the neighborhood, sending fire into the air. A long, narrow staff of lightning struck a vehicle twenty feet away with a crack of sound, the force pushing it onto its side, where the vehicle shook with power and stank of burning rubber and bad magic.

If this was a ward, was the demon near?

"There's someone in there!" a voice called out, and I jolted from thought, ran forward to help them roll the vehicle over again.

"On three!" I said, as we grunted and strained to right the car.

It had only just bounced onto all four tires when Black shouted my name. And there was warning in it.

"Elisa!"

I had no time to react. And then Black was on me, shoving me down onto concrete. I hit the sidewalk hard enough to rattle my bones, and felt the angry pop in my foot as my boot struck a wedge of concrete. His body fell atop mine some milliseconds later, and I instantaneously wondered if he was fighting me again. Until lightning struck the spot where I'd been standing, fracturing and buckling the asphalt so planks of it stood up four feet in the air.

I'd have been disintegrated.

"Damn," I said quietly, my gratitude at being shoved aside dulling even the new pain in my foot.

"Sorry," Jonathan said, rolling off me. He sat up, rubbing the elbow where he'd probably struck concrete. "Are you okay?"

"I'll live," I said. "Thanks." And felt momentarily guilty for assuming he'd tried to take me out.

He nodded. "I owed you one."

"Yeah, you did." I stood up, felt the sharp pinch in my foot, could feel it swelling in my boot. Broken, but I was alive, and I'd heal in a few hours. I could ignore the pain and hobble until then.

I glanced back at Black. "You okay?"

He nodded. "Is this one of those demon protections?"

"That would be my guess."

"Then where's the damn demon?" he asked.

"Nearby" was all I knew. But I was beginning to wonder if the Guardians' bark was worse than the demons' bite. After all, the demon hadn't harmed us, at least not yet.

Instinct had me looking up, and I saw the woman standing across the street in heels and a long coat. Monster felt the magic an instant before I did, and I felt its shuddering fear.

The demon, its camouflaging magic now gone, was ringed in sharp and grating and sulfurous magic. It had shed its disguise.

Connor had been right. We'd missed the obvious demon candidate.

It was Rose.

NINE

She stood beneath the stretching arms of a tree denuded of leaves by the coming autumn. She wore a short black dress and high dark heels beneath a long, fluid jacket that shimmered like bronze and shifted in the wind. It had a high collar of delicate feathers that wisped around her face. Her hair was down and waving now, and new highlights gleamed in the streetlight. The injuries we'd seen a few nights ago were gone now. Had she healed quickly, or had they been faked?

I stared at her for a full twenty seconds, trying to make sense of the last few days. And hoping against hope I was wrong. Or, if I was right, that she wore her sigil on a chain, and I could simply snatch it away.

Then I was running toward her, darting around people in the street. I reached her, stopped short. If she was surprised to see me, she didn't show it.

"At least your message to Roger was honest," I said flatly. "You're clearly alive."

"Clearly." There was no fear in her now, no trembling. But she glanced at the sky, then again, as if waiting for lightning to strike, figuratively and literally. "I plan to stay that way."

"You lied to us," I said. "You lied to Roger." And I already knew the debriefing was going to suck.

"Everyone lies," Rose said. "I just happen to be especially good at it." She lowered her gaze, glanced at me. "Combine a convincing backstory and a pitiable character, and humans will believe it. I had plenty of time to plan while I waited for my chance."

"To use us to cross the gate? You thought, what, that we'd battle our way through for you?"

"The timing wasn't by choice," she said. "I was discovered, you might say, by my former colleagues. I needed out of Edentown and knew I'd need help. Or ballast, at any rate. The time I'd spent nurturing my relationship with the Ombuds' office paid off. You battled, so thank you." Her smile went thin, and the loathing in her eyes had goose bumps lifting on my skin. So very different from the last time I'd had that reaction. There was nothing similar between her magic and that of the Pack's.

"How did you know the gate would keep you out?"

"I'm a demon. I can tell."

"How?"

She rolled her eyes.

"Why are you here? What do you want? Why did you wait so long to come back to the place that exiled you?"

"Do you really think I'm going to answer those questions? Like some spineless human criminal in an interrogation room?" She leaned in, and I felt the hot and bitter edge of her magic. "I'm here because you let me in," she said, each word an indictment of me. And I felt the truth of it in my gut.

Mechanical thunder rumbled. "But I'm afraid I don't have time to talk right now. The weather has taken a turn."

With a *ping* of steel, I unsheathed my sword, extended it. "You'll be going nowhere but a cage."

She laughed, the sound hoarse and smoky. "You're fighting alone, and we're surrounded by humans I'm sure you don't want damaged in the onslaught. What risk could you possibly present to me?"

It was my turn to feel that spark of concern. Not because I was alone; this wasn't the first time my sword would be the only one swinging. But because I didn't know the full extent of her power, and that made me nervous.

Of course, my fear didn't really matter. She was here, and it was my job to stop her—while injuring as few people as possible.

I flicked the tip of my blade, snagged one of the feathers around her face. Her gaze followed as it floated through the air. "Would you like to see what I can do?" I asked. I figured my best bet was keeping her contained—or keeping her from doing any more damage—until backup arrived.

"I have seen it," she reminded me. "You served your purpose, but it wasn't especially impressive."

She cocked her head, stared at me with focus so sharp it felt she might incise my very soul. She took a step toward me, each moment sending a wave of perfume in my direction. It was strong—rich and musky. But beneath it, ashes—dark and bitter. She sniffed delicately, as if scenting the air.

It wasn't the first time I'd seen a Sup wrinkle their nose and lift it to the wind. I'd done it myself, and I was dating a wolf. Magic had scent, undeniably. But this didn't look like mere curiosity, more a searching of her own. She was looking for something. Trying to find something.

And then joy blossomed on her face, and her smile widened.

"You're the one. The vampire who popped out of her mother like Venus from the foam. You are chaos," she said, narrowing her gaze as she looked into my eyes.

Monster skittered backward. I also wanted to shrink back from her intrusive stare but refused to move.

"The first vampire to be born," she continued. "The most unique. The change. The mutation." She smiled thinly. "The cataclysm. Vampires will never be the same. Not now."

She was right that I was different; I was the only vampire born, not made from another human by biting and blood.

"I didn't choose how I came into this world."

"Perhaps not." She watched me again, and I wondered how much of monster she would see. "I bet the Masters hate you, don't they? You interrupt their order, their understanding."

"None of that matters here," I said. But, oh, how right she was.

"Of course it does. I want to see what happens when I throw chaos your way. When everything is taken away from you, as it was for me. For I see you, girl. You like your rules. Your boundaries. Your space. You try to inflict order. But you can't order chaos. And I don't even need to move mountains or drown the sun. I only need to let humans do human things."

The scents of smoke and sulfur rose. Demon scents, which meant she was doing something again.

"Put down that fucking sword!" a human yelled, and I looked back.

Two guys, both bulky gym types, were barreling down the street toward us. The one on the left pushed a man out of his way, sending him sprawling over a park bench.

I'd have thought they were demons, given the self-centeredness, if I hadn't smelled the human on them immediately, at least behind the pulsing of demonic magic.

"Help," Rose said weakly when they reached us, using the same voice she'd used in the SUV. Fury curled my lip.

"The fuck is this?" one human asked, gesturing to my sword.

"Everything's fine," I said. "I'm from the Chicago Ombudsman's office, but I can't get to my badge right now. She's the one who's caused all this damage. And I'm going to take her into custody." Or, god help me, I was going to try.

The humans looked between us, from the woman in leather with a weapon to the woman in feathers and heels and spot-on lipstick. And they chose to glower at me.

"What's with the sword?" one of them said. "You some kind of samurai?"

Monster wanted to show them exactly what kind of Sup she was. But this was not the best time for paranormal show-and-tell.

"I'm a vampire," I said flatly. "She's a demon, and she's wanted for the destruction at South Gate."

"Doubtful," said the guy closest to me. Average height, stocky of build, square of jaw. He didn't believe me, and there was a glint in his eyes that I didn't much like. Why the hell was he targeting me?

"She's a demon," I said again, pouring as much soothing glamour into the sentence as I could, until my skin fairly rippled with magic.

But instead of soothing him, his lip curled and his gaze went hotter. He looked even angrier, which wasn't how glamour was supposed to work.

Chaos, came monster's explanation.

The demon is doing this? I asked, trying to calculate how that could have happened. *Did she make them angry?*

"You think you're better than me because you have that sword?" the human asked and, without waiting for a reply, started forward. I held out a hand to him so I could keep my sword pointed at Rose, but he slapped my hand away.

My anger was rising, too, so I let him see the silvering of my eyes—the sign of a vampire in high emotion. Maybe he'd get the warning, and that would be enough to work through whatever magic Rose was using.

"Back off," I demanded, but he roared his apparently endless fury and swung out. The shot glanced off my arm, and would have done a lot of damage if not for my late pivot. But I'd focused on him, not the second guy, who managed to grab my arm.

The first guy came in again. I jerked my arm away, and before I could give him a shot of my own, he was flying through the air. He hit the sidewalk with a thud, looked up once, and then his eyes rolled back.

I looked back, found Black shaking his fisted hand.

"Thanks," I said, still trying to understand what the fuck had just happened.

"Is she—" he began to ask, but someone revved a vehicle behind us, loud and insistent, and the sound drowned out the rest.

And then it was barreling toward us. I pushed the other human out of the way, landed hard on the sidewalk, which wasn't any better than the asphalt. Black dragged the unconscious one out of the way just as the car struck a gleaming yellow hydrant on the driver's side at just the right angle to send it into the air.

"What the fuck?" the human I'd saved murmured, staring as we all did as the car rammed into the scaffolding and then through it, burying itself in the corner of the building. Bricks toppled, and the scaffolding's supports began to buckle at the point of impact, and the metal began to whine as physics and gravity worked their particular magic.

There was a tremendous *groan* of failing steel, along with *cracks* as loud as gunshots as the brackets that temporarily tied scaffolding to building began to burst, sending bolts through the air like bullets. They smashed car windows, plate glass in buildings across the street. Humans screamed, began running.

"It's going!" someone shouted. "Get out of the way!"

The scaffolding's lower level began to fall like dominos, bringing the upper floors of metal with it.

Someone else screamed, and I looked down, saw the vehicle's passenger-side door open a foot. A woman reached out. "Please!" she yelled.

I didn't have a choice.

I ran away from Rose, whom I could still feel behind me, and wrenched open the door, pulled the woman bodily out of the car—ignoring her screams and the screech of falling metal—and heaved us both to the sidewalk.

I was making a career of falling down. And that shit was beginning to hurt.

I covered her head with my torso, covered my head with an arm, and nearly lost my breath when something hit the back of my hip in the cascade of falling brick and steel. Glass added a high note, probably the building's first-floor windows.

The crash and vibration unsettled more of the building, which was apparently in need of rehab anyway, given the scaffolding, and slabs of brick began falling, tossed down into the pile like boulders in an avalanche.

The sound was tremendous, and it was followed by a moment of equally stunning silence and thick dust that scattered the streetlights and covered everything. And then the shouting began again in earnest.

I heard a sob and pushed up—and was nearly sent to the ground again by the bolt of pain through my hip. A rod of scaffolding lay nearby, the apparent perpetrator. Tears flooded my eyes, but I sucked it in. Pain and feelings later. For now, survival.

Black offered me a hand. I took it, climbed to my feet, looked down at the woman. Tears had tracked clean lines in her dusty face, and she was scraped all to hell and would have a rainbow of bruises tomorrow. But she looked to be in one piece.

The building, on the other hand, had seen better days. The front half had all but collapsed, and the rest didn't look especially stable.

"Slowly," Black told the woman, and we each offered her a hand as she sat up, her movements slow and deliberate even as people swarmed around us to remove rubble, to help others. And in some cases, to fight over damaged cars or loot pulled from the building's smashed windows.

"Just breathe," I said. She nodded, and I could see the gratefulness in her eyes. And then she glanced back and saw the destruction she'd escaped from—and the pile of rubble that now contained her car. And would have covered her.

"You're okay," I said as the sobs began in earnest, and waved an arm at a nearby med tech. "She was in the car," I told them. "She needs to be looked over."

"You look pretty busted up yourself," he said, with typical midwestern frankness.

"I'll heal," I said, and limped back to the spot where I'd left Rose and was baffled to find she was still there. She hadn't so much as moved from her position, despite my giving her ample opportunity to get away.

That surprise faded when I saw the hunger in her eyes—and recognized it. As Patience had said, she was feeding off the chaos—the pandemonium she'd spawned with a flick of her hand. This was her power, I thought, as two women pushed a gurney between us and settled the woman from the vehicle upon it. This was the destruction she could wreak. This was the power that had her exiled from Chicago.

That should have been enough to have me turning back or looking for backup, because what could a bit of steel do against her? But I didn't stand still, because that wasn't my nature. And I was too furious anyway. I walked forward, one slow step after another, until only five feet separated us.

She was scenting the air again. For what? Is that why she'd come back to Chicago? To claim some treasure she'd left behind? Or find some treasure she hadn't been able to claim the first time?

"Get out of my city."

It took a moment for her to drag her gaze away, look at me again. "No. I entered here, and my business is not done."

"I don't care. Either you leave, or I'm going to send you back to wherever you came from. I'm going to be the one who stops you."

The dull roar of the magic machine began to sound again, recharged and ready for another round of lightning. Based on the last one, we had only a couple of minutes before lightning groped for her again.

I couldn't tell if Rose was aware of the danger or was worried about it. She cocked her head at me, brow furrowed as if I were a puzzle she didn't know how to solve. "Why would you try to stop me? Why do vampires hate other supernaturals so much? Is it because they aspire to be human? Because they miss being human? That self-loathing is a very unattractive quality."

"We don't hate all supernaturals," I said with a thin smile. "Only the assholes."

The roaring grew louder, and this time Rose glanced up and looked mildly concerned. I had a visceral memory of her screaming and sobbing from the back of the SUV, and my anger sparked again.

She flicked a hand again, and I went on guard.

Behind me, a human screamed, then slammed a tree limb into the window of a building to our west. Then again, then a third time, until the glass spider-webbed and cracked and imploded inward. Others picked up bricks and chunks of asphalt deposited by damage to building and street, began heaving them at each other.

"Stop," I said, looking back at Rose, and tried to appeal to her self-centeredness. "If you destroy Chicago, what kingdom will be left for you?"

Her smile was . . . malevolent. "There will always be a human looking for a fight," she said. "And they're rarely the only ones."

I assumed she meant Sups and realized I hadn't seen any others beyond me, her, and Black in this chaos.

And then I heard a new sound. A different sound.

I spun around, sword raised. This time, it wasn't humans or vehicles aiming for me.

It was a very big cat. Tall and sleek with black fur, and nearly eight feet of muscled power. A black panther, or so it looked to me.

I froze, trying to understand what I was seeing. Was it a shifter? A hallucination? Because I hadn't seen many panthers in the South Loop recently. I swallowed as it advanced, teeth bared and hissing, and maybe for the first time thought fondly of the smaller Eleanor of Aquitaine.

"Stay back," I said, and sliced my katana through the air, the move sending a fresh wash of pain through my hip.

The panther ignored it, swiped (its paw as big as my head), and made an unearthly sound that was eerily human and had the hairs on the back of my neck lifting.

Zoo, I belatedly thought. The South Side Zoo. I hadn't been there in years—there weren't many animals left out after dark— but they'd had big cats. Had Rose managed the zoo escape? Or had she somehow directed the panther here to this spot and made it eager to attack a person?

Or was it just more of the improbable being made . . . actual?

Monster was eager to fight this one and tried to urge me forward, dared me to slice the panther through.

The cat swept its paw through the air again, this time catching me on the arm, raking its enormous claws across tender skin. I must have screamed and loosened my grip enough to allow monster to take control, to turn my eyes red.

The panther hesitated only for a moment before stalking toward me, hunger in its eyes. Monster spun my sword as my blood *plinked* to the sidewalk. It managed a slice against the panther's front leg, putting the scent of new blood into the air.

But that only pissed it off. Its growl was low and deep, the warning obvious.

Another sour breeze lifted—the scent of demon magic. And chaos struck again.

Something hit me in the back, sent me stumbling forward. The bright shock of pain sent monster into the back corner of my consciousness. A brick, I thought. I'd been struck by a human with a damn brick.

I nearly dropped into the panther's waiting jowls but managed to pivot and hit the ground on my back. Close enough to smell the musky tang of its fur. It screamed again and bounded.

I managed to get my sword up, its spine against the panther's belly, pushing with all my strength to keep its snapping teeth and those damned claws off of me. I gathered all my strength—and the strength that monster could contribute—and shoved it off me. It struck concrete, then rose again, limping on its wounded leg and hissing with fury. Rose might have been directing it before, but now it was genuinely pissed.

I kept my sword in front of me, climbed to my feet, and waited for it to launch.

And then there was a different sound, a new smell.

The padding of heavy feet. A low growl. And suddenly beside me, the thick fury of a gray wolf.

Connor, I thought with a mix of relief and fear.

"Rose is the demon," I said. "I think she's influencing the panther."

He sniffed, raised his muzzle toward me, noted the blood on my arm, and snapped his head back to the panther, lips pulled back and teeth bared with obvious fury.

I looked back at Rose. Once again, she hadn't moved, presumably because she'd been busy drinking in the energy from the cacophony she'd orchestrated. But she did look surprised, and not a little worried. Patience had said demons didn't like dogs. I guess that feeling extended to their lupine cousins. Was it Connor? Did the wolf frighten her? Because we could use that.

The panther screamed again as it faced its new foe. Connor was bigger than the cat, but they were both plenty large. The cat bounded and Connor followed suit, so they hit each other midair. The panther clawed and Connor snapped, tried to catch the nape of the panther's neck in his own enormous teeth. They grappled, and the panther screamed its disturbingly human sound.

The air snapped with energy, and the ward unleashed its wrath.

"Take cover!" I screamed, and huddled back against the building's wall beneath a narrow ledge that extended over the sidewalk.

Even the panther could feel the energy in the air. It wrenched itself from Connor, slunk behind a stand of shrubs. Connor came to me, crouched at my side beneath the overhang.

The lightning came at us like a barrage of arrows: fast, furious, and deadly. Maybe because the three of us were so close to each other—demon, shifter, vampire—the barrage seemed worse, stronger, more than the others. Concentrated weaponry intended to annihilate its target and damn the consequences. The bolts speared into buildings, sidewalk, road, vehicles—sending concrete, asphalt, glass, and metal flying. I heard a human's cry some yards away, knew they'd been struck, and was newly furious at the Guardians and the demon who'd tripped their infernal "defenses."

Rose had gone absolutely still, but either the lightning or the beam of light had given her skin a strange green cast. To make her noticeable, I guessed. Either for the ward to identify her or for humans to know she was *other*.

A bolt struck a plot of brick town houses across the street from where I crouched, right in the seam between the last two houses, as if trying to shear one away like a slice from a loaf of bread. Occupants screamed as they ran outside to escape, only to be faced with the torrent outside. They huddled as we all did, hoping the odds were in our favor.

A final crackle, and the attack stopped.

I looked up toward Rose.

She was gone.

"Shit," I said, and ignored the lightning, climbed to my feet, and took off, darting through humans and overturned vehicles and fires now burning from direct magic strikes, and the officers and rescue crews who'd finally made it through traffic to help with the turmoil behind me.

I chased her down the block past more town houses, realized her legs and feet barely moved; she was doing a horror movie glide that was infinitely creepier. Connor ran beside me, and his low growl seemed to agree.

I circled around, making my way through an alley to shorten the distance so I could flank her from behind and use my surprise as an advantage.

She turned when I was only feet away. She breathed deeply, her eyes brilliant and shining as she replenished her energy from the turmoil in the streets.

She watched me move toward her—hobble toward her—as she waited on her still-perfect heels. She held out a hand, poised to use her magic again. "You take one more step, and I see how much more trouble I can cause."

So much trouble already. Buildings crumbling. Streets and vehicles destroyed. Humans fighting. Cars reduced to rubble. The poor lost panther.

If I followed her, she'd do it, causing what damage she could. And the machine would fire up again, doing its own damage to Chicago. I didn't know the machine's range, but there was no doubt in my mind she'd cut a path through the city if she could. She'd bring Chicago down around us.

Fuck, I thought. Because there was only one option. I had to let her go.

She smiled, realizing her victory, and brushed grit from her coat. "Thank you for helping me come home again. This fits much better than Edentown."

And then, with a hot burst of sour magic, she was gone.

TEN

Fuck," I said. *"Fuck."*

Connor trotted over, nudged my hand with his nose. I gave him a neck scritch. "I'm okay. Change back when you're ready," I said.

He put a few paces between us, let the magic build around him. Light flashed as the magic became visible, a tornado that swirled around him as his body transformed from wolf back to human again. And then the light and magic faded, and he stood before me—and was very, very naked.

Shifters removed their clothes before shifting, or they'd be shredded during the transition. Moto leathers were much too expensive to waste, so they were usually naked before and after. Like a reverse Clark Kent.

The humans were beginning to stare.

"I've never seen that before," said Black, who'd caught up with us. "It's impressive."

Honestly, I wasn't sure if he meant the magic or the man. He wouldn't be wrong either way.

Connor strode toward us—strong and substantial—prince in bearing but with fury in his eyes. And then he was on Black and had the man by the shoulders.

"What did you do to her? Why is she limping?"

"Shit," I said, and moved forward, shoved a hand between

them, put the flat of it against Connor's bare abdomen. And in doing so, became the target of those fiercely blue eyes. "He didn't do this. He saved me."

Connor arched his eyebrows dubiously, slid that gaze back to Black. "Did he?"

"He did," I said again. "He pushed me out of the way of the lightning."

Connor watched him again for a moment. Black, for his part, knew better than to take on Connor, at least physically. We'd both beaten him at hand to hand.

"All right," he said, and let Jonathan go. He didn't stumble back or put space between him and Connor. He stayed where he was, straightening his shirt. Uncowed or unwilling to show it.

I cleared my throat. "You might want to find some clothes."

Connor glanced down at himself, then up at the humans who were now watching with unhidden interest. He grinned that wolfish smile, and a few of them sighed.

Alexei found us then, a pile of fabric under one arm. He held it out. "Clothes."

"Perfect timing," I said, and glanced away to give Connor a moment of privacy while he pulled on gym shorts and a tank.

"Let's give them a minute," Alexei said, as he led Black a few feet away, shielding us from the humans.

And then we were mostly alone, and Connor's arms were around me, his mouth on mine, to the mostly amused shouts of the humans around us. The kiss was a brand, a claiming. It was confirmation that we were safe and we'd made it through.

"You sure you're okay?" he whispered.

"Honestly, maybe not," I said, and my voice wobbled. Pain flooded back—emotional and physical—the entire, miserable night of it. "Crap."

He kissed the top of my head. "You want me to tell you to buck up or let it out."

"Let it out," I mumbled into his shirt.

"Then do it," he said. "I've got you."

So many hurt. So much destroyed. So much fear and anguish and anger. And, I knew, so much more of that to come. I gripped his shirt with white-knuckled hands and let go of the emotions and the helplessness.

After a moment, when I'd let out all that I'd been holding, I took a haggard breath, wiped my eyes, patted half-heartedly at the tear stains on his shirt.

"It's dark," he said. "It'll wash out." He sniffed his shoulder. "Although I'm pretty sure Alexei found this shirt in the dirty laundry pile at the NAC gym."

"Lies," Alexei said, still nearby, and I decided not to mind that he'd seen me be vulnerable. He was a friend, too.

"So Rose is the demon. How did she do all this?" Connor asked, worried gaze on the chaos.

I moved, and the pain nearly buckled my knees. The hip was going to take some time. "I need to sit," I told Connor when he reached out a hand to steady me. "I'll tell you all about it, but I need to sit."

I didn't bother walking back to the warehouse. Instead, I sent the Ombuds a ping to signal my location, warned them to beware of the panther, then sat on the curb and put my head between my knees while my body righted itself.

Footsteps sounded nearby when Theo, Roger, and Petra came toward us, Gwen behind them, and this time in a suit the color of red wine. Her detective's shield gleamed gold at her waist.

They were all here. They were all safe. That helped. Because this was going to hurt.

Roger stepped forward and offered me a bottle of blood. "Thought you might need this," he said, and my heart clenched with appreciation and guilt at the pain I was going to have to inflict. That *she* would make me inflict.

"Thank you," I said. "If you'll just excuse me . . ." Without waiting for a response, and ignoring the little voice that told me to hide what I was doing, I drank the bottle in a single breath, and felt the power of it immediately as pains began to dull.

"Thank you," I said again when I'd capped the bottle. "I took a couple of hits, and healing takes a lot of energy."

"Hits?" Theo said, alarm in his voice, and crouched in front of me.

"I'm okay. Or will be." The dull aches were already beginning to ease. I looked at Roger. "Do you want me to start at the beginning or get to the important part first?"

He paused and visibly prepared himself. "Hard part first."

"Rose is the demon Eglantine."

Silence followed that revelation, and it seemed the city hushed around us, too. Gwen was already pulling out her screen, probably sending instructions for a BOLO.

"You saw her?" Theo asked quietly, breaking that hush.

"I *talked* to her," I said. "We can pick through the details later, but here's the gooey middle of the brownie: She wanted back into Chicago. Her companions made a move on her sooner than she wanted, and she decided the time was now. She knew the gate was magicked, so she called in her marker with the Ombuds' office, hoping she'd get muscle to get her through. Which she did."

I looked at Roger. "I'm sorry for the part we played in this. In making this happen."

"Not your fault," he said, voice hard and jaw rigid. Battling many emotions, I guessed. "Keep going."

"I didn't get any details about where she'd been since the gate, but she probably took that trail back to the road, either had a vehicle waiting or called another accomplice in the city."

"Why did she want to come back?"

"She refused to tell me," I said flatly. "I think she may be looking for something. This sounds ridiculous, but she kept sniffing the air."

"Like you do?" Petra said.

"Like I— What? I don't do that." The lie popped out automatically. I guess I wanted to distinguish myself from her.

"You do when you think there might be coffee, doughnuts, or magic."

"Quite a list," I muttered. "But yeah, it was like that. I don't know what she's looking for, though. Something around here, or else the ward wouldn't have been triggered." I pointed to the warehouse. "That's your ward."

"It makes lightning?" Petra asked. "I didn't see much before it stopped."

"Yeah. It projects a beam of light that generates lightning. I think it's intended to strike the demon. And it made her look a little green."

"Green?" Roger asked.

"Not quite a glow, but a strange tint to her skin. Maybe designed to make her stand out."

"Very different from the first one," Roger said.

"Maybe that's part of the strategy," I said. "Each defense challenges her in a different way, like looking for a weak spot."

"There's millions of dollars of property damage out there," Gwen said grimly. "They couldn't have picked a better spot for a lightning rod?"

"We're within the boundary of the Great Fire," Petra said. "This area was annihilated. They probably wouldn't have thought more than a century would pass before it was triggered."

Gwen nodded. "I know we can't blame them—they did the best they could with the technology they had and while trying to predict the future." She looked around, kicked a bit of glass off the curb. "And sometimes getting it very, expensively wrong."

"Is that what did all this damage?" Roger asked. "The lightning?"

"No," I said ruefully. "That was mostly Rose."

"She did this?" Roger asked, awe and horror in his voice.

"Not directly. Chaos demon does chaos," I said.

"Like the butterfly effect," Theo said.

"The what?" I asked.

"You know, something minor happens over here, and it makes something big happen over there." He moved his hands together as he explained. "Throw a rock in the water at Navy Pier and deer turn blue in Sheboygan."

"That's not how it works," Petra said.

"Close enough," I said. "Her magic is . . . chaos. Making the improbable happen. A vehicle skids into scaffolding, which damages the building, which begins to fall. It almost makes me miss good, old-fashioned fireballs. Oh," I said, "what about the panther?"

"Zoo staff are already on scene," Gwen said. "They'd been tracking it. It really attacked you?"

"Not on purpose, so this shouldn't be held against it." I didn't want it put down because it had "attacked" me, when the attack hadn't been its fault. "The demon magicked it. Another chain reaction." I looked at Gwen guiltily. "I had to give up the chase. I was afraid she'd bring down more buildings."

"Every cop has pulled off a chase," Gwen said. "Sometimes you have to protect the city and hope you get another chance at the bad guy. I don't suppose you got a picture?"

"If you've seen a picture of Rose, you've seen the demon," I said drily. "Just imagine more lipstick and better clothes. But I bet some of these buildings have camera security, especially with all the bars. Maybe there's video?"

Gwen gestured to an officer, who understood the implicit instruction and hurried out.

"If she was in this neighborhood to find something," Roger asked, "did she know the ward was here?"

"If she could feel the first ward," I said, "I'd think she could feel this one, too."

"So," Connor said. "Which came first? The demon or the ward?"

Gwen looked at him. "What do you mean?"

Connor looked at her. "Was the ward in this neighborhood because the Guardians thought she might come here, or was Rose in this neighborhood because of the ward?"

"In other words," I said, "we're back to asking what she wanted."

"I don't suppose you saw the sigil?" Petra asked.

"She was not wearing a sigil necklace," I said ruefully. "Or anything else with a sigil on it."

"Knew that would have been too easy," she said, "but had to ask."

"Let's go take a look at the ward," Roger said.

We walked together back to the warehouse. That's when I realized Jonathan Black was gone. In fairness, he didn't need to be here. We'd moved on to the investigation part of the drama, and he didn't have any lines in this particular scene. But it was weird that he hadn't said goodbye. I still didn't have a read on him, lifesaving or not.

Gwen walked beside me. "Officer Glenn said it was your idea to set up the triage area. Nicely done."

"Thanks. I had good training," I said, and meant that literally. Roger had made us watch a video produced by Homeland Security on responding to paranormal attacks. He'd sprung for doughnuts, and I was still finishing the first glazed when the speaker got to establishing a treatment zone for humans.

A dozen cops were posted outside the police tape that surrounded the warehouse. Protecting people from the machine and the machine from the people.

Gwen had ordered stands of floodlights, which were now shining through the empty window frames to illuminate the machine inside it. The building's doors had survived the initial blast, so the CPD had to pull a ram to blow down the door. When it was open and out of the way, we walked inside. Glass and metal crunched under our feet, and the air smelled of dust and oil and heat. Like a cast-iron skillet ready to char.

I'd expected to see a jagged breach in the roof where the light had punched through, but the builders had planned for that. A sliding metal cover was currently pulled back from the opening where the shaft of light had risen into the city. Remnants of magic still peppered the air, and I could smell sour milk again. No cold. No ghosts. But an olfactory echo of whatever the Guardians had done.

The warehouse was three stories, but the middle of each wooden floor had been cored out to make room for the machine that rose nearly to the roof. It was easily twenty feet across—a complicated nest of metal gears, levers, and pistons. The components looked to be made of iron, with fittings in silver and gold and probably thousands of rivets holding it all together.

Roger whistled. "This is—I suppose the word would be 'impressive'?"

"Imposing," Theo said, neck craned and squinting as he peered up at the machine. "There's just . . . so much of it."

"How did they do this in 1872?" Gwen asked, directing the beam of a flashlight to a set of golden gears near the top of the machine. "And how long did it take them?"

"Depends on whether they used magic," I said. Although I didn't know what kind of magic could form the components of a giant machine, assemble them with what looked like obvious care and skill. "However they did it, it looks like they did it well."

"It's lasted more than a century," Connor agreed.

"I'm a tech person," Petra said, glancing around. "But Victorian machinery isn't my bag. Can anyone else help interpret this?"

"I'm no engineer," Connor said. "But I work on bikes. I know my way around an engine."

"Then let's interpret," Petra said. She put her hands on her hips, frowned at the machine.

"So," Connor began, "we're looking at a machine that generated a pillar of light and sent out lightning when triggered."

"Keep going," Petra said.

"You'd need a sensor—something that could identify the demon or Sups in the first place, and possibly track them once the machine is on. And you'd need a source of power."

"Ley lines," I said, thinking of Black's comment. "The wards probably used ley lines to maintain a ready state and power them up if and when she got close."

"Damn," Petra said. "I bet you're right. I think the north-south line runs pretty close to here. But you'd need something to transfer that energy into the machine." She frowned. "The ley lines are, like, powerful, though. I don't know how you could just slap a machine on top of one."

Connor smiled. "So you'd need a transformer—something that could make the energy usable by the machine."

"Exactly!" Petra said. "And you'd need a component that would change the energy created by the machine into visible light—since that's its weapon."

"That's a lot of tech for the Victorian era," Roger said. "They were a steam-engine society."

"Yeah," Petra said, "but magic cures a lot of ills."

"Lis," Connor called out, and I moved to where he stood, pointing at a flat iron panel that covered some other moving parts. Petra was already crouched and taking pictures of the symbols that had been etched into the metal. There were two rows, with maybe twenty symbols in each row, one above the other, and neatly engraved in a tall, spindly script. Each symbol was made up of two or three lines, dots, or circles.

"Part of the spell," I guessed. "Something used to power the machine or give it instructions or link magic to metal."

"Agreed," Petra said. "I don't recognize the language, though. I'll run it through SpellCheck."

It took us all a minute to get that one. "Like, a place to check a spell. That's seriously a thing?" Theo asked.

"Where do you think they got the word?" she asked with typical Petra exhaustion.

"Learn something new every day," Theo said.

"I've learned entirely too much today," I muttered. "Send it to Paige and the Librarian, too."

Petra gave me a thumbs-up.

I moved closer, reached out to touch the blunt tooth of a gear taller than me, then looked at my fingertips. There was no grime. Just a thin coating of clear oil.

"It's old," I said. "Like 1872 old. So why does it look like this?" I showed them my fingers. "Not even a mote of dust. It was oiled and ready in case she got too close."

"Someone's been maintaining it," Connor said. "Someone with ties to the wards."

"A century plus of ties," I said. "A vampire? Wouldn't we know that, though?"

"Memory spell," Connor reminded me. "Maybe they don't know anything about the rest of the plan or the machine's purpose. They just know they have to maintain it."

"Possible," I said. "We need to find out who owns the property. Maybe that will lead us to the custodian, which will lead us to . . ."

"To?" Connor prompted.

"I have no idea. Information we need to stop this asshole from destroying Chicago?"

"I'll take that," Petra said, gaze on the machine. "I love a property record deep dive."

"I know none of you have been sitting around," Roger said. "But the mayor's going to increase the pressure on us to find and stop the demon."

"If she's got any ideas," Theo said, drinking from his own bottle of water, "we're happy to hear them."

"She'll probably get them from the feds," Roger said. "And we won't like it when the suits come in."

"Freaking G-men," Petra said. "That's all we need."

We walked back outside and watched the cleanup begin.

"I'm beginning to think they weren't good at ward building," Roger said.

"It was probably that one guy," Petra said.

"What one guy?" I asked, thinking she'd made some big headway in her research.

"You know, that asshole in every group project whose ideas are ridiculous, but he throws such a damn fit that everyone basically has to go along with it."

"There's one in every government committee," Roger said.

"Maybe he's the reason why there's no manual," Theo muttered. "Total asshole move."

Petra nodded. "I bet he was all like, 'Who cares about collateral damage?'"

"There was a lot of it," Roger said, then looked at me and Theo. "You're both injured. Go home. If you want to work from there, fine. But go home."

"I'm fine to keep working," Petra said, still taking photos of the machine.

Roger nodded. "Then we'll meet at dusk tomorrow."

Theo cleared his throat. "Boss, we'll need to review your files. Anything she gave you, if you've got it written down. Any files of the ones prosecuted because of information she gave." The apology was thick in his voice. "They could give us something to start with. A way to find her."

"I'm already making a mental list," Roger said, and sounded as tired as I felt.

* * *

Connor had arrived in an SUV, and we walked back to the vehicle at a slower pace than usual. This was the time to heal for the next round, not push. Because I knew there'd be a next round.

"She triggers another ward, and she might bring down an entire neighborhood," I said.

"She's shown herself now," Connor said. "Used her magic. You'll get her."

"I damn well will. And I hope it's before she does more damage. But I don't think it will be. We don't have enough information. We don't know how to stop her—and we certainly don't have a giant demon-killing machine."

We reached the car—and saw the Leo's coffee truck parked a half block farther down.

I made a noise. No coherent words but definitely noise.

"You've earned it," Connor said.

I agreed, so I got the largest they offered. And also a churro, because churros are amazing.

We walked back to his SUV and sat on the curb.

"Late-night human partiers," Connor said after taking a bite of my churro, "and hungry Sups make the perfect food truck Venn diagram."

"I'm happy to share the bounty," I said, sipping my drink. There was a chill in the air—due to weather, not demons—and it paired nicely with hot coffee and the warm shifter beside me. I stretched out my legs, winced at the jolt of pain.

"I still don't like him."

I presumed the "him" was Jonathan Black. "This isn't his fault," I said. "And he did save my life."

"I like that less."

I lifted my brows at the growl in his voice. "You don't like me being alive?"

He gave me a Very Dry look. "I don't like you being in danger, but I accept that you will be. I really don't like a grifter thinking you owe him a favor. He's dishonest about who and what he is, he has shady clients he won't identify, and he attacked you."

"He sounds like a member of a supernatural mafia."

"I wouldn't put it past him. I don't think it's a coincidence that he asked you to come to his place and then the demon appeared across the street."

"I hadn't even thought of that, actually. I just figured it was right place, right time. Besides, it wasn't that close. It was like half a mile away. Don't look at me like that," I said, and nearly flicked him. "I really don't think he knows the demon. His clients, maybe. But that's another issue. The point is we don't have any evidence he's directly involved, and he saved my life. In the meantime, we'll tolerate him."

"For now. And only for that reason." He leaned in, pressed a kiss to my forehead that lingered, as if he needed to maintain the contact to assure himself that I was safe. "If he touches you, I will break his fingers."

"If he touches me, *I'll* break his fingers, thanks. I can fight my own battles. Did Cade show his face again today? And the other interlopers?"

"Of course," Connor said. "They were in the bar when I got there and in the bar when I left."

"Getting drunk, playing cards, or fomenting rebellion?"

"Is this the shifter version of coffee, doughnuts, and magic?"

"Yes. At least we can be insulted together."

"You're such a comfort, Lis. And yeah, they were doing at least the first two. Probably also the last one."

"You think they're waiting to make a move?"

"I'm not sure they have a move in mind. I think they probably bragged to their asshole friends in Memphis about how they were going to drive to Chicago and stand up to the goddamn Apex. And they did that, and they're probably now messaging their asshole friends about how they did it *and* they're drinking in the Apex's own fucking bar." He took a sip of his own—much smaller—coffee.

"I feel like there's a punch line here."

"Yeah, but the joke won't be very funny."

I leaned the churro toward him. "Bite?"

"Yes, please," he said in a low growl that had my blood thrumming despite the pain and general suckage of the last couple of hours. He bit in, chewed.

I finished the last bite, then licked the sugar from my fingers. Connor rose, took our cups and paper to the recycling bin, then offered me a hand. "Let's go home."

I let him pull me up, then against the warmth of his body. He was solid, stable, gorgeous. *Mine.* My blood began to thrum in a very different way. But I had other obligations right now.

"I need to check on Lulu."

"I think she went back to the loft," Connor said. "She said she wanted to do some work. Something about mock-ups for a mural?"

"Shit," I muttered. "I should have asked about that. I think it's because of a guy she met at the gallery opening."

"Which you were at," he reminded me. "You're doing what you can."

"I need to do more in between demon slaying. Other than demon finding. And I need to warn her about that. So I'm apparently going back to the loft tonight."

"You aren't going home with me?"

"I'm doing what I can," I repeated.

"Okay. In that case . . ." He slid his hands into my hair, closed his mouth over mine, and kissed me with enough passion that I had very little doubt about his interest in me. And I could barely remember my name. But I did remember something important.

"Also, could you give me a lift?"

His smile went wicked.

"To the loft, puppy."

"Arf," he said, and nipped my earlobe.

The loft was quiet but for the low hiss that rose up from the hallway just inside the door. Eleanor of Aquitaine waited inside, her sleek, dark tail switching.

"I probably smell like demon and old magic," I acknowledged, crouching down to look at her. "And I'm going to vanquish her as soon as I find her and figure out how. In the meantime, I'm here to check on Lulu. Truce?"

She regarded me for a moment. Then began to lick her butt.

"Yeah," I said, rising again. "That checks out. Good to see you, too."

Lulu was in the main living area, using a small brush to put flicks of color on a wide canvas. It was a rainbow of joy—bodies dancing among rising flowers.

I sidled up beside her. "I hear you've got a big secret."

Lulu screamed so loudly I thought my eardrums might burst, and an outflung hand sent a cup of paintbrushes scattering across the floor.

"Damn, Lis," she said, then pulled music buds from her ears. "What the hell are you doing here? You scared the devil out of me."

"Funny you should say that," I said, and helped her gather up the paintbrushes.

"Is it?" she asked, and nearly spilled the paintbrushes again.

"Let me do that," I said. "I'm sorry I scared you. I didn't know you were listening to music."

"It's okay," she said, and took the cup I handed back to her. "What secret are you talking about?"

"How many do you have? Never mind," I said, waving that away. "I meant the mural one."

She looked at me for a second. "The mural one. Oh! For Clint Howard. Yeah. It's this." She gestured to the canvas.

"Yeah, Connor said you were coming back here to work on something. Did he already request something from you? Because: amazing."

"We batted around some ideas. I'm still playing with them." She stepped back a few feet, gave it a look. "He wants big and bold, and different, but in my style. I'm trying to figure out how to do what I do without doing what I do."

"I like what you've got there."

"Thanks." She dipped a paintbrush in something to clean it, then slapped it on the side of the container. "I think I'm going to take a break. Want some wine? There's a bottle of rosé on the counter."

I walked over to it, picked up the bottle. "It says 'strawberry wine-drink.' I don't think that counts as rosé."

"It's close enough," she said.

Since I tended to agree, especially on nights like this, I poured some into two glasses and carried them over to the couch. I handed her one and took a seat with the other, sipped.

It had the complexity of a melted red popsicle. "I'm not even sure that's wine-drink," I said, smacking my lips together.

She took a very long drink, then nodded. "Melted cherry popsicle."

"Right?"

"You said something about the devil?"

"The demon is, in fact, in Chicago. And it's Rose, of 'Hi, we're coming to rescue you' fame."

Lulu blinked. "I—she. She's a demon?"

"She is," I said, and gave her the overview. "So be careful out there, Lulu. The damage she did was . . . overwhelming. You'd have to be in the wrong place at the wrong time, but—"

"But chaos demon," she finished.

"But chaos demon. So be careful out there," I said again.

"I will," she promised.

She went to sleep before I did. When I opened the door, I found her sprawled on her bed like a four-legged starfish. She'd started leaving on a radio during the day as white noise, and someone with a deep voice crooned softly while she snored.

Part of me wanted to watch her sleep—creepy as that sounded— as if that might ensure she was sleeping well and I could rest easily, too. And part of me wished the sun wouldn't rise, that I could sit in the quiet and the dark and just . . . be.

I left Lulu to sleep and went to my room next door, closed the door against the rising sun, and wished peace for us all.

ELEVEN

Dinner, we were informed by my mother, would be at 10:00 p.m. Fortunately, sorcerers, vampires, and shifters all kept the same hours. Connor and I would bring wine, which made me feel very adult. Lulu offered to bring a side. Since she didn't cook, I was betting on potato salad from the deli down the street. But she'd surprised us before.

Unfortunately, they hadn't found anything else in the archives, nor had Paige had much luck with the old documents they'd located. She thought the writers had used alchemy as a sort of magical cipher, but she hadn't been able to decipher much yet. I had to pin that hope on Mallory and Catcher. Paige had contacted the Order, but they'd burned any materials relating to Chicago's sorcerers and had no records from any other supernaturals in the city at that time. Uncle Malik was trying to track down two vampires he'd known in Chicago, but vampires historically changed their identities every few decades to avoid detection, so he hadn't yet had luck.

So I had basically nothing to offer the team as I badged my way into the former brick factory that served as the Ombuds' headquarters, nodding at Mr. Pettiway, the guard who'd done his duty at the door for years, and heading down to our administrative offices. Theo, Petra, and I shared an office between Roger's and a conference room. Where the conference room was sleek, the

designers had kept some of the original features of the building—
brick walls and hardwood floors—for our office. We had a couple
of long work tables with screen stations, a large overhead wall
screen, and a couple of tables that held snacks and equipment—
usually gadgets Petra was working on.

"Good evening," Roger said. He leaned a hip on the edge of
Theo's desk.

"Hi. How are you?"

"Still trying to readjust my mindset."

I nodded, squeezed his arm in support, then glanced at Theo.
"How's the arm?"

"Itchy. But less achy."

I took off my leather jacket, slung it on the back of my chair.
"That's something, at least."

"Your foot? Your hip?"

"Foot is fine. Hip is achy but better than yesterday." I gestured
toward Theo's cast. "So that still makes me feel a little bit guilty."

"Ah, but I can go out in the sun anytime I want."

"You work the night shift," I pointed out.

"That is a pisser."

"Eat a doughnut," Roger said.

"I don't want a doughnut." I paused. "What kind of doughnuts?"

Roger walked to the table, flipped open a white box. It was
loaded.

"Damn," I said, staring at glossy pink frosting and sprinkles.
"Why are there so many?"

"Jonathan Black," Petra said, gaze on me as she swiveled in her
chair. "Had them delivered."

I'd reached in to grab one, then paused, hand poised centime-
ters above glossy pastry. "Why?"

"He said he had a better appreciation for the dangers of being
an Ombud after yesterday. You told him the pastries at that place
down the street were good, so he obliged."

"Hmm," was all I could think to say. A thoughtful thing to do, but so unnecessary it seemed . . . sycophantic. But since there was no need to punish a doughnut for the acts of its purchaser, I plucked one out, took a bite.

"I don't suppose he decided to suddenly share the details about his 'clients'?" I asked.

"Nope," Petra said. "Any news on your end?"

"Absolutely none. Everybody is reading and researching and looking, but we have bubkes. Lulu's parents are coming into town tonight. I'm hoping they have something."

"Ah, for the big deciphering," Petra said. "Could I visit?" She squeezed her hands together like a woman in prayer. "I've never met them."

"I think dinner tonight is just for family, but I'll let them know you're available for consultations."

"*Cooool,*" she said, drawing out the word, made a complete rotation in her chair.

"Since we're all here," Roger said, "let's get started. The mayor is estimating more than eight million dollars in damage due to the combined efforts of the Guardians and Rose. Eglantine."

"Rosantine?" I offered.

After a moment, Petra nodded. "Rosantine. That works. And believe me, boss, she's our first priority."

"Anything new from the CPD?" I asked.

"First," Roger said, "since I have 'Rose's' number, I sent it to Gwen. It's got some kind of anti-tracking device, so we can't use that to trace her."

"And second," he said, then nodded at Theo.

Theo did some swiping, and a photograph appeared on the large wall screen. It was the purple car that had chased us toward the gate. And it had been flattened, and metal curled from its edges, as if something had tried to pry it apart.

"No more running board lights," I said. "The driver?"

"And passenger, both dead on scene."

"Where?"

"Not far from the gate. On the Chicago side."

"Probably at a prearranged spot," I said, and glanced at Theo. "You said the car pulled in behind us—had been waiting for us to pass."

He nodded. "She probably told them to wait there."

"And they chased us toward the gate," I finished. "Because she wanted us to fight that battle."

"Something's bothering me," Petra said. "Why couldn't she just go around it? Like, if she really knew the defense was there, why not come in from some other direction?"

"A very good question," Roger said. "Add it to the list."

I looked back at the car. "Did she kill them?"

"Not exactly," Roger said. "How did you put it? Chaos demon does chaos. A combine rolled over onto their vehicle."

The room went dead silent.

"Damn," Petra murmured. "Miserable way to die. And 'don't do business with demons' is the moral of that story."

"Yeah," I said. "They find anything on them or at their residences that might tell us where she is or what she's looking for?"

"Nothing yet," Roger said. "But crime scene guys are still looking."

Theo cleared his throat. "Would this be a good time to mention your files?"

"No, but there's no good time. And that's my problem, not yours. I found nine cases in which she provided information. That's been over the last three years."

He put a new image on screen—a chart of allegations, dates, and results. "Five led to arrests," he continued. "Fraud, burglary, gambling."

We read through the data quietly. There was a mix of dates,

responding precincts, incident locations. And nothing obvious stood out.

"I don't see any patterns," Theo said.

"There may not be one," Roger said. "I think I'd have seen it over the years."

"Other than her," I said, and they both looked at me. "She's the pattern—the connection, I mean. She's a demon, and she was a criminal, right? Some may have been rivals. Some might not have given her the respect she thought she was owed. Some might have been just for fun."

And I didn't see anything here that would help us.

"What about the information you gave to her?" Theo asked. "Did she ask any pointed questions about Chicago, magic, sorcerers, anything like that?"

"I reviewed my notes," Roger said. Then he walked to the table, propped a hip on the corner. He looked tired, and I guessed he'd spent many hours on those notes. "Our conversations were usually short. She provided information. I noted it, reported it. If a case involved supernaturals, she might ask about them generally. I was friendly because she was useful. But I only gave her public information. Nothing that she wouldn't have been able to find online."

"Maybe you were her thermometer."

"What?" Roger asked, head snapping over to look at Petra.

"She might not have been using you for information, but to get a read on things. Maybe she hoped that if something important happened, you'd tell her. Or she'd read your excitement."

Roger stood up again, frowning as he considered that. And it seemed to lighten him.

"I didn't give away any state secrets," he said, as much to himself as to us.

Theo snorted. "You barely tell us anything when we're in the same room, and we're on the same team. You're not going to hand over the details of our work to an informant."

"A week ago, he didn't want to message his lunch order," I said, "because he got the chips *and* the sandwich."

"Exorbitant spender," Theo said with a rueful nod of the head.

"Rude," Roger said, but with a relieved smile.

"We're all trying to do the right thing here," Theo said. "That includes you, boss."

"All right," he said, and waved away the sentiment. "Back to demons."

"I've been waiting for, like, ten minutes to use this segue," Petra said, and cleared her throat. "*Speaking of things that demons entail*, let the teaching begin."

She changed the image on-screen to a vintage photograph of a teacher in front of an old-fashioned blackboard. On it, in white letters, was "Real Talk About Demons."

"From a Western religious standpoint, they're usually considered evil minions of Satan, wreakers of havoc, et cetera. Other religions don't necessarily consider them evil but different. Troublemakers sometimes, but not inherently bad. Most of them were sealed long ago by King Solomon and his acolytes. Some managed by their wiles—or their chaos—to escape that punishment, hiding in the human world."

"Relatable," I murmured, since vampires had done the same thing. Assimilation was the only alternative to death, and usually a very nasty one.

"Solomon," Petra segued. "Supposedly, demons were a scourge on the populace. Solomon was dedicated to eliminating them, but he decided they had some uses. He supposedly identified seventy-two demon aristocrats, most of which had their own legions, and figured out their skill sets. One might help you predict the future, help your finances, tell you about science, get your son a wife, act as a demon notary."

"The last one's a lie," Theo guessed.

"It is absolutely true. Bureaucracy is eternal, as you should know. Anyway, Solomon figured out how he could call up one particular demon at a time, depending on his needs, then send them back to their plane when he was done."

"So, it's minor league baseball," I said.

"Not far off," Petra said with a grin. "If pitchers and catchers reported to help you with some horse thievery or transmogrification."

"I doubt that's in the standard contract," Roger said with a little smile.

"Probably not," Petra said.

"And what did he use to call them up?" I asked.

"There were several methods," Petra said. "Sometimes you did a chant, a little alchemy, or even a little religion. And each one required something very specific." Another image flashed on-screen—a black geometric symbol on a white background.

"The sigil, right? That's what Patience said they needed but didn't have."

She nodded like a pleased teacher. "It is."

"It looks kind of like a stave," I said. Staves were also simple geometric symbols used in Nordic magic to construct spells. The witches in Ariel's coven had used them, and Ariel had had one tattooed on her arm.

"Staves are spells," Petra said. "Sigils are more like . . . secret monograms. It's the secret symbol for each demon that locks or unlocks their power."

"Not so secret if Solomon found them all."

"Not all, unfortunately. She's not one of the demons whose sigils he identified."

Theo sat up. "Wait. She's not even an aristocrat—just some demon schlub slumming it in Chicago—and she can bring down buildings?"

"Unfortunately."

"So we need her sigil," I said, "but the Guardians didn't know it, and it's not written down anywhere that we've been able to translate, and we can't find anyone alive who knew anything about it."

"Hey," Petra said. "The Guardians didn't have the Internet. Hope springs eternal."

"Do all the demons have assigned traits—like chaos or whatever?" I asked.

"She wants to know if there's a coffee demon," Theo said with a grin.

"I mean . . . is there?"

"There's a demon for every desire," she said. "And demons of desire. At least, that's according to the texts. It's hard to tell how much is folktale versus actual documentation."

I flicked an errant doughnut sprinkle off my sleeve. I'd paired a short, fitted black jacket with fitted jeans, a white fitted tee, and black booties for the dinner with my parents, and I shouldn't show up covered in doughnut castoffs. "This conversation is depressing."

"So, let's think of her like a superhero," Theo said, rising from his seat and lifting his hands like he was pumping up the team before a big game. "Just like superheroes, supernaturals have their strengths, their weaknesses. If we figure out her kryptonite, maybe we'll get closer to stopping her."

"Good thought," Petra said, and added a "Strengths" column to her on-screen presentation. "Elisa, this is your territory since you've seen her in action."

"She's fast, strong. Typical supernatural stuff. Except that she makes chaos happen."

"What's her mechanism?" Petra asked.

"Her mechanism?"

"What does she do to make this happen? You said no fireballs, so we talking verbal spells, or is she drawing symbols on the ground, or what?"

I closed my eyes, tried to remember what I'd seen of her. And given the aforementioned chaos, that hadn't been much. "Hand flicks?"

"Hand flicks," Petra said. "Like, just . . ." She flicked a hand in the air like she was dismissing something.

"Yes?"

Petra just looked at me.

"I was trying not to get hit by magical lightning and flying cars."

"Did she look supernaturally constipated?"

I just stared at her. "What?"

"You know, when Sups doing magic squinch up their faces." She gave me an example, tensing her eyes, lips, and cheeks into an expression that did look . . . frustrated.

"No. It looked . . . easier than that."

She turned back, added "Creates chaos with hand flick" to the screen. Which sounded like very good observational reporting to my mind.

"Weaknesses," she said, turning back to us.

"Canines," I said. "Patience said demons don't like dogs, and she seemed very nervous when Connor joined the fight."

"Inferior coffee, sunlight, Eleanor of Aquitaine."

I looked at Theo, brows raised.

"Oh, sorry. Those are *your* weaknesses. I got confused."

I gave him my blandest stare. "Is that cast itchy?"

"Snap," Petra said with quiet awe as Theo he grabbed a pencil and started scratching.

"Is that glamour?" he asked.

"It's the power of suggestion," I said with a smile. "Partner or not, I'm not taking you back to the ER if you get that pencil stuck in there."

"I'll take an Auto," he said, eyes closed in scratching bliss. "And it will be worth it."

"Back to the demon," Petra said. "Weaknesses."

"I'm guessing she doesn't like ghosts," I said, "given that's the tool the Guardians decided to use first. And lightning, obvs."

"Excellent thoughts," Petra said, and added those to the list. "And the big thing: the sigil. Being controlled and sealed by it."

"We have to find her damn sigil," Roger said.

"Maybe we can trick her into it," Theo said.

Petra snorted. "Like demon phishing?"

"That's not a bad idea," I said. "Except we'd have to lure her out, and we don't know what she wants."

Theo glanced at Roger. "If she has an anti-canine thing, can we adopt a pack of coyotes? Corgis? Wild dogs?"

"Not in the budget," Roger said, gaze on his screen.

"I hate to pile on the good news," Petra said, "but even if we figure out the stuff—the sigil, the spell, the chanting, whatever, we need serious power to make it work."

Roger looked up. "Define 'serious power.'"

"Permanently sealing a demon is no joke. Solomon had a lot of juju. Supposedly he got his magical strength directly from god, but I don't think we have any of those connections?" She looked around the room. "Direct line to the universal font of power? No? Didn't think so."

"You don't think Mallory could do it? Or Mallory and Catcher?"

Petra winced. "Do you think they'd want to dabble with demons?"

She had a point. "Is making a demon go away technically 'dark magic'?"

"That's a question for Catcher Bell. Isn't he really into the divisions of magic?"

"That sounds vaguely familiar," I said. But he was my friend's dad—my friend who avoided magic. It's not like we talked about it a lot. "I can add that to the dinner list. If I can figure out a way to make it not awkward."

"You know what's not awkward?" Theo said. "Coyotes."

"No," Roger said.

"Well," Petra said, turning off the screen. "Here's something positive: Ask me about the landowner."

"What landowner?" I asked.

She paused, gave me a dry look. "The one who owns the machine building."

"You found him?"

"I did. His name is Hugo Horner. He's the current owner, and his mother before him, grandfather before her, great-grandfather before him, et cetera. The deed is traceable through multiple generations of Horners."

"Back to 1872?" Theo asked, and Petra put a finger on her nose. "Bingo."

"Let's go see him," Theo said, and gestured to me. "Saddle up, partner."

I swallowed the last of the doughnut. "Okay. But I'm taking another doughnut."

TWELVE

Forty minutes later, because traffic was miserable, we pulled up in the Ombuds' van in front of a tidy white house with a bare but tidy yard.

We climbed out.

"Anything?" Theo asked.

"No magic," I said quietly, but belted on my katana just in case. I glanced at Petra. "You?"

"No. But someone's barbecuing down the street." She closed her eyes, pointed to a house. "There."

"Excellent detective work," Theo said with an eye roll. "We can all smell that."

"Let's play this hard and official," Petra said, adjusting her white gloves as we tromped down the sidewalk.

I glanced at Theo. "You do it. You're the cop."

He snorted but took the steps to the front door, pounded it with his non-casted fist. "Mr. Horner. Ombuds' office. We need to talk."

Okay, he did actually sound pretty official. But there was no answer, even to the second or third round of poundings. The fourth had the door swinging wildly open, and me putting a precautionary hand on my sword.

"For Horguh's sake, what? We finally reached Korkath the Demogorgon, and we're trying to strategize, so this better be good."

The man in the doorway was tall and thin, with pale skin and dark shaggy hair that stood up where he'd pushed fingers through it. He had a couple of days' worth of stubble on his chin and shadows under his eyes, and he wore a sleek headset and a T-shirt with an enormous JQ across the front.

I glanced behind him, wondering if there was a Demogorgon somewhere in the house. And wondering what a Demogorgon was. That was snake heads, right?

Petra snorted. "It's a game, noob," she said, and bumped me with her shoulder. "Horguh is a god in *Jakob's Quest*. Korkath is a ninth-level boss."

That explained the JQ on the shirt. Actually, I think Connor— who was much more into geek culture than I was—played *JQ* occasionally, including a game with Theo once or twice.

"Mr. Horner?" Theo asked.

"Yes?"

Theo held up his badge. "We're with the Ombudsman. You're going to need to take a break from *Jakob's Quest* for a moment. We need to talk to you."

His face lit with purpose as he looked us over. "Theo and Petra and Elisa, right? I wondered if you'd ever come looking," he said, and bid us inside.

The house was sparse, but tidy for a bachelor/gamer. The front parlor was his *Jakob's Quest* headquarters, complete with a wide screen, a chair that looked skeletal in its construction, and a table of gaming accessories and empty drink bottles.

"This is gonna take a few," he murmured into the headset, and sent a flurry of messages scrolling across the comp screen. Most of them very unhappy he was skipping out on the quest.

"Okay," he said when that was done and he'd pulled off the headset. "What do you want to know?"

"Tell us about your property in the South Loop," Petra said.

His face lit up. "You've been there? That's amazing. Did you find the machine?" The smile dropped away. "Did something happen to it? Did someone break in?"

We weren't going to have a problem getting this one to talk.

Theo held up a hand to stop the barrage. "Hold up. You're confirming you own the property?" He listed off the address.

"Well, sure. That property's been in the family since the 1870s. We're the Machinists." He said that with obvious pride.

"What do you mean?" Theo asked.

"Well, we keep the machine in order, right? That's, like, my family legacy. I go in weekly, make sure everything is clean and oiled, make adjustments if necessary. Sometimes I have to replace a spring—Victorian-era metal can be finicky—and that means machining a new one. It's my job."

"Your family is involved, too?" Petra asked.

"It's just me now," Hugo said. "My parents passed."

"I'm sorry to hear that."

He nodded. "It's been a few years, but thanks."

"Are you paid to do this work?" Theo asked.

"Well, sure. There's an annuity. A trust was created when the machine was first built. The bank's the trustee, and I get paid to keep the machine ready and in order. The bank handles the insurance and property taxes and that kind of thing." Hugo swayed a little.

Theo reached out a hand to steady him. "You okay?"

"Sorry, yeah." He breathed in and out a couple of times. "We've been running this game for, like"—he checked his screen—"dang, twenty-eight hours. I think my blood sugar's low."

"How about I get you some juice or something?" Petra offered, gesturing to the hallway. "Kitchen that way?"

"Yeah, that would be great. Kale-pear juice, please."

She curled her lip but disappeared down the hall.

"Let's sit," Theo said, and pulled the gaming chair over for him. Hugo took a seat, ran a hand through his hair.

"Thanks."

"So twenty-eight hours," Theo repeated. "You haven't checked the screen or your . . . machinery . . . in the last day?"

"Nah. Questing takes all the attention. We've got twelve in our band, and we've been working toward this for a while now."

Petra came back with the drink, offered it to him. He took it, sipped, and seemed to steady himself.

"Thanks. Too much caffeine, not enough real food. Anyway, why are you here about the machinery? Are you checking the ward? Nothing's happened in the entire time I've monitored—or for a couple of generations back. One of the great-great-greats had an attempted breach, but it's been a while."

That explained why he'd felt comfortable going off-line to go online for a full day.

Petra flipped through her screen, found what she needed, then offered the screen to Hugo. "Does she look familiar?"

Hugo leaned forward, gave the photo a look. I saw no recognition in his face.

"No. She's pretty. Who is she?"

"She is a demon." Petra put her screen down. "Her demon name is Eglantine. She's gone by Rose Doerman lately. Hugo, the machine was triggered yesterday. She triggered it."

He looked a little—I think "puce" was the word—about the face. "Are you kidding me?"

"No," I said, and told him what we'd seen. By the time I was done, his face had lost all color.

"I'm sorry, I don't understand. She triggered the machine?"

"She did," Petra said. "There's a proximity trigger, yes?"

He nodded, tears glistening in his eyes. "Yeah. That's how it works."

"She got close, and the machine triggered."

"Was anyone hurt?"

"Some injuries and a lot of property damage. No one was killed."

"What about the demon? Did it get her? Is she dead?"

"She isn't," Petra said. "She was able to get away. I'm very sorry."

He looked away, blinking hard against those tears, and my heart ached for the loss in his expression. "I'm sorry," he said again. "I'm having trouble getting this. This was my job. My mission—that's what my dad said—to make sure she was captured. And I guess I failed?"

"You didn't." I waited until he looked at me. "Your family has helped keep Rose out of Chicago since the ward was put into place. But Rose is wily. This time, she beat both of us. At least so far."

He nodded but obviously wasn't convinced.

"You knew our names when we came to the door," I added. "Why haven't you contacted us?"

He made a motion like he was zipping his lips together. "Sworn to secrecy. I mean, you come and ask me about it, and I can talk. But I can't spill the beans unless someone asks. Blood oath," he explained.

I frowned. "And in all the years you've been the Machinist, no one asked?"

"Not me or my dad, as far as I'm aware. I'm sure someone asked one of the greats all those years ago, but I don't know what they were told. As long as the demon doesn't get in, people lose interest."

I glanced at Petra, who was making a low growl, and wearing the same scowl as yesterday. "We're aware efforts were undertaken to keep the wards secret," I said. "So you don't know where or what the other ones are?"

"Not a thing. We were supposed to be separate to be incorruptible."

"What about other people involved?" I asked. "Other Machinists?"

"There's no one outside the family who's involved," he said. "Other than the trustees I told you about. But the original paper records were lost in a flood in the early 1900s."

"What about the ley lines?" Petra asked. "How are they involved?"

For a moment, Hugo just blinked at her. "Seriously? I mean, the Cornerstones, right? That's the whole point."

We just looked at him.

"I don't know what those are," Petra said. And if she didn't know, Theo and I certainly didn't.

"Magical tablets buried in Chicago?" Hugo said, looking between us. "They were put underground and spelled to regulate the power coming from Chicago's ley lines and power the wards."

It was Petra's turn to blink in obvious shock. It wasn't often that someone surprised her with information. "Magical tablets?"

"Well, yeah. Really big rocks?" He stretched his arms in a wide circle.

"You said they regulate the power of the ley lines," I said. "So they're kind of like electrical transformers?"

"Sure. Like that."

"Did the Guardians put them in place?" I asked.

"Yeah. I think it was a two-birds-one-stone kind of deal. Regulate the ley lines as Chicago's human population increased to make everyone safer."

"Because less powerful ley lines meant less powerful supernaturals?" I asked.

"I think that was the theory, yeah."

"And one of the Cornerstones powers your machine?" Theo asked.

Hugo nodded.

"How many Cornerstones are there?"

"I don't know."

Petra sighed. "And I guess you don't know where they are?"

"Well, no. I mean, I don't know where all of them are. I know where mine is. You want to go see it?"

We did. We did want to go see it.

But first, we made Hugo eat and hydrate.

When he was steadier, we let him join us in the van, and Petra drove while he directed us to a short, squat building only half a block from the warehouse.

"Damn," he said as we passed the damage Rosantine had done. "She's really here, and it really activated."

"Yeah," Theo said. "Plenty of footage online if you want to see it."

"Yeah. When I'm ready, I probably will." He tapped his head. "I'm still kind of processing, you know?"

To have been the guardian of nearly two centuries of history and out of commission for the two hours the history happened had to be a punch.

We parked on the street and followed him around the building, all of us watching for Rosantine. She'd been looking for something in this neighborhood. Why not this?

"Insurance agency rents out the main building," he said. "They're good tenants." He walked to an unassuming shed, maybe a few yards from the main building, pushed against a concrete wall that separated this lot from the one behind it.

"It's in here," he said. "We've replaced the shed a few times over the years, but this one's been in place since my grandpa put it in. I added a few layers of security, though."

He used a key to open a small box by the door, then pressed his thumbprint against a small screen inside it. He pulled out his personal screen, then entered a code there. "Triple authentication," he said when whirring began to sound within the shed. The doors popped open, revealing a steel layer inside the wooden shell. A light flickered on, sending cool blue light across the only object inside it.

It was . . . a rock.

A big rock, sure, of a dotted stone I guessed was granite. The edges were rounded, and there were symbols etched into the surface that looked like the same language we'd seen on the machine. It sat on the dark earth, as it apparently had for nearly two centuries. And that was it.

Yeah, it was called a "Cornerstone," but I guess I'd expected something more ornamental. Or larger. Or studded with crystals. I'd also have expected a giant magical rock to put some residual magic in the air. But there was nothing. It felt completely inert, and if Hugo hadn't told me its purpose, I'd have assumed it was decorative.

Petra pulled out her screen, began snapping pictures.

"It's kind of like a rune," Theo said. "Or at least the ones I've seen in *The Revenge of Freja*."

"Such a great flick," Hugo said. "And yeah, they do look similar."

"Phenomenal flick," Theo said.

"It doesn't feel like magic," I said.

"It was spelled to be neutral," Hugo explained. "Designed so it doesn't emit any magic as it does its thing."

"So Sups can't sniff out the Cornerstones and manipulate them."

"That's the theory," Hugo agreed. He leaned forward, brushed away an invisible bit of dirt from the stone with obvious care and attention.

"The Cornerstones may be neutral," I said, "but I don't think the wards are. I think that's how Rose figured out where the South Gate and the machine were."

"Do you know what the symbols say?" Theo asked. "Or how the magic works?"

"No. They didn't give us any of that information, at least as far as I was aware. Only how to clean and oil the machine. I had a schedule to follow, and I've only missed it twice. I broke my collarbone a few years ago, and it was a couple of weeks before I could really get in there. One year I had pneumonia, and I was down for nearly a month."

Those both sounded like normal human things. Not demon interference or manipulation.

"Did anyone ever fill in for you?" I asked.

Hugo's eyes widened with surprise. "Well, no. I couldn't tell anyone else, so they couldn't, like, show up and do it."

Theo caught on to my line of questions and where I was going with them. "Did anyone ever ask you about it? I mean, people asked about your job, right? Just in casual conversation, and you told them—what—that you worked on a machine?"

"Well, kind of. Folks I game with have known me forever." He blushed a little. "But I didn't give them any details. I make a little extra money streaming my games on the side. Some just assume that's my real job."

"Anyone ever follow you here? Or have you seen anyone suspicious hanging around?"

"No," he said with a laugh, but his expression sobered. "You think someone caught on, or maybe she had someone follow me or become friends to find out where the Cornerstone was? But how would she find me in the first place?"

"Just eliminating possibilities." I looked at Hugo. "What's the machine's range?"

"What?"

"I think she's asking how close the demon has to be for the machine to trigger," Petra said, and I nodded.

"Oh, well, I don't know." Hugo ran a hand over his hair. "Anywhere within its perimeter, I guess."

"Which is?" Petra asked.

He winced. "I don't know that, either. I'm sorry. I've never seen it work before. I just know it was supposed to target the demon if she got close."

I didn't detect any magic in his lack of knowledge. If Petra was right, and some kind of memory spell affected Patience's ability to remember or talk about the wards, it hadn't affected him. Maybe because he hadn't been alive at the time.

"Run us through how the machine works," Theo said. "Lay-people's terms."

He blushed. "It was . . ." He cleared his throat as if embarrassed. "It was explained to me in a song when I was little, to help me remember. They didn't want to write it down."

"Could you give us the lyrics?" Petra said.

Hugo cleared his throat and stared up at the shed's metal ceiling, a flush riding high on his cheeks. *"Ley line to Cornerstone; keep the magic calm. Cornerstone to feed the ward; keep the city safe. Machine to light the city; make the demon seen. Plasma flash to bring her low; eliminate the scourge."*

Theo blinked. "Went a little dark at the end there."

"That last line's a little harsh," Hugo agreed. "When I was a kid, I thought 'scourge' meant 'dirt' or something."

"Demons are harsh," I said. "And the song nailed it. The light from the machine turned her kind of green."

Hugo's gaze snapped back to mine, curiosity now replacing the embarrassment. "Green?"

"It put a weird cast on her skin. Made it clear she was different."

"To make the demon seen," he said again. "Maybe to help the plasma flash—the lightning—identify her."

"Here's the problem, Hugo," Theo began, "which you might have guessed. The demon is powerful. She is a literal agent of chaos. Snaps her fingers, and very bad things happen."

Hugo looked distraught.

"The machine worked really well," I reminded him. "The system kept her out for more than a hundred years. Unfortunately, she's just stronger than the wards. She might have gotten stronger while she waited. And there's something in Chicago she wants very badly."

"The Cornerstones," Petra guessed.

I nodded. "That's what I'm thinking."

"How does she know they exist?" Hugo asked.

"That, I don't know," I said. "But she's had a long time to look for them, to puzzle out the possibility."

"What happens if she gets to the Cornerstones?" Theo asked.

"That would be bad," Hugo said. "First thing is she could manipulate the wards." He scratched absently at his arm. "She could turn them off—like unplugging a toaster."

"Would she have to destroy the stone for that?" Petra asked.

"Or just change the spell." He pointed to the symbols. "The power of the stone is in the symbols. If she did that, who knows what she could do? Power whatever she wanted using the ley lines, I guess?"

"And that's why the Cornerstones are magic neutral," I said, "and why so few people know about them—so they don't become objects of supernatural lust.

"We need to find her before she gets to one," I continued, "and we need to stop her. Is there anything else you can tell us about where you think she might go, or where the other Cornerstones might be? Anything that might help us take her in before she hurts more people?"

"No. But if I think of anything, I'll let you know."

I didn't doubt he would. He'd been entrusted with the care of a magical object, and he seemed to take that obligation very seriously. The problem was, based on everything we knew, he wasn't going to have any more information.

Hugo ran a hand through his hair. "What should I do now? I mean, it's my job to maintain the machine."

"The machine is cordoned off while the investigation is under-way," Theo said, tapping fingers against his cast as he considered. "But there's going to need to be repairs and cleanup."

"There's a fund for that," Hugo said.

"A fund?" Theo asked.

"It's part of the trust. The Machinist gets paid, and there are funds for repair."

"We're going to talk to the CPD," Theo said, "and get you in touch with the right people so you can coordinate the repairs." He pulled out his screen, started sending a message.

"Oh. Cool."

Petra nodded. "We'll need your expertise if there's any hope of getting the ward up again."

Hugo perked up now, straightened his shoulders. He'd been given another task, a new mission, and that eased his guilt. "Yeah, yeah, whatever you need."

Theo nodded. "Good. I'm also going to get some guards over here now. Plainclothes so they don't draw too much attention, but we need someone keeping an eye on this stone and making sure she doesn't come near it."

"Sups would be best," I said quietly. "They'll be able to sense her magic."

"Yup," he said, and tapped at his screen.

"Could I go see the machine?" Hugo said. "I don't have to touch anything, but if there are parts that need repair, I could maybe make some sketches?" He sounded hopeful.

"We'll see what we can do," Theo said.

We locked up the shed, then walked Hugo to the warehouse.

"Wow," he said, staring up at the broken building. "Wow."

"We think it broke out the windows when the machine started," Petra said.

Hugo looked at her, confusion in his eyes. "No, it wouldn't

have done that. It does the beam of light, but that's only vertical, and there's a door for it."

Petra, Theo, and I looked at each other.

"Then it was probably due to fighting humans," I said. "She's a chaos demon, after all."

"CPD is working on getting surveillance video," Theo said.

"I can do that for you," Hugo said brightly. "For my building, anyway. I've got cams, and I'm sorry I didn't think of it."

"We'd appreciate it," Theo said.

Gwen emerged from the building, looked around, spotted us.

"Wow," Hugo said quietly. "She is really pretty."

"Yeah," Theo said, chest puffing out a little. "She is."

Gwen reached us, nodded. "You must be Mr. Horner. I'm Detective Robinson." She tapped her badge. "I'll take you inside, and you can take a look."

"Sure, sure."

She looked at us. "Plainclothes officers, a few Sups who keep their magic under the radar, are on their way to the spot you identified. They'll let us know if they see anything even potentially odd."

"Thank you," I said, and looked at Hugo. "And thanks to you, too. You've been a real help, and you're going to help us nail her."

And maybe that would help him exorcise the guilt.

We left Hugo in Gwen's capable hands and looked around for a spot to discuss. There was an old-school coffeehouse a block away—scuffed floors, raggedy furniture, burned-in coffee smell, and demon-undamaged—and we walked over for a cup.

It was mostly artists and students that filled the tables, studying over screens or working together on projects. And the inevitable guy in the corner with glasses and a dog-eared paperback, reading as he sipped from an enormous mug. There was one in every coffeehouse.

"Cornerstones," Petra whispered as we took rickety seats at a small round table. "We got that, at least."

"Patience didn't mention them," Theo said. "So she didn't even know that much."

"There had to be so much coordination to get this done," I said. "It's an entire system of defenses—levels of wards. How could the Guardians have done it all without talking to each other? Without writing anything down?"

"Maybe that's what's on the documents they found at Cadogan House."

"I don't know," I said, and glanced at Petra. "I think you were right about the memory spell. I think they knew Rosantine was manipulative and might try to make her way in again, so they gave Patience only just enough information to explain the reason why they built the defenses."

"The ward makers might have been separated while they worked," Petra said, "or spelled afterward so they couldn't talk about what they'd done."

"And Rosantine couldn't find them, force them to tell."

We all needed a moment of quiet sipping after that.

"So what is on the documents at Cadogan House?" Theo wondered.

"I have no idea," I said, "or who wrote them. I'm hoping Mallory can shed some light on that tonight."

"We need to find the Cornerstones," Petra said. "Find them and secure them."

"The first one will probably be near South Gate," I said. "Maybe there are property records that would help?"

"I'll get Gwen on it," Theo said. "If she finds anything, the CPD can send out uniforms to check the site and secure it."

I smiled at Theo. "Is that just a convenient excuse to talk to Gwen again?"

"It doesn't hurt," he said with a sly smile.

"The problem is finding the rest of the wards before she finds a Cornerstone or triggers a ward and hurts more people," I said. "We need the sigil. We have to find the damned sigil and seal her." I rubbed my temples at the brewing headache.

"We'll have to find her first," Petra said. "At this rate, that's the only way we're going to find the sigil."

"Then we assume she'll go for another ward, and we figure out where the wards are. But the locations so far don't make sense to me."

I pulled sweetener packets from the dish on the table, put one near the table's bottom edge, another near the middle. "South Gate," I said, pointing at the lower one. "And lightning machine," I said, pointing to the other. "We know there's a Cornerstone near the lightning machine. We're checking to see if there's a Cornerstone at the gate, and probably there is. Rose said she found South Gate because she could feel the magic. She was sniffing around the lightning machine for magic, too. So even if she couldn't detect the Cornerstone, she could detect the wards."

"But?" Theo prompted.

"How do wards in these two positions keep out a demon? Why didn't she just come into the city somewhere else? Not through the gate but across the lake, or from Evanston. Couldn't she have just walked into the city literally anywhere else?"

"Not very good wards if that's the case," Theo said.

"Exactly. They'd be really crappy wards."

"Maybe they're concentric rings," Petra said. She opened a sweetener packet, drew a wide circle in white powder that intersected with the gate. "Cornerstone fuels the ward, and the ward is basically this big ring. So the ghosts appear wherever the demon pops up along that ring."

"Okay," I said. "That makes sense. Except for here." I pointed at the lightning machine. "It's nearly downtown. That's a long way from the gate. If the wards are in concentric rings, why didn't she trigger something in between?"

"Maybe it's broken," Petra said. "It's been a long time since they were established. Maybe they didn't all survive the intervening years."

"Wouldn't there be more than one, though?" Theo asked. "Otherwise, the gap is too big. And I think you'd only build a defense in rings if you're protecting something in the innermost ring. Like a castle. Moat, wall, keep, et cetera."

"There's nothing that says Rose is targeting something downtown," I said, "or what used to be downtown in 1872, anyway."

"Maybe there are only two Cornerstones," Petra said. "Imagine the planning and magic that would go into something like this." She tapped a finger—which I just realized was inset with tiny gold stars—near the outer sweetener ring. "Maybe this was all the time or energy they had."

"I don't know," I said. "They went to a lot of trouble to hide their plan. That says complexity to me. But what do I know? This all happened years ago. Maybe we're totally off track."

"How about this," Petra said. "When we get back to the office, I'll start on a map. I'll mark out the incident locations, the Cornerstone locations as we find them. Maybe if we start looking at it that way—not in sugar on a table—we'll see some kind of pattern."

"And we're going to need to give the servers a very big tip," Theo said, sweeping sweetener into a napkin.

"I'm suddenly craving a Chicago dog," Petra said. "Anyone else interested?"

"Not me," I said, and checked the time on my screen. "I have to get to Cadogan House."

"Forgot," Petra said. "You eat good over there?"

"Honestly, it's probably pizza." We were talking about my mother, after all.

THIRTEEN

I rode to Cadogan House in style—in the back of the Ombuds' van, while Petra listened to a podcast about the extraterrestrial creatures living in our midst.

When she stopped to let me grab a bottle of wine for the party, she was talking about conspiracies. She was still talking about conspiracies when I got into the vehicle again. Petra was brilliant, creative, and skilled. And she'd never met a conspiracy theory she didn't love. I still wasn't sure if she believed any of it or just enjoyed the wackiness.

We pulled up to Cadogan House to a surprise—nearly a dozen of them. Shifters on bikes idling outside the gate. Including the three interlopers who'd invaded the Pack.

"Who's the hot brunette?" Petra asked, obviously checking out Cade.

"One of the Pack troublemakers," I said. I climbed out of the back of the van with my bottle of wine and felt very uncool. And like I was in high school again.

"No vampire-on-shifter violence, please," Theo said. "And let us know the second you learn anything."

"I will." I closed the door, put on my blandest vampire expression, and walked toward the bikes. The interlopers were positioned near the back of the group, and I doubted that was an accident. There was still a hierarchy.

"You have business at Cadogan House?" I asked Cade, who sat astride a red lowrider with high handlebars.

"We were out for a ride," he said, casting a warm glance over the other shifters like they were family and besties combined.

Miranda, bless her this once, met his gaze with an explicitly chilly one.

"Shifters love the air. The metal. The night. I'm treating them to drinks," he said.

"So you're trying to bribe them?" I asked.

I saw the hitch in his gaze, but he recovered, and the smile he gave me was thin. "Maybe I'm just showing them the way."

"Maybe you are," I said. "But they know what Connor can do. And he doesn't have to bribe them." I kept walking, but the commentary kept coming.

"Vampires think they live in castles," said the female interloper as I passed her.

I stopped, just as she'd intended, but kept my gaze neutral. "Your name is Brandy, right?"

Temper flared in her eyes. "It's Breonna."

"Right. Breonna. Vampires live in houses together, just like the Pack. And the NAC owns a huge corporation and pays shares to its members. What's your point?"

She muttered something uncomplimentary.

I cocked my head at her. "Isn't that a name for a female dog?"

Her magic flared, fingers around the bike's handlebars going white.

And with that preface to violence, monster's interest flared.

"I've had a shit night," I said quietly, "in a pretty shitty week. A little hand to hand might make us both feel better." Both, of course, meaning me and monster. On this, we were aligned.

A whistle split the air. I looked up, found Connor on a bike at the front of the group. He wore jeans and a snug T-shirt, his strong thighs still straddling Thelma. She was low and dark and matte, and finally back in fighting trim after a crazed vampire had nearly run him over while he returned to Pack HQ one night.

"I guess we're out of time," I told Breonna, and didn't wait for a reply. But I felt the hot itch of her magic—and her angry stare— as I walked past the rest of the bikes and shifters to where Connor waited.

His smile was slow and confident. "Hey, brat."

"Hey, puppy," I said, then took his face in my free hand and kissed him hard.

When the kiss was done, he whistled again, held up a fist. Apparently taking the cue, the other bikes roared to life and took off single file down the road. That left only three bikes: Connor's, Alexei's, and the bike I thought belonged to Connor's father.

"Your parents?" I asked.

"Inside. They got a late invite. I hope you don't mind."

"The more the merrier." And the more minds focused on our demon problem, the better off we'd all be.

"Wine?" Connor asked.

"Yeah. And not just strawberry wine-drink."

"I don't know what that is."

"You're better off for it."

Alexei already stood with Lulu at the curb. She waved at me, the handles of a brown paper bag in her other hand. The appetizer, I assumed.

"Are they on an actual date?" I whispered as Connor climbed off Thelma and took my hand. We fell into step behind them.

"Emotional support," he said. "He's trying to walk a very narrow line."

"That she's drawn."

"Yep. Her prerogative to set boundaries. My enjoyment to watch him dance around on them."

"Like a mating dance?"

"I mean, if the shoe fits."

"I didn't get a mating dance." I bumped his arm. "I think you're more the preening type."

"I have many skills," he said with that utterly confident drawl of the shifter prince.

I heard a rumble, automatically glanced at the sky. It was clear, the moon an embiggening crescent, and I figured it was just the bikes roaring down the road. For reasons I didn't understand, louder bikes were better bikes where most shifters were concerned. Thelma had more of a deep purr, which I appreciated.

"Does anyone else smell garlic?" Alexei asked, and his stomach audibly rumbled. Alexei was an omnivore's omnivore and seemed to find pretty much everything digestible.

"Pizza," I said. "Or maybe pasta." Gastronomic obsessions were as immortal as vampires.

"Weird either way," he said. "Vampires being freaked by garlic is a tradition."

We reached the gate. A human guard waved me through, and we started down the sidewalk toward the House's front portico.

"Yikes," Lulu said, wrinkling her nose. "That's not garlic."

A hot breeze stirred, and I could smell smoke . . . and the sulfurous tang of brimstone. It was like evil had exhaled across the House's lawn.

I put a hand on the handle of my sword.

"Lis?" Connor said.

"Demon," I said, and everyone went on alert.

That rumbling sound tumbled across the neighborhood again, and this time the ground shook with it. Light cast from the House's windows shifted as chandeliers shook inside; Connor took my free hand.

Another rumble. Another vibration, and the House itself seemed to waver, like the image on a screen with a bad connection.

"What the fuck?" Alexei murmured.

There was a crinkle of sound, like crumpling paper. No, I thought with horror—as yellow flames suddenly flared where the House met the ground and began to climb the stone—like the snapping of a fire. In seconds, the forks of fire were crawling upward, more like grasping fingers than actual fire. But there was no heat. Only the smell of char, of sulfur, of demon.

I looked around and didn't see Rose. Wherever she was working, she was staying hidden this time. But the magic was undeniable. This was demon magic. Not just enhancing chaos, but active and purposeful. But what was she doing?

"Get help!" someone called. Maybe one of the guards. "Call 911!"

I knew that wouldn't help. The brick wasn't singed, and the shrubs around the House hadn't caught. This wasn't fire—or at least not as we understood it—so water wouldn't extinguish it. A sword wouldn't slice this. A shifter couldn't claw it back. A sorceress might have been able, but Lulu didn't use her magic.

"Mom!" Lulu screamed, and tried to launch forward as the magic reached the second floor. Alexei grabbed her arm, pulled her back toward him, even as she screamed to be loosed. "Let me go!"

But he held her tightly, bound his arms around her to keep her safe and out of the magic's reach.

She wouldn't have made it anyway. In seconds, the House was wrapped in those magical flames, and the entire House flickered again.

For a moment, I'd have sworn there was no House at all.

Then I felt the pull, like something had reached into my body and was trying to draw my bones into the maelstrom of magic. I instinctively braced my knees and sucked in a breath, trying to fight back against the tug of power.

It took a moment to realize the magic wasn't grasping for me, but for monster. Even though I stood outside the House, the magic somehow sensed monster's presence and was trying to draw monster into its domain. Maybe because of the connection to my mother's sword?

Monster had no interest in being dragged. It reeled back inside me, as if trying to squeeze itself into a secure corner. The magic didn't care about its wishes, or the fact that monster was bound to me. Suddenly, it was yanking my entire body forward, dragging me toward the flame-wrapped House. I bore down, my boots digging furrows in the dirt as I tried to scramble back and out of its grasp.

"Elisa!" Connor yelled my name. He jumped forward, grabbed my arm; Alexei took the other.

"Shit," I said, kicking against grass and pulling on their arms as we fought—all three of us—against the strength of it. The power of the magic was tremendous; the pressure intense enough to roar in my ears.

"Not a fucking chance you're getting sucked in there," Connor said, sweat popping on his forehead as he strained to hold me back.

"Apologies in advance," Alexei said, and jumped around to straddle my legs, holding me down to keep me stationary. Changing the center of gravity gave Connor a chance to get a better grip.

Connor hit his knees in front of me, gripped my forearms. I did the same, my fingers white from the strain. We'd have bruises tomorrow . . . if we survived this.

"Not a fucking chance," Connor repeated, arms corded with effort, reading the fear in my face.

The air pressure suddenly changed, and the magic released me. Connor fell backward as the tension was released. Alexei stood up, offered me a hand. I took it and rose to my knees, and when I couldn't avoid it any longer, looked back. Streaks of magic flashed, stuttered. And disappeared.

And when they did, they took the House with them.

*   *   *

Cadogan House was gone.

I don't know how long I kneeled in grass damp with dew, hands shaking from magic and effort, breathing air that smelled of flame and demon, and trying to comprehend the fact that the House—and all its inhabitants—were simply . . . gone.

I stood up, pushed away the hands that tried to stop me, and walked to where the House had been. The shrubs that had edged the House were still there. The sidewalk still existed. But the House itself—the building—was gone. And in its place, in its footprint, was only darkness. A void of inky black. Not liquid. Not solid. Not smoke. Just . . . nothing. It was *absence*.

And she had made it happen.

I knew the flames hadn't been real, that the House hadn't really burned. But that was just mechanics. The House was gone, and with it our families: my mom and dad, Lulu's parents, Connor's parents. And every other person, vampire or otherwise, who had been in Cadogan House.

Rose had taken them away. And I was torn between absolute fury and sobbing grief.

I heard footsteps beside me and knew without looking it was Connor.

"I don't know . . ." I said, trying to breathe through the band of fear that tightened my chest. "I don't know what to do. Or what I could have done."

Connor said nothing, and I looked at him, saw the same emotions in his eyes. Rage that someone had taken his family. Fear and grief about whether they'd survived.

Wordlessly, he turned and wrapped his arms around me—leaned against me, as if he needed someone to help shoulder the weight of his sorrow. It was doubly heartbreaking that, as a prince, he was so rarely able to ask for that help.

"I thought you were going with it," he said.

"I didn't," I said. And felt momentarily guilty for wishing I had—that I'd gone with my parents. Because then they could tell me how to help them. "I didn't," I murmured again.

As if sensing my thought, my regret, his arms tightened. A refusal to let me go.

"I should have done something," I said, tears slipping down my cheeks now. "But I don't know what I could have done."

"Nothing," said Alexei behind us. He held Lulu in his arms.

We looked back. "What?" I asked.

"You could have done nothing. There are Ukrainian stories about the brimstone flames that don't burn. And none of us had power enough to stop it."

Lulu cried harder, and he whispered something into her ear; her pain and his compassion had my tears falling again. "They can't be gone," she said. "They can't be."

"Maybe they aren't," Alexei said. "A spell can always be undone. You will figure out a way."

Connor looked down at me. "Can you feel them? Or the House?"

"I . . . don't know," I said. The air was thick with magic and emotions, and I wasn't sure if I could separate them out. "I can try."

He let me go and I stepped forward, putting a few feet of space between me and the others so I was clear of their magic. I closed my eyes, blew out a breath, and tried to center myself, to push away the distractions. The fear. The grief. The fury.

I made myself think of the House itself, of the buzz of magic and scent of gardenias, of the flowers that always waited on the table in the foyer. Of the old-book smell of the second-floor library. Of my mother's perfume and the feel of curling up beside her to watch a movie. Of sitting in my father's office, eating pizza. And, for better or worse, of the sword in the armory and the tendrils it seemed to stretch out to monster, drawing it near. But even monster went still now, offering me the quiet to reach out and feel what I could.

In the mental quiet, through a tunnel of darkness that led to a place I couldn't see, I could feel the faint and familiar buzz. The magical heartbeat of my home, my family, and the vampires I'd grown up with.

They were alive, I thought, with gasping relief. But they were far away, their connection to me as faint as a whisper. And streaked across that thin connection was a smoky, bitter stain that was becoming all too familiar.

Demon.

Rose.

I hadn't had any doubts that she'd done this. But sensing her mark on the magic was another slap, another wound atop the damage she'd already inflicted.

I opened my eyes and felt the tears, already fallen, cold on my cheeks.

I turned back, looked at Lulu, trying to reassure both of us. "I can feel them," I said. "They're alive. They're just somewhere else."

"Where?" Connor asked, his voice low and deep and full of mingled hope and trepidation.

I shook my head, wiped my cheeks. "I don't know. But the House wasn't destroyed, right? It wasn't exploded or burned down or dismantled. It just isn't here anymore. So we figure out where they are and we bring them back."

"How are we going to figure that out?" Lulu asked.

I didn't know that, either. "We'll either figure out the magic on our own, or we'll capture the demon and make her do it. One way or the other, we'll fix this," I said, forging the promise.

Lulu nodded. "It almost sucked you in." She swiped at tears.

"Yeah."

"Maybe because you lived there?" she said. "Maybe because of the binding spell that made you."

"Maybe," I said, and slid my gaze to Connor. His face was carefully neutral, but his expression said he understood what had happened. What the magic had targeted and tried to pull away. Monster was still reeling from the attack, still in shock about the absence of the House and the sword.

There were lights and sirens behind us. We glanced back, watched Gwen, Theo, Roger, and Petra emerge from vehicles and run toward the House they expected to see. And then stop and stare at what wasn't there.

"I heard," Roger said. "But I didn't believe it. And seeing it—I still don't know what to believe." He looked at me and my tears nearly welling from concern. Family came in all forms. "I'm sorry," he added.

I nodded and tears welled again. Roger offered me a handkerchief, which was so thoughtful, if old-fashioned. I had a really great boss.

"Thanks," I said, and wiped my eyes. "I think they're still alive. They're just . . . wherever the House is."

"Then we'll bring them back," Roger said simply, as if it would be so easy. A gentle squeeze of my arm, and then he moved on to Connor, to Lulu, offering what solace he could.

Theo gave me a one-armed hug, the other still casted. "We'll figure it out," he said quietly. "I promise that."

Petra waved her gloved hands. "Consider this a hug."

"Considered," I said with a slight smile.

"Then let's get to the business of figuring." I appreciated that her mind went directly to solving the problem. "There's definite demon involvement," Petra continued. "You can smell the bitterness."

"Yeah," I said, anger blooming. "You can."

She frowned. "Since when do demons do portal magic?"

"Portal magic?" I asked.

"If the House isn't here, and it's somewhere else, that's basic portal magic. The House is probably wherever that"—she pointed to the well of darkness—"used to be. They switched places, like the world's worst parent trap. Demons aren't known for portal magic."

"Maybe someone helped her," Theo offered.

"It's possible," Petra said, "but who'd want to help a demon?"

"Her criminal accomplices," I said. "She ran with a bad crowd."

"True," Petra said.

"Why was she here?" Theo asked, gaze scanning the landscape. "There's no sign of a triggered ward, right? Why come to Cadogan House otherwise?"

"Maybe she thought there might be a ward and a Cornerstone," I said. "There's a lot of magic in and around Cadogan House. Maybe she just guessed wrong."

"That's logical," Petra said. "But why toss the House? What does she get out of it? Maybe it was a defensive move when she saw you walk up?"

I liked the word "toss." It made this feel more like a puzzle and less like a horrifying tragedy.

"We didn't see her," Connor said. "There was no need for a defensive move."

"So she wanted the House gone," Roger said. "Why?"

"There were powerful people in that House," I pointed out.

"And powerful things," Lulu said. "The library."

"The library," I said slowly, nodding. "And the spells Paige and your mother were going to translate. But she couldn't know what's in the library. Not in any detail." I looked at Roger. "Did she ask you about it?"

"No," Roger said. "But it's easy enough to figure out the House has a library. That information is public and online. If she's been preparing all this time, and knew at least one of the defenses existed, she might have been researching the city, trying to figure out where . . ." Roger trailed off and closed his eyes as we all realized the implication.

"Which is one of the reasons Rose was talking to you," Theo concluded. "She wanted to know where to look."

Roger's jaw tightened, and he held up a hand, then walked a few feet away, paced. Still feeling guilty about Rose, I guessed. I opened my mouth to tell him not to blame himself, but Theo put a hand on my arm.

"Let him work it out."

Petra cleared her throat in the awkward silence that followed. "Oh, I forgot to tell you—the CPD found the Cornerstone by the South Gate."

That wasn't the good news I'd have preferred to hear, but it confirmed we were on the right track. And that was something.

"Where was it?" Connor asked.

"Buried in the median," she said with a grin. "The easement is still on record. The CPD has uniforms around it."

"Can we search for similar easements?" Connor asked.

"Unfortunately not. I mean, we can search the records, but there are literally tens of thousands of easements in the city, and this one wasn't searchable in any unique way. We only found it because we were looking at that particular plot of land. But we can check the property records for Cadogan House just in case there's something unusual."

"Do that," Roger said, walking back to us. Then he looked at Lulu, Connor, and me in turn.

"I'm sorry again for whatever part I've played in this. For whatever help I gave her."

Lulu stepped up to him, pointed a finger. "No," she said, eyes still red and swollen. "You don't take the blame for this. *She* takes the blame for all of this. *She* does."

Then she turned and strode toward the House—where the

House had been—and screamed at the top of her lungs into the chilly darkness.

"We are going to find our parents, Rose, and bring them back! And then we're going to find you, and you will never see the light of day again!"

I'd have sworn I felt magic in her words.

Connor took on the miserable task of explaining to the Pack that its Apex had disappeared—while also grieving the loss of his parents. Alexei accompanied him back to Pack HQ, and I expected the Pack's reaction would be . . . strong. Not just the worry or pain, but suspicion that vampires had been the cause. And the interlopers would probably add their own conspiracies.

Because my coworkers were kind and generous people, they offered to help out any Cadogan vamps who'd been away when the House disappeared, taking their home and belongings with it. They'd be grieving, too, and would need clothes, food, and shelter from the sun's inevitable rise.

I was too numb to do anything but stare at the spot where the House had been. Lulu sat cross-legged on the sidewalk that led to the House's portico, staring at it like she might simply conjure it back into existence. I stood beside her like a guardian. I don't know how long we waited, watching for some change as members of the CPD moved around us, carefully recording the scene and canvassing the grounds for any sign of Rose.

I jumped when vehicle doors slammed, and looked back to find a cadre of strangers coming toward us. This time, it was vampires. Given my recent experiences with unfamiliar vamps, I went on alert and put my hand on my sword.

The vampire in front was a tall man with tan skin, a lumberjack's build, glasses, and dark blond hair in a topknot. "Hi," he said, and looked at me. "I'm Micah. Washington House's Second."

His voice was deep, quiet.

I knew him only by name; I'd met the vampire who'd stood Second before him, but he'd vacated the position before I'd come home from France.

"Washington House," I repeated lamely, as it took a moment for my brain to compute what that meant. And then my heart sank all over again. "He was in the House? Uncle Malik?"

He nodded. "For dinner with you and your parents and the Bells."

"Oh, my god," I said, tears welling again. "I'm so sorry."

"No need for that," he said quietly. "You didn't do—whatever this was."

"It was a demon," I said, and told him what we'd seen. "We're figuring out the rest, but"—I cleared my throat and felt awkward and a little sad saying this—"I can sense them out there. Somewhere else but alive. So we'll figure out how to get them back."

Micah looked at me for a very long time, then swallowed hard. "Thank you for that."

Nodding was all I could manage without more tears.

"I'm going to take a look. I just—I feel like I need to."

I nodded, and the group split to allow him through. I looked back at the vampires who'd accompanied him. There was devastation in their faces as they watched their Second move to the spot where their Master had disappeared.

The bond between Master and Novitiate was an important one. Not one I understood well, because I didn't have a formal House or a Master. But Uncle Malik had turned most of the vampires in his House, and he'd handpicked the others to join him.

Micah stood in front of the void for a while. By the time he came back, his expression was grim. There was sorrow in his eyes, and I heard more than a couple of sniffs from his other vampires.

"We're going to get him back," I said, and wondered how many more people would have to hear that tonight. Would have to deal with the consequences of what Rose had done.

"Are you?" It was an honest question, earnestly asked.

"Yes. We're working out how to track her, how to seal her, and how to ensure she can never hurt this city again."

He watched me for a moment, nodded. "I believe you will." He cleared his throat. "He'd wanted us to meet," he added.

I blinked. "Uncle Malik?"

Micah nodded. "I think he wanted us to . . . connect."

It took a moment to realize what he meant. "Wait—what? He did?"

"That was before the shifter." He lifted his hands, smiled earnestly. "And I'm not trying to hit on you. You two are obviously a good team, and I don't poach. I just thought you'd want to know that he cared that much."

"I appreciate it," I said with an answering smile, surprised and pleased that Uncle Malik had given it thought. "Damn it," I murmured, as tears spilled again. I looked up, focused on the waxing moon, which hung bright and white in the sky.

"Hard night all around," Micah said. "I may need some extra Babu time tonight."

"Babu?"

"New House mascot," he said, then pulled out his screen, showed me a picture of what I was confident was the ugliest dog I'd ever seen. It was a bulldog of some sort, wrinkly of face and drooly of mouth, with a rather remarkable underbite.

"Babu is . . ." I struggled for a compliment.

"A face only a mother—or two dozen vampires—could love," he finished, saving me. "He comforts all of us."

"Then I'm glad you have him," I said.

He put his screen away again. "The vampires who weren't in Cadogan when it disappeared?"

"The Ombuds are making sure they have what they need."

He must have seen my face. "If you're feeling guilty, don't. Your job is to get the House back, and I'll wager that's not going to be easy. I'll talk to Roger and we'll help with the displaced vampires however we can. We've got plenty of room in the House, and I'm sure Grey and Navarre will help, too."

Those were Chicago's other two vampire Houses.

"Thank you," I said, and began to understand why Uncle Malik had selected him as Second. "We'll keep you updated on this."

"Do that," Micah said. "And if you need some time with Babu, you know where to find us."

By the time the moon had arced across the sky, I was exhausted. There were still two hours before dawn, but I felt like the sun was already on the rise.

Connor and Alexei pulled an SUV to the curb, which they'd switched out at Pack HQ so we could travel back to the town house together.

We said our goodbyes to the Ombuds, and I took one last look at the grounds. CPD uniforms had been stationed around the House, as if Sentinels to replace the one—my mother—who was currently missing.

I turned back to the SUV, where Connor held open my door. He hadn't mentioned yet what had gone down at Pack HQ, but his face was hard and tired.

"How bad was it?" I asked quietly.

"As bad as it gets. We'll talk about it tomorrow. We're going to get something to eat, then we're going to sleep. We all need our strength," he added, anticipating my argument that we didn't have time for anything else. "Without it, you won't do your parents any good."

I climbed in and he closed the door. I had no energy to argue, so I didn't try.

We were silent as Connor drove to a silver bullet of a building that apparently housed a twenty-four-hour diner.

"Just a minute," he said, then went inside and picked up an order that smelled, frankly, delicious. We rode to the town house in a fog of food smells.

I changed clothes and came back downstairs to find dinner on the table—assorted containers of soup. Someone had added a box of crackers, a bottle of ketchup, bottles of small-batch soda made in Chicago, and a bottle of blood for me.

Lulu was already seated, arms crossed and staring blankly across the room.

"Eat," I said, taking a seat next to her. "It's probably going to be a long few nights, and we might need your strength. Have you been practicing with those throwing knives Alexei gave you?"

I was trying to shift the mood from grieving to planning, hoping that giving her a goal, something to focus on, would help dilute the sadness. She picked up her spoon, at least, dabbed it into the soup.

"Some," she said. "I'm more comfortable with guns."

Lulu might have avoided supernatural drama, but she had no issues with weapons. Weapons were her father's magical specialty, so she'd been taught how to use a variety of them. And there was nothing supernatural about an M1911.

I pulled the lid off my container, found chunks of beef in a thick potato- and carrot-filled stew that made my stomach rumble. I could eat, even if the act felt selfish because it wasn't laser-focused on getting our parents back.

"Taking care of yourself isn't selfish," Connor said, as if he could read my mind.

When I gave him a narrow stare, he just smiled. "It was written all over your face, Lis. And it's going to take time and energy to fix this."

"Will we fix it?" I hadn't meant to express that as a question. But my fears were real.

Alexei leaned over, snatched a cracker from Lulu's plate, chomped it.

Lulu gave him her driest look. "Could you not?"

By way of response, he took her soda and nabbed a solid swig of that, too, all the while meeting her gaze. Then he put it down again, went back to his soup with a sly little smile. He was trying to make her smile, I thought, even through the pain.

"They'll be working on getting back," Connor said, and waited for Lulu to look at him.

"What?" she asked.

"Our parents. They solved a lot of problems together in Chicago in their day. And they were already planning on helping with the demon. They may be somewhere else, but they're researching a way to get back. To reverse what was done."

"Yeah," she said, frowning as she considered it. "Yeah," she said again, this time more sure. "And the Librarian, Paige, the guards. Everyone. They'll all be working on it."

That seemed to lighten her mood, even as it depressed mine further. Everyone I loved was either at this table or totally unreachable.

"Maybe it's Candy Land."

We all looked at Alexei.

"What?" Lulu asked.

"Maybe they're in Candy Land. Or a world made of steak frites, theirs for the taking."

"Dad would like that," I said. "Mom would prefer deep dish and chocolate."

"Does she still have that drawer in the kitchen?" Connor asked. "The chocolate drawer?"

"Yep. At least, she did the last time I was in there."

Connor smiled. "You'd want, what, a world of coffee?"

"And good boots," I said, trying for a smile. "Lulu wants a giant art supply store. You want custom bike parts as far as the eye can see." I looked at Alexei. "You'd want a refrigerator that never empties."

"Accurate," Connor said. "All the way around."

"We'll get the asshole demon," Lulu said, clearly trying to make herself believe it. "And we'll see what wishes she can grant."

FOURTEEN

The sun rose and set again. And even with the beginning of a new night, everything seemed wrong. Off. Tilted and unbalanced. I didn't know if that sensation was the working of the chaos demon, or just the fact that sometimes life was a pile of hot, buttered garbage. That was life, for better or worse.

So I ran away.

Running through the neighborhood in the dark, with the half-moon shining above me and the city mostly quiet, had become something I actually looked forward to. Because I had to concentrate on my speed, my breath, the inevitable gaps and cliffs in Chicago's frost-heaved sidewalks, it helped me clear my head of worries.

I was nearly a mile from the town house when the rain started—a soft mist that quickly turned to a downpour.

Maybe it would be a cleansing rain. Maybe it would wash away the dregs of demon magic, the shards of glass, the bloodstains. But it wouldn't bring Cadogan House back again. I still had no idea what would.

I was drenched by the time I made it home again and trudged back up the stairs. This time, running hadn't made me feel better. I didn't feel anything, really. I felt numb; grief was a weight that pulled me down, stripped me bare. I felt aimless and hopeless . . .

and guilty, I realized. Guilty that I hadn't stopped Rosantine before she'd taken my parents, Lulu's parents. Guilty at the possibility she'd taken the House because we'd been the ones to go after her. We'd been the ones to chase her.

And I'd been the one to taunt her.

Was this payback for what I'd done?

I moved through the town house like a zombie, but managed the basics. I showered and dressed for a night of work—boots, leggings, fitted long-sleeved top, vest. Then I checked my screen. Micah had sent a message checking in, and assuring me that the fourteen Cadogan vampires who lived in the House, but hadn't been there when it disappeared, were safe at Washington House. I also found messages from vampire friends in Minnesota offering their condolences and any help they could provide.

I responded to both, then went downstairs, intending to go immediately to the office. But I found bustling in the kitchen.

Connor stood in front of the stove. He wore jeans that traced the lines of his body beautifully and a favorite gray T-shirt.

"What's this?" I asked, trying and failing to sound even slightly enthusiastic.

He looked back at me from the stove, smiled. "Waffles. Bacon. Eggs. And there's blood in the fridge. You didn't eat much yesterday. I thought you might be hungry."

That he'd taken the time to ensure I ate even as he was grieving warmed me up a little.

"Come here," he said, and opened his arms. "Just take it one night at a time. One hour at a time. That's how you'll figure out how to bring Cadogan back."

I looked up at him. "What will you be doing?"

"Trying to hold the Pack together."

"How can I help?" I asked, since we hadn't talked about it yet.

Something seemed to blossom in his eyes, and he lowered his forehead to mine. "I don't think you can. And I'm afraid I can't, either. The Pack is scared. Furious. Pissed at the demon. Pissed at me because I didn't stop it. Pissed at vampires because it happened on their watch."

"And the interlopers?"

"They were surprisingly quiet," he said. "Maybe felt some actual concern that their Apex was gone. But more likely just planning their next move."

"How . . . vampiric."

He made a sound that might have been a chuckle but stood there for a moment. I rubbed his arms, trying to soothe him, and could feel the tight tension in his muscles.

"You can let it out," I said. "It's just us right now."

He shook his head, a lock of hair curling over his forehead. "If I put down this weight," he said, "I'm not sure if I can pick it up again."

I knew what it cost him to make that admission, even to me.

"The world needs to change," I said quietly.

He looked down at me, tugged on a lock of my hair. "We'll change it when we're in charge. But we aren't in charge yet."

I ate, less because of the enjoyment of food than because I knew I'd need the energy. I'd either be fighting a demon or hunting one, and that was going to require every skill at my disposal. I added two bottles of blood and was feeling nearly (un)human again.

I was cleaning up—it seemed only fair given he'd done the cooking—when Connor's screen rang.

"Alexei," he said. "What's up?"

I hadn't even known he'd left the town house. I'd assumed he was still asleep upstairs.

Alexei must have requested Connor put him on speaker, as Connor swiped the screen, and Alexei began talking. "Lulu left the town house a couple of hours ago. She was crying. I don't think she slept last night."

I didn't know she'd left, either, and I really didn't like the sound of this. "Do you know where she went?"

"Yes, I followed her in an Auto. She was crying," Alexei said again, as if that fully explained and justified his behavior. And maybe it did. "She rode around for a while in an Auto. And then she went to the fairy castle."

I froze, even as my heart began to pound. Chicago's mercenary fairies were dangerous and sly as vipers. They weren't exactly evil. But they were powerful and old and arrogant, and they didn't much care how their plans would affect others. They'd once guarded Cadogan House during daylight hours—until they'd sold out the House. One had nearly destroyed Chicago in their effort to bring back the green land—their homeland—and return the fairies to power.

"Why the hell is she there?" I finally said when I'd wrapped my brain around what Alexei had said. Lulu had been to the castle before, with me, just after I'd come back from France. It was after that trip that she'd re-upped her decision to avoid magic.

"I think she's convinced they made Cadogan House disappear— and she's going to make them pay for it."

The rain kept coming, creating a terrific noise in the SUV that Connor drove while I passed messages—to Theo, to Gwen— advising them what Lulu had done and promising an update as soon as possible.

"She could start a war," I muttered when I'd gotten their acknowledgments and put my screen away again.

"How?" Connor asked. "She doesn't use magic."

"Humans don't, either, and how many wars have they been involved in? Consider history—and fairies."

"Right." He hit the accelerator. "We'll get there," Connor said, putting a hand over mine. "We'll get there, and we'll stop her. We'll stop all of it."

I hoped he was right.

The fairies had once lived in a dilapidated, but heavily magicked, tower that was the only remaining bit of a Gilded Age mansion. But they'd upgraded a few months ago, exchanging the tower for a castle they'd built along the south fork of the Chicago River. It was a behemoth of stone, tall and imposing, with towers and a crenellated wall—very medieval—at the end of a long expanse of grass and a white stone drive.

We drove toward the building, my sword already in hand, watching for signs of attack. They were called "mercenary fairies" for a reason. And that reason was fierce and calculated violence.

We stopped ten yards from the two-story gatehouse that allowed entry through the structure's defensive wall. The doors were open, but fairies stood guard outside—and they had daggers trained on Alexei.

"Well," I said. "I guess keeping him alive is the first step."

"That would be preferred," Connor said dryly.

We climbed slowly out of the car, careful not to make any sudden moves.

The rain had slowed to a sprinkle, but it didn't disguise the fairy magic in the air. It seemed stronger now than the last time we'd been here, when Ruadan had nearly killed Claudia in his effort to revive the green land. I could feel Alexei's magic on the edge of it. But his wasn't the only power I felt. And I was afraid I knew exactly where it had come from.

"Did Lulu . . . ?" Connor began, and that's all he needed to say. He felt it, too.

"We'll see." I resheathed my sword; we were outnumbered, and I didn't want them getting itchy with their blades.

"Bloodletter," one of them said. "She has not invited you."

"She" was Claudia, the queen of Chicago's fairies.

"No," I agreed. "She has not. But the woman who came here without her permission is our responsibility. We will apologize and pay the debt incurred by her intrusion." I looked down at Alexei. "And the debt incurred here, as well."

Because there was always a debt. It was something vampires and fairies had in common.

There was a beat of silence, and then a woman stepped into the doorway. A human, albeit one dressed in a long tunic-style dress of chalky blue that was more fae than Fifth Avenue. Her skin was pale, her hair cropped and silver, her expression blank.

She stepped up, whispered something to the guards.

After a moment, they resheathed their own blades, stepped aside.

"I am Daphne, Herself's handmaiden. You may follow me."

Connor and I looked at each other and stepped into the gatehouse, Alexei behind us.

"Human, but servant to a fairy queen?" I asked, as we were led through the gatehouse and across the bailey.

"I am here to learn," Daphne said. "I was offered the opportunity, and I took it."

"And why did you get the opportunity?" I asked.

She glanced back at me, amusement in her eyes. "You are inquisitive, as Herself has said."

That was probably the nicest thing "Herself" had said of me. I hadn't heard that particular title for Claudia before. Maybe it was a human thing.

The castle had been nearly empty the last time I'd been here, most of the fairies having followed Ruadan in their ill-fated quest. But the bailey was alive with activity now, even at night. Torches were lit, and fairies worked at small garden plots, pulling the season's late vegetables. A smithy worked near the far corner, preparing metal in a forge that appeared to be heated by magical bellows.

No tech was needed for what magic could do instead.

Daphne led us into the keep, through the large common room with its rush-strewn floor and car-sized hearth, and up a set of winding stone stairs.

"Your friend has caused a bit of chaos this night," Daphne said, and Connor and I exchanged looks at the use of the word. Then Daphne opened a set of carved wooden doors and stepped aside.

It was a throne room. A fire burned at one end, and the wooden ceiling vaulted overhead. The throne itself sat at the other end beneath a bower of flowering trees that appeared to have grown from the wide-planked wooden floor. Fairy magic filled the room, old and iron heavy. Monster was intrigued but stayed down. It loved a fight, but was becoming more discerning about its opponents. And it knew better than to tangle with fairies in their own home.

The queen sat her throne. Beneath the arc of purple flowers, she was statuesque and strawberry blond, her long, wavy hair nearly reaching her waist. Her dress was layers of a gauzy material that left little of her body beneath to the imagination. Her feet were bare.

She was guarded by a line of fairies who looked like the others we'd seen: tall and fit and paranormally beautiful, with strong cheekbones and wide eyes. They had pale skin and wore black pants and tunics; their subdued clothes were a strange contrast to Claudia's lush throne and wispy gown.

Lulu stood in front of them, pixie petite, shaking with anger, and covered in the magic I'd felt outside.

Lulu's magic.

I knew she'd been trained when she was younger, and I'd felt her magic as a child. But she'd made the decision not to use it more than a decade ago, and I had no real idea what she was capable of as an adult sorceress. I wasn't sure she did, either.

"Lulu," I said behind her, lifting my sword from its sheath just enough to show steel. "We're here. Step back."

"Bloodletter," Claudia said by way of greeting, then cast her gaze slowly over the shifters who'd come in with me.

"Claudia," I said, inclining my head in what I hoped was a respectful manner. "My apologies for the interruption."

The queen's brows lifted.

"They did this, Elisa," Lulu said. "Petra said it was portal magic—the house was moved through a portal to some other world. They're the only Sups who can use portal magic, so they must have been involved."

"It was demon magic," I said. "We could feel it. We could smell it."

"I can smell it on you now," Claudia said mildly, her ring-laden fingers glinting in the firelight.

Lulu lifted her chin. "Then they must have worked with the demon."

Claudia's brows—perfect arches—lifted elegantly. "We do not consort with demons."

"Who else can do portal magic?" Lulu insisted. "Who else could have done this? Did you send Cadogan House away?"

"Why would we have done so?" Claudia said. Her tone was still mild, but I could tell her patience was waning.

"Enough of this," Lulu said, voice rising. "Bring back the House and my parents. Immediately."

Claudia rolled her eyes, waved Lulu off. "I have done nothing with your parents."

Then I felt the hot spark of magic coming from Lulu. "Then one of the fairies did it," she said, the words lower and more serious than any I'd ever heard from her. "Like Ruadan."

I heard Alexei's murmured "Oh, fuck" and agreed with the sentiment. The reminder of the fairy who'd violated his loyalties wasn't going to go over well.

Claudia's eyes went hot, and the room began to fill with stifling magic. "You are lucky that I do not disappear you where you stand."

"Try it," Lulu murmured, and then her hand was up, and there was a glowing orange fireball in her hand.

She'd start a war, I thought again, and she'd never forgive herself.

So I launched myself between them . . . and the fireball she threw toward Claudia hit me square in the back.

The pain was terrible, remarkable, and all-consuming. Like every bone had been simultaneously broken, as the magic spilled from nerve to nerve. My knees buckled, and I hit the wooden floor, tried to suck in a breath. But I couldn't remember how to make my lungs work, and it was a terrifying thirty seconds before my lungs inflated again.

"Elisa!"

Someone called my name, the sound of it staticky as magic echoed around in my head. I felt the trickle on my face, swiped beneath my nose, found blood. Maybe she'd actually rattled my brain.

I heard someone move forward, saw the offered hand. I ignored it, looked up and into Claudia's eyes, and climbed shakily to my feet.

Then I glanced back at Lulu. She looked shocked, afraid, defiant.

Lulu didn't just have magic. She had *powerful* magic. And she'd used it on me.

I knew it was accidental—or accidental that it had hit me instead of Claudia—but I was still thoroughly pissed about it. Messing with fairies was no joke; we didn't need more supernatural enemies right now. So I gave Lulu a look that promised A Very Long Talk Later, then turned back to Claudia.

"You move quickly, Bloodletter."

"Practice," I managed, and that single word took effort. Sparks of pain were still echoing through bone.

"I must thank you for allowing me to avoid that pain." She cast her gaze back to Lulu. "And the battle that would have followed it."

Lulu began to speak, but I pointed at her. "No. You are done."

Claudia's smile was wide. I didn't like that, and I especially didn't like the groveling and negotiating that I knew were going to follow Lulu's show-and-tell. But that's where I was tonight.

"Connor, take them outside, please."

I could feel him pause, unsure if he should leave me alone. He respected my skills, but he was also protective. It was the alpha instinct.

So I glanced back, met his gaze, and let him see that I was confident. I nodded. "I'll handle it," I said quietly, and that was enough for him.

"Come on, Lulu," Alexei said, taking Lulu's arm. "Let's get some air."

It was to her credit that she didn't argue or pull her arm away. Of course, that still wasn't enough to clear away the debt of *fireballing her best friend*.

Connor gave the fairies one last long look before following Lulu and Alexei out, leaving me alone with them.

Time to break out those Cadogan House diplomatic skills. "I'm sorry she interrupted your evening," I repeated.

That had Claudia blinking back surprise, and I liked that. Surprise was an advantage.

"She is powerful, your friend," Claudia said.

Which was mostly news to me. "She is. You said you agree this was portal magic. Do you have any idea who could have done it?"

Claudia's brows lifted. "You believe that we did not."

"Not your style," I said. "Not anymore."

She inclined her head. "We cannot forge a bridge to all the worlds that may exist. Our connection is only to the green land, which you have seen."

"Could a demon have done it alone?"

She nearly answered, then paused, seemed to consider. And in doing, began drumming her fingers on the arm of her chair. "I do not know the skills of all demons, and demons are legion. Before, I would have said it was impossible. But the demon's was the only magic I felt."

So Rose had acted alone. Good, in that we were only looking for her. Bad, in that she was more powerful than we'd known.

"Were you in Chicago when the demon made trouble the first time?"

"We were here but not aware. Our connection to the green land was stronger then, and we were not actively involved in the human world."

"So you don't know where I could find the demon now?"

Her brows lifted. "How would I know where to find a demon?"

Fairies and their nonresponses. "In that case, I will leave you," I said, and inclined my head.

"Ah," she said, sitting forward, avarice in her eyes. "But there is the cost of the intrusion. What will you give me?"

"I took a shot for you."

"That addresses your intrusion, but not hers."

Damn it. "What do you want?"

"You may take a drink."

A long trestle table that nearly filled one side of the room was suddenly groaning with platters of meat, potatoes, bread, silver chalices, and golden wine. But fairy food and drink was not to be trusted in the best of times, much less when they'd been offended. They were tricksy folks.

"No, thank you."

She watched me for a moment. "I will accept a secret," she decided. "From you."

I watched her carefully for a moment, debated which secrets were safe enough to share. Not that I had terribly many. The obvious one wasn't fully mine to share; monster was its own consciousness, or so I believed, and the fairies' knowledge that it existed could have repercussions I didn't have time to consider now.

On the other hand, Claudia's moods were erratic, and she was getting impatient. The longer I stayed here, the more dangerous this visit would become. So I made the invitation to monster.

Shall we?

When monster agreed, I glanced at Claudia again. "You agree the fae won't harm, or cause to be harmed, anyone because of our intrusion, or any acts committed on your property tonight?"

Her smile was slow. "Your bargaining skills have improved, Bloodletter. Your mother was rarely so careful. And I agree."

I gave monster the nod, let it stretch into me, sending warmth through my arms and legs and enjoying for once the buzz of fairy magic. My eyes turned red, the color of blood and rage, and curiosity rose in Claudia's.

I felt the tendrils of her magic, heavy as iron, cold as a hilltop spring. But unlike the ghosts' fog, hers was alive with growth and desire and dancing.

"Bloodletter," Claudia said, and the word was almost tangible with power. "You are a surprise I did not expect." She rose and walked toward me, magic swirling in the room, and peered at me like a carnival curiosity.

"Our debt is clear," she said, and it felt as if the room's magic lightened a bit. "But as you have done a turn for me in moons past, I will offer you one now."

"At what cost?" Nothing was free.

"At no cost," she said, "because to be silent is to damn us all." She paused. "You can hear them, far away," she said, and my throat went tight. I knew she meant our parents.

"Yes."

She nodded.

"Do you know where the House is now?" I asked.

"Only that they are safe where they are. I can hear them, too, although the sound is faint as dew. But their time is limited."

"Limited?"

"She has made happen that which ought not happen."

"She," I presumed, was Rosantine. "The improbable," I said. "The unlikely, coalescing together."

The chaotic.

"Yes," Claudia said. "The magic she has wrought is old, and it is inflexible. There are ties that will not bend. They will *snap*," she said, and the power in that word seemed to shake the entire castle.

She waved a hand toward the table. The food and drink disappeared, replaced by a floating and three-dimensional visage of the waxing moon, the far side shadowed, the near side glowing.

"There are limits to even a demon's power in this plane, and soon the choice will be irreversible. Soon," she said again, and the shadow across the moon shifted, grew smaller, disappeared, leaving a glowing silver orb.

"The full moon," I said quietly, and was suddenly heartsick. "That's only in a few days, right?"

"Three. On the third day, the die is cast."

"And the House stays where it is." I looked back at her. "If we don't bring them home before then, they don't come back at all."

She inclined her head. "We will both of us remain out of phase. The consequences will be fast."

"I don't suppose you know how to stop her?"

"Demons are untrustworthy, immortal, and amoral." (Honestly, I'd have said the same things about the fae, but probably best not to voice that aloud.) "They have no care," Claudia continued, "for that which does not serve them and them alone. And they care not what consequences their actions bring."

That matched my experience but didn't help us.

"Do you know her sigil?"

"I do not." She glanced at her handmaiden, then back at me. "But beware. You cannot command by words that which will not be commanded. You must feel your way."

I had no idea what that meant, but I wasn't about to stay and ask questions. I practically ran out, hustling before another debt was incurred.

The three of them waited by the SUV on the white stone drive. I wasn't sure which thing I should be mad about first—the fireball or the confrontation. But I could feel the fury rising up from my boots as I stalked toward them.

"Are you okay?" Connor asked.

"I'll live," I said, my gaze on Lulu. "We need a minute," I said, and Connor and Alexei stepped eagerly back, giving us room.

"What the hell were you thinking?" I demanded.

"Portal magic," she said again, as if that was the only excuse she'd needed—this woman who'd avoided the supernatural for years—to threaten some of the most powerful Sups in the city. "It was logical they'd done it."

"No," I said, "it was *possible* they'd done it. But we know the demon was there—and felt her magic. Even Claudia said she only felt the demon's magic; no one else's."

"She might have lied," Lulu said, but weakly.

"And even if the fairies wanted to make Cadogan disappear," I continued, rolling over her objection, "that would start another war in Chicago they couldn't win. They wouldn't do that, much less use portal magic to do it. It's too obvious."

Lulu opened her mouth, but closed it again, swallowing whatever sarcasm she'd intended to serve.

"You are my sister in all the ways that matter," I said. "But I swear to god, Lulu, if you pull a stunt like this again"—I groped for an appropriate punishment—"I will tell my dad you wrecked his Mercedes."

"That was in was the *ninth grade*," Lulu said, but with fear in her voice. He'd loved that car.

"Wait," Connor called out. "That was her?"

"That was her." We'd blamed it on the weather. "And he still talks about it." I pointed back at the castle. "How the hell did you even get in there?"

She swallowed, made an effort to straighten her shoulders, but embarrassment or guilt still weighed them down. "I charmed the fairies."

I just stared at her. "You charmed the fairies."

"I've been here before, so I knew my way around. It was a pretty simple spell."

"Was it now?" My voice was dry as day-old toast.

"I'm sorry," she said. "I was just . . . I felt desperate."

"And you didn't trust me to do my job."

She opened her mouth, closed it again.

I put my hands on her cheeks, waited until she met my gaze. "I'm going to get them back, and I'm going to fix it. I swear to you." And I hoped she didn't see my own fear that we'd run out of time first. "But we're going to have to talk about the magic."

"Yeah," Lulu said. "I know."

"Like, tonight. And no magic in the meantime."

She nodded.

Thinking we'd worked out our mad, or at least some of it, Alexei and Connor walked back.

"You," Lulu said, narrowing her eyes at Alexei, "are a traitor. Did you follow me?"

"Yes," he said, without even a hint of apology in his face. "You needed to be followed. You've barely eaten. You haven't slept. But you run off to attack the fae."

"You aren't my keeper."

Alexei just lifted his brows. "Aren't I?"

Entertaining as it would have been to watch them keep fighting, this wasn't the time or the place. "Focus," I said, and they both snapped to attention. "Claudia says there's a time limit here. When the moon goes full, the magic will be irreversible. That's all the time we have."

They all looked at the sky, the glowing moon mirrored in their eyes, and calculated.

Lulu was the first to meet my gaze again. I saw the panic flare in her eyes, watched her work to control it. "That's, like, a few days."

"Three days. We now have a very specific deadline."

Somehow, that made me feel better. Why did that make me feel better?

Connor must have seen the confusion in my face. "Because it's a line in the sand," he said. "A goal line. You know exactly what you have to do and when. You like rules, brat."

He was right. "But we don't know how," I said. "That's the part that worries me."

"We'll figure it out together," he said, drawing me toward him. He gave Lulu a look. "Without confronting any more supernaturals with fireballs, maybe?"

"Yeah," Lulu said.

I sighed, looked at Lulu. "I need to get to work. You're going back to the town house—or the loft if you want to check on the cat—and you're going to stay there until we can talk about"—I waved my hand toward the castle—"all of this." I shifted my gaze to Alexei. "I know the Pack has its own issues to deal with, but can you go with her? Stay with her?"

He looked at Connor, got the nod of approval.

"Yes," Alexei said.

"I don't need a babysitter," Lulu said again.

"It's not for you," I said. "It's for me. The fairies may retaliate. I don't think Claudia has the hold on them that she used to, so you need to stay inside and stay put. Alexei will see to it, and that will make me feel better. Take a nap, get something to eat. Paint, mop the floor, run the stairs. But stay in the building. Please?" I added.

Lulu sighed, ran a hand through her bob of hair, but nodded. "Fine. But I would like some food." She put a hand on her stomach. "Doing magic really makes you hungry."

She'd be all right, I decided as they climbed into an Auto, and we climbed into the SUV.

"She's still has some mad in her," Connor said.

"Yeah," I agreed. "I won't judge her for having the magic. I'll judge her for acting like an idiot, which is right and proper." But we'd damn well talk about the magic. Oh, yes. Words would be had.

I rolled my shoulders, felt magic bubble out. And did not care for that sensation.

"Is she using?" Connor asked quietly.

Using dark magic, he meant. Tapping into the old and dangerous and deadly stuff that left scars on the sorcerer and the surroundings. "I don't think so. I mean, she's been a little off, but I think that's because of the demons and her parents disappearing and all that jazz." I ran hands through my hair, tugged a little. "I like to think we're aware enough to have seen some sign, and I haven't. God, I hope it's not that. My schedule is full up on emotionally exhausting supernaturals."

Connor's screen buzzed. He pulled it out, checked it, and swore as he all but threw it into the center console. "Fucking assholes," he growled.

"What's happened?"

"Cade," Connor said. "He's announced vampires are to blame for the Apex's disappearance."

"Because it happened at Cadogan House," I guessed. "Not entirely surprising."

"No, it isn't. But according to him, the Ombuds, CPD, and

vampires are part of a massive conspiracy intended to bring down the Pack by installing a puppet as Apex."

That had me laughing aloud.

"Is that funny?" he asked, looking at me slowly, his voice a little more testy than it usually would be.

"I'm assuming you're supposed to be the puppet. Which proves how little they know you. You are no puppet."

He grunted, which I took for general agreement.

"What do your uncles say?"

He rolled his neck. "They're walking a very careful line between telling me to do what's best for the Pack and telling the interlopers, as you call them, to pound sand."

"They've put you in the middle." I reached out, took his hand. "I'm sorry about that."

"I'm in the middle because I'm the prince," he said. And there was no joy in it.

FIFTEEN

Connor dropped me off at the office. Theo and Petra were out of their seats as soon as I walked in.

"She's all right?" they asked simultaneously, reinforcing the fact that I'd made the right call by joining this team.

"She's fine. And she picked a very bad time to restart using the magic that she's spent a very long time avoiding."

"Is Mercury in retrograde?" Theo asked. "What the hell is going on right now?"

And the answer was so obvious I was embarrassed not to have thought of it. "Well, there's a chaos demon in Chicago."

Theo opened his mouth, closed it again. "You think the chaos demon made her start practicing again?"

"I think the chaos demon is throwing a lot of magic into the air, which means unusual things are happening." And I didn't like the implication that decisions we made were only the result of her magical whims. How could we ever be sure we were making our own decisions, and not just doing what she'd influenced us to do?

Roger stepped into the doorway. "The fairies?"

"Situation contained for now," I said, and took a seat. The adrenaline was gone, and I was suddenly exhausted. "Lulu is freaked out and worried for her parents. Because this was portal magic, she decided the fairies had to be involved. So she confronted Claudia at the castle."

Theo whistled low. "How'd you maneuver your way out of that one?"

"I took a Lulu fireball meant for Claudia. And yes, it hurt."

"You need medical attention?" Roger asked, brow furrowed with worry.

"I'm already on the mend. I got Lulu out of there, and I think I defused the situation. I will be talking to Lulu at length later tonight."

"Did you learn anything from Claudia?" Theo asked.

"I don't think the fairies had anything to do with Cadogan House's disappearance. Claudia was insistent fairies only have a connection to the green land. I tend to believe her. I don't think she's going to be playing around with portal magic for a while—or letting her people do it—given what happened the last time."

"Could it be another rogue fairy?" Theo asked.

"Is it possible? Yes. But what's the benefit to fae of sending Cadogan House somewhere else? That's just negative attention on the entire group, with no obvious benefit. Claudia didn't think a demon would need an accomplice. But we do have a bigger problem."

I told them about the time limit.

"Two seventeen a.m. on the nineteenth," Petra said, looking at her screen. "That's the exact time of the full moon."

"So we've got, like, three days," Theo said, then blew out a breath.

"Yeah," I said. "So let's get on it?"

"Our best bet to get Cadogan House back is to get the demon," Petra said. "And our best bet to get the demon is to find the Cornerstones first and trap her when she tries to get one." She put an image on the overhead screen. "Here's the map we discussed."

We all looked at it in silence: the wards, the Cornerstones, and the ley lines.

"The warehouse Cornerstone is pretty close to the first ley

line," I said, "but South Gate's nowhere near one. So that's one theory out."

"That's good news," Petra said. "We know the Cornerstones aren't literally on the ley lines. Think of all the points we don't have to search now."

"It's probably another defensive consideration," Theo said. "Ley lines are the first place anyone would search." He gestured to all of us. "Case in point."

"Unfortunately, it doesn't give us any better idea of where the Cornerstones actually are and why." I looked at Petra. "What about Cadogan House?"

"Gwen didn't find anything in the property records," Petra said.

"We only know of two Cornerstone locations," I said, "but I'm not seeing anything that suggests there's some obvious pattern. Like we discussed, if the Guardians wanted to build concentric defense rings, these positions don't make sense."

Theo nodded. "There'd have to be an intermediate ring, but she didn't trigger one."

"What about neighborhoods?" I asked.

"Neighborhoods?" Theo asked, frowning.

"Like, community areas or political wards? Maybe it was one ward per area? Can you get a map of legislative districts from 1872? Add a layer for that?"

"Hmm," Petra said, but she was already looking. It took less than a minute for her to find a map, and less than that for her to superimpose it over the ward locations.

"There were twenty political wards in Chicago in 1872," Theo said. "That leaves eighteen more potential Cornerstones, if they used those boundaries as a guide."

"That's too many," I said, scanning the map. "I don't think they have the magical resources for that. Not without sorcerers."

Petra narrowed her gaze in what I'd decided was her Thinking Stare. "Maybe math can help."

"Math?" I asked.

"An algorithm. We calculate the distances and angles between the Cornerstones and ley lines that we know about, and we predict where the other ones might be. I've got a cousin who's a mathematician."

"Do you have any below-average cousins?" Theo asked. "Who aren't mathematicians or doctors with generously portioned wedding parties?"

"I *am* the below-average cousin," she said. "At least if you ask the other ones. Personally, I think it's Ralph."

"What does he do?"

"Electrical outlet magnate. Like, the plastic covers for outlets," she added at our blank stares.

"He's a *magnate*, though," Theo pointed out. "That implies a certain level of success."

"If you care about financial resources, well, sure." Petra growled, pulled out a smaller screen, began tapping. "I'll work on this with Armin—the mathematician. And let you know."

That would have to work for now.

Gwen stepped into the doorway. Theo stood up, straightened his jacket, which was adorable.

"Hey," he said. "What brings you by?"

"So, I did some thinking about Rosantine," she said. "And about Edentown. And I did some research."

"We're listening," I said.

"So," Gwen said, "while I was looking through the land records, I started thinking about Edentown." She glanced at me. "Had you ever been to Edentown before you picked her up?"

"I had not," I said.

"Me neither," Theo said.

Gwen nodded. "The town's only a few miles from Chicago, but if you search decades of stories from the *Tribune* and *Sun-Times* archives—which I did—you know how many times Edentown is mentioned?"

"No clue," Theo said.

"Six. In all those years."

Roger moved closer. "That seems low. Especially if it was supposed to be a bedroom community for people who work in Chicago."

Gwen nodded. "Exactly. And that's not all." She gestured to the overhead screen. "Can I—"

"Sure," Petra said, and fiddled with the controls. "Go for it."

Gwen swiped her own screen, and a series of headlines appeared overhead:

FIRE BURNS EDENTOWN CITY HALL AND RECORDS

SINKHOLE KILLS NEW HOUSING DEVELOPMENT

CHEMICAL SPILL EMPTIES TOWN

LOCUSTS DESTROY CROPS FOR FOURTH CONSECUTIVE YEAR

CITY COUNCIL KILLED IN FIREWORKS TRAGEDY

"Damn," I said. "A city can have back luck, but all those tragedies happening to one relatively small town? That seems . . . very improbable."

"Chaotic even," Theo said.

"And then I found this." Gwen swiped again, and the headlines were replaced by images of people. Some old, black-and-white, grainy. Women in high-necked Victorian garb like what Patience had worn, or in sleek flapper-style dresses from the 1920s. A color photograph of a social gathering in the 1950s. Hippies in the late 1960s.

A woman's face had been circled in each one.

Petra sat straight up. "That's her. In each picture."

"Yup," Gwen said. "We assumed she was hanging out on the edge of the city because she was waiting for her opportunity to break into Chicago. She was apparently there long enough to basically ruin the town. To keep anything from growing, to destroy everything. But even still, even when the town is toast, she stays there."

"So why didn't she just leave?" I asked. "That's the question, right? Why did she stay in Edentown for so long?"

"Oh snap," Petra said, sitting up straight. "Because she didn't have a choice."

"That's what I'm thinking," Gwen said with a satisfied smile. "Maybe she didn't leave—despite how crappy the town became—because she couldn't."

Roger got it, too. "You think she has some kind of geographical limitation."

"Like a djinn in a very big bottle," Theo said with a nod. "Huge bottle, Chicago, but still a boundary. She's still contained. It still takes away her choice and her freedom."

"Why would there be a geographical limitation in the first place?" I wondered.

"I think I can answer that one," Petra said. "She told you she came into the human world in Chicago, right?"

"I think she said she 'entered' here, but yeah. Close enough."

"We know she's been here since at least 1872, and Chicago wasn't very big then, at least by modern standards. And most of it was contained . . ." With a dramatic pause, Petra put a new image on screen.

"Within the ley lines," I said. "So she's got some connection to Chicago's ley lines, and she's stuck near them."

"Bingo," Petra said. "We know she can go at least to Edentown, so she's got a little perimeter beyond this central triangle. But not much of one."

"She's been waiting," Theo said. "Not just for her opportunity to get into Chicago short term—but to get *out* of Chicago long term."

"And then the wards get weaker," I said. "She thinks if she gets back into Chicago, she can draw on the ley lines, maybe, and use that power to break her bonds."

"Or she figured out the Cornerstones, somehow," Petra said.

There was a knock at the door. We looked up, found an admin in the doorway. She looked at me. "Someone's here to talk to you."

"To me?" I rose, flipping through possibilities. Jonathan Black. The demon. Connor. "Who is it?"

"A shifter. Called herself Breonna."

"Interloper," I said with a curled lip. "I'll be there in a minute. Keep her in the lobby, please."

The admin nodded, clipped back down the hallway in sensible shoes. I ran a hand through my hair, then rolled my shoulders, tried to shake out some of the building tension. "Do they seriously not understand the deadline we're under?"

"I bet they do," Theo said. "And I bet they're fine if it passes."

I glanced back at him. "One less Apex to worry about?"

Theo nodded sagely.

"Assholes," I said.

"You need backup?" Theo asked, voice carefully neutral.

"No, thanks. I'll take care of it."

I was glad the hallway was empty, because I was perilously close to fanging out and letting monster play with Breonna awhile. But that wouldn't help Connor and the Pack. So I'd keep my cool as long as I could.

I found her in the lobby in workout gear. Leggings and a sports tank in a gleaming pink that showed off toned muscles. Her usual style of dress or just part of the display?

"Breonna," I said blandly. "What do you want?"

"Dating a shifter, but you aren't even going to bother with politeness when one of his Packmates comes to see you?"

"Are you his Packmate? Last I heard, you and your buddies are doing everything you can to tear the Pack apart."

"We're asking important questions," she said. "Questions we have every right to ask."

"About whether I hurt my parents on purpose?"

"How do I know they weren't in on it?"

"Logic, for one. What do you want?"

"You're an obstacle, and I want you out of the way."

The straightforwardness was almost refreshing. "An obstacle to Connor—or the Pack?"

Her smile was mild, as if we were businesspeople discussing a transaction. "Both." She leaned in. "The man you've gotten your fangs into is a wolf. An animal. You need to grow up and face the truth. Maybe Connor likes you. Hell, maybe he loves you. Doesn't matter. The Pack will never accept you. You should step aside. Do you even care what you're doing to the Pack? What that will do to Connor?"

It was a question I didn't like, but it also wasn't the first time Connor and I had discussed it. "Doesn't that help your cause?" I asked. "Increase the odds the Pack rejects him as Apex?"

"It's useful in one scenario," she said with a sly smile. "But I'm also considering taking the more direct route. Taking him for myself."

Monster and I became enraged at the same moment. "Lay a finger on him," I said, and felt my eyes silver, "and you will feel my wrath."

She snorted. "As if there's any chance he'd pick a vampire over the Pack. He just hasn't met the right shifter yet."

I gave her a flat stare. "And you think you're that one? A shifter who's trying to break the Pack apart instead of focusing on getting the Apex back? On getting his mother back? Do you think he's going to thank you for that?"

It was her turn to look furious.

"Spoiled little vampire," she said, stalking toward me, her eyes flashing gold like a wolf in the night. "Too used to getting what you want. We're going to change that. And you'll never interfere with the Pack again."

She turned and left, leaving her last words floating in the air.

"Fucking shifters," I said loud enough that the admin poked her head around the doorway.

"Everything okay?"

No, I thought. No, it really wasn't. But it wasn't her fault, so I gave her a nod. "Fine, thanks."

I needed air. I waited until Breonna was gone, then walked outside to a spot beneath some trees—where I couldn't be seen by anyone else—and breathed. I needed darkness and cool air and the sounds of creatures scurrying in darkness, a reminder that drama and treachery weren't the only parts of life.

When I was calmer, I went back inside. Gwen was already gone, and Roger was back in his office. Theo and Petra were at workstations and swiveled around at my entrance.

"What's the story?" Theo asked.

"Basically, she told me to drop Connor so she could have him, which is her backup plan in case the interlopers don't win the Pack the old-fashioned way." And I was going to have to warn Connor about the nonsense, which just infuriated me more.

"What the hell?" Petra said. "Do they not have enough going on? That's such an asshole move."

Theo leaned forward. "Want me to have Gwen pull her over for bad plates or something?"

"No," I said with a smile. "But I appreciate the gesture. You're the best coworkers a girl could have." I sat down at my workstation, shoulders slumped. "Sometimes it feels like we're pieces on a chessboard. People using us to get to our parents. To get revenge on our parents. To take the place of our parents."

Petra made a sound of agreement, and I looked at her. "Did you have drama, too?" I asked.

"Well, sure. I love my parents, but they both have magic. There were plenty of expectations about what I should be able to do. And how much control I should have."

"'Should' can do a lot of damage," I said, thinking of what Breonna had said. *You should step aside.*

"So," Theo said, "are all kids of powerful parents or grandparents just destined to have supernatural drama?"

"You mean, did our parents screw us up?" I asked with a smile. "Or did we do it to ourselves?"

Petra snorted. "Objection. I'm not screwed up. I'm just . . . a Sup."

Theo snorted. "That sums it up pretty well. So let's get back to work and prove them all wrong. Who wants what?"

"I've got Armin," Petra said.

"I'll dig into this ward pattern idea," Theo said. "Maybe there's some thread that links them all."

"I'll continue the eternal search for the sigil," I said. And turned back to my screen.

Two eye-blurringly long hours later, our screens began to ring simultaneously. I got to mine first. NAC PACK HQ. CPD NEEDS ASSIST.

My first reaction was concern about whether Connor was okay. Which Roger anticipated.

CONNOR NOT INVOLVED. NO INJURIES—YET.

That was something. But I had a feeling I knew exactly who was causing the problems.

SIXTEEN

Theo and I drove to Ukrainian Village; Petra would stay at the office and keep working on the demon. Alexei was with Lulu, so I sent Connor a message en route: WHERE ARE YOU?

HELPING WITH A DELIVERY, he said. DRIVER FORGOT A PAN OF BEANS. WHERE ARE YOU?

Catering parties in Chicago was a big part of the Pack's food business. And it meant Connor wasn't involved in whatever was going on, which was a relief. Although probably not to him.

ON WAY TO NAC PACK, I messaged. OMBUDS GOT CALL FROM CPD NEEDING ASSIST. SITUATION UNKNOWN.

There was a pause that made me think he was swearing, turning a vehicle around, or hustling to get the job done. TWENTY MINUTES, he promised.

It took nearly thirty for us to reach the headquarters building, and we hit a standstill two blocks away. We could hear the noise from there, and found its source to be a two-block-long morass of shifters and magic leading back to HQ.

We don't have time for this, I thought, fury rising, and knew Connor was being played. Again.

"The fuck?" Theo said.

"Demon influence?"

"I don't think they need it," I said.

Two CPD officers approached. We held out our badges.

"Thanks for getting here fast," said the one on the left. "Officer Padwicky. That's Officer Jones."

"Sullivan and Martin," I said. "What's going on?"

"Anger, as far as I can tell. It started at the NAC Industries building," Jones said. A rookie, I guessed, as he was brimming with nervous energy.

"Fight started inside, spilled onto the sidewalk, then the streets, then . . . this," Padwicky said, gesturing. "Neighbors got nervous when the fighting started. And they've been chanting."

"Chanting?"

"Honestly, it sounds like conspiracy theory–type stuff? A lot of 'Tell the truth' and 'Release the Apex.'"

Theo climbed onto the bed of a truck parked beside us, looked over the crowd. "Eighty or so shifters. Couple circles of fighting." He narrowed his gaze. "And you'll never guess who's leading the party."

"The interlopers," I said, anger rising again.

"Your eyes are a little silvery," Padwicky said in the same tone a trusted friend would let you know you had lipstick on your teeth.

I nodded, blew out a breath, tried to calm down. Escalation wasn't going to help.

Theo jumped down from the truck. "Didn't you stop a Pack fight recently?"

"Yeah. I got a shifter the opportunity to help Connor work on his bike," I said.

"That's not going to help here," Theo said.

"No," I said. "They don't seem like the teamwork or manual labor types."

The sound of breaking glass echoed from somewhere in the crowd. "We need to get this contained," Padwicky said, "before it spreads or becomes a full-on riot, or someone ends up dead."

* * *

I didn't see any sign of Connor, and I didn't get a response to my messages to him. So we were going to have to start without him.

The street the shifters had picked for their near riot was bounded by town houses on both sides, and the crowd flowed nearly to the fronts of those buildings. We sent CPD officers into the crowd to thin it out at the edges and locate any shifters or humans who needed help. Theo and I would work our way to the front the only way possible—through the morass of shifters who were busy hiding their fear with booze and screaming.

But they didn't want to stop the party; they didn't even want to move aside as we tried to press through them, and I knew I'd have bruises tomorrow. Instead of cooperation, there was plenty of booze, plenty of anger, and more than a few shouted conspiracy theories and insults. A few knives strapped to belts, but no larger weapons that I could see.

"Fucking asshole cops," a big man murmured.

"We aren't cops. We're Ombuds," Theo said. "Here to serve and assist supernaturals. And I'm feeling real good about that career decision right now."

Someone threw out an elbow toward me, and I instinctively grabbed it, twisted it away. "Hands to yourself," I said to the responding shout before letting him go and moving forward again.

They'd put a table on the sidewalk in front of the building, which Cade, Breonna, and the other one—Joe—had mounted to spread their particular gospel.

"We don't really know where he is or what they've done with him!" Cade was saying with the thrill of conspiracy in his eyes.

With an electric screech, someone pulled the plug on the amps they'd set up, and the microphone went silent. A cop directed the interlopers off the table.

"Oops," Theo said as a cop who'd come through the building to meet us handed him a bullhorn.

"Party's over," Theo said, stepping onto the table and holding up his bullhorn with his non-casted hand. "Disperse. You don't have to go home, but you can't stay here."

"First Amendment, asshole," someone called out. "We have rights to say what we want."

"Yeah, but not to say them loudly in the middle of the night while your neighbors are sleeping. There's a noise ordinance."

"Fucking cops," someone called out.

"This is a vendetta!" someone said. "You've got it in for the Pack! That's why our Apex was disappeared!"

Someone in the crowd threw a punch, nailed another shifter. That started a scramble that rippled through the crowd like a pebble thrown into a stream.

"Cut out the fighting!" Theo said. "Or you'll be spending the night in lockup, and that's no way to party."

The roar of a bike and the squeal of brakes cut through the crowd. I felt his magic before I saw him; Connor stalked toward us with fury in his eyes and magic in his wake. He glanced at me, nodded, then walked up to Cade, met him toe to toe.

"Give them room," I said to the officers who moved toward us. "And work on getting the crowd dispersed."

But Connor's focus was on Cade. "What the fuck are you doing?"

"Pack has a right to speak its mind," Cade said with an arrogant drawl.

"The Pack will end up behind bars because you're itching for a fight."

"Do they look like I forced them to be out here?" He nudged close. "Your daddy's gone, friend. And all these people want to know exactly what happened." His gaze skimmed to mine. "And how the vampires were involved."

"You're spreading lies."

"I'm asking questions."

I watched Connor wrestle for control. "There's a goddamned demon running loose through Chicago. She is the Pack's enemy."

"The Pack decides who its enemy is. And who its leader is."

"You want a fight?" Connor said, magic spilling around them, taut and angry. "I'd be happy to oblige."

"A fight wouldn't be enough, would it?" Cade asked, his own power surging now and fighting back against Connor's—a battle within a battle. "Not without making it official."

That's when I realized this was exactly what Cade had planned. It was smart; I hadn't given him enough credit.

Connor realized it, too, his jaw quivering from the effort of not saying the word that Cade longed to hear. The word that held power.

Challenge.

The crowd moved behind me, but I ignored them and kept my gaze on the men. This fight would inevitably affect all our futures.

Connor watched Cade, eyes glittering, and grabbed the bullhorn from Theo, thrust it toward Cade. "Say the words, big man."

Cade took it, and there was only a moment's fear and hesitation in his eyes before he raised it. "I, Cade Drummond, hereby challenge Connor Keene for the throne of the North American Central Pack."

The world went silent.

And then wheels began to squeak.

We looked back, found Dan pushing a stainless cart topped with catering pans through the garage doors. He wore an apron—and made it look stylish—and used two fingers to whistle so loudly half the shifters covered their ears.

"Dinner's ready!" he called out. "And it's on the house!"

I wouldn't call it a stampede, which was probably fortunate. But more than a few shifters ambled—some drunkenly—toward the intoxicating smell of barbecue.

Connor watched them for a moment, something softening in his eyes. Then he took the bullhorn from Cade, handed it back to Theo, nodded.

Theo held it up, turned it on again. "You get off the street and eat this, or you go into the tank until you're sober. Make your choices."

A few threw punches at the CPD officers who maintained order; they'd be spending more than a few hours in a cell. But most went quietly, opting for pulled pork and brisket. Cade, Joe, and Breonna went off in their own direction. They had preparations to make, no doubt.

Connor stood in the street until every shifter was in the building or out of the neighborhood, and the lights in the town houses went dark.

I went to him, took his hand. He interlaced our fingers, squeezed tightly.

Together, we stood in silence, and considered what might come next.

Because after this, nothing was going to be the same.

The night felt so long, and dawn was nearly here. But it wasn't over yet. I still had to talk to Lulu, and that needed to happen tonight.

She'd opted to go to the loft so she could feed the cat, so I left Connor at the Pack and took an Auto back to our neighborhood. I stared morosely out the window the entire drive. And was alternatingly worried, sad, and furious.

I keyed into the loft and found Alexei on the floor at the end of the hallway dangling a toy that Eleanor of Aquitaine was dancing to get at.

"Hi," I said, and closed and locked the door. "You heard?"

"I heard," he said as Eleanor of Aquitaine pawed at a bobbing feather. And looked really cute doing it. That was undoubtedly a ploy. A distraction. Or maybe she just liked him.

"Have they set a date for the fight?" Alexei asked.

"Not yet. The family needs to talk, make some decisions since the Apex isn't back yet. How's Lulu?"

"She's . . . doing some reading."

"Ah," I said, as if I understood. But I didn't. Lulu wasn't much of a reader.

"I'll take over here," I said. "He needs you tonight. He needs Pack."

Alexei nodded and rose and put the toy on a console table in the hallway. Eleanor of Aquitaine sat down obediently, waited for him to reengage. Seeing good behavior from her was just . . . spooky.

Alexei looked at me. "Don't worry about him."

I gave him a half smile. "I have to. It's my job now."

He nodded, smiled back. "That's why he loves you. But worry isn't going to change anything. Not where a challenge is concerned."

"What's all the—" Lulu stepped into the hallway, a book in hand, open like she was going to show a page to Alexei. "Oh," she said. "Hi."

"Hi."

"Alexei told me about the challenge."

"Yeah," I said, toeing off my shoes. "It's been a night."

She nodded, and we all looked at each other awkwardly for a minute.

"I'll get going," Alexei said. He nodded at her, then offered me a wave and left us alone in more awkward silence.

"Hi," I said again.

"Hi." Then she turned and went back into the living room.

I followed her, noticed the stack of books on the coffee table that she became very busy gathering up. I moved closer, glancing at the stack. They were all books about demons and demonology.

"What are you doing?" I asked, looking up at her.

"Researching," she said, and cleared her throat. "My parents can't. Librarian and Paige can't. There's no one else. So I'm doing what I can to help."

She cleared her throat. "I know the timing is bad, but with me fireballing you and all, and the odds things are going to get worse . . ."

I nodded, sat down on the couch. There was fear in her eyes, and I braced myself for what was coming next. And felt guilty that I had no intention of spilling my own secrets.

"I'm tired, Elisa. I'm tired of lying."

"Okay," I said.

She blew out a breath. "Here goes. The thing is—I don't avoid magic because I'm embarrassed by my mother or because she did dark magic."

"Oh" was all I could think to say, as that was the last thing I'd expected to hear from her. "Okay. So why do you?"

"Because dark magic is the only kind I can do. And I'm really, really good at it."

SEVENTEEN

I'm not entirely sure what I thought she'd say. But it certainly wasn't that.

I stared at her for a full minute, trying to think how to respond. "First of all," I said, "I love you. So let's just establish that and get it out of the way." That had her tears already welling. "Second, what the hell, Lulu?"

"I know." She pulled a pillow over her face, hiding it. "I know. I should have told you."

"I mean, yes? How long have you known this?"

She lowered the pillow, winced. "Since I was like, I don't know, fourteen."

"Lulu Clarissa Hannah Montana Strawberry Shortcake Bell!" Only one of those was her actual middle name, but I needed the emphasis. "That's nearly a decade!"

Pillow up again. "I know," she said, the words muffled.

"You'd better start at the beginning," I said, and recalled Petra saying nearly the same thing to Patience. Had that been only a few nights ago?

"So, I guess the beginning isn't very interesting. When I was little, I tried to use the magic my mom promised me I had. We tried tricks, charms, potions. Alchemy. This one that uses hand movements." She extended her hands, clapped them together, and then did intricate movements with her fingers, like she was weaving a cat's cradle without the string. "I couldn't make any of it work."

"How old were you?"

"She started me at five. She didn't want me to stumble into my magic like she did. But I wasn't able to repeat the things she showed me how to do. They—my parents—were convinced I was just a late bloomer since mom didn't know she had magic until she was in her twenties."

I had no idea about any of this. "I just thought you weren't interested in it?"

"I mean, I wasn't. I'd gotten used to the idea that I couldn't do anything. I wasn't, like, stoked about that, but it was what it was. And my parents believed I'd come around eventually and didn't want to pressure me." She exhaled. "And then came Carrie Witshield's fourteenth birthday party."

"That wasn't the twist I expected," I said.

Carrie was one of the few humans we spent time with as kids; we operated on wildly different schedules than humans. Slumber parties—where we were all expected to stay up all night—evened the odds.

"We'd kind of paired off at the party, and Julie what's-her-name was being bitchy to that Meyer girl. I forget her name."

"Natalie, I think?"

"Sure. They were doing that stupid prank where you put someone's bra in the freezer."

"Cool boobs are happy boobs."

"Agree to disagree. As did Julie what's-her-name. She threw a total fit, threw hands at Natalie. Ended up gouging the crap out of Natalie's arm."

"I remember. Julie drew blood." And I looked at Lulu, and understanding dawned. "She drew blood," I repeated. "And you felt something."

"Julie's reaction was over the top, and it was the final straw. I was already mad, and I was sitting next to Natalie when it happened. It . . . kindled something in me. Like magic that had been waiting around finally got the green light. I could feel the spark in my hand, and that scared the shit out of me. There's no *Are You There God? It's Me, Margaret* for newly onboarded sorcerers. I was afraid I'd hurt someone, or worse. So I made a joke of it and went outside and jumped in the pool."

"I remember. We thought you were the wild, artistic one. But you'd been cooling off. Literally."

Lulu nodded. "I convinced myself I'd imagined it. But then, a couple of years later, we read *Macbeth* in English class. 'By the pricking of my thumbs,'" she recited, "'something wicked this way comes.' I was curious and braver than I had been. So I pulled a thumbtack from my corkboard, pricked my finger. And everything went . . . floaty."

"You felt dizzy?"

She looked up, her smile wry. "No, I mean literally. The spark appeared again. Instead of extinguishing it, I let it live. And everything went floaty. Comp, screen, notebooks, books." She wiggled her fingers. "Those little plastic people they gave away at Saul's Pizza for a while? I had like forty of those in a box."

"I remember," I said with a smile.

My parents loved Saul's, and they had a basket of plastic trinkets that kids waiting on pizzas could choose from. Lulu always took the figurines; I took the temporary pizza tattoos.

Tears welled at the memory of my mom, and I brushed them away.

"At first, I thought the city was under attack or my mom had done something magical downstairs. But then I pricked my finger again. And all the spells I hadn't been able to do, all the charms that hadn't worked just . . . did." She looked down, frowned, as if revisiting those memories. "I sat there for a long time, once I'd figured out what I'd done. And not entirely sure what I was going to do about it. I was, like, crazy relieved that I could do something. That I wasn't just a family aberration. But I also felt . . . abnormal."

That word—so full of meaning—was a vise around my heart. Because I knew exactly how she felt. I'd felt that way, too.

"They were both good witches, right? And I was . . . not."

"You told your mother?"

"Didn't have to," Lulu said, taking a drink. "She felt me doing it in the house. Dark magic has its own kind of shadow about it. Something you can feel. She guessed what I'd done, and then I showed her."

"Did she freak out?"

"She was actually really cool about the whole thing. But you could see there was a part of her that wanted to dive into it—to start using again. And part of her—I guess recovery—was to learn to sit with those feelings. Acknowledge them and experience them until they passed. So we sat with it. We just, I don't know, felt our emotions about it. Sometimes we talked about it. Mostly we didn't. We just—tried to adjust. And then the job opportunity came up in Oregon, and they thought it was best to put more space between us, and I agreed."

"That was a really adult decision."

She rolled her eyes.

"I'm serious, Lulu. I mean, not just avoiding magic altogether—the teetotaler's approach—but putting space between you and your mother. The easy thing would have been ignoring the risk—pretending everything was fine. Instead, you did something hard in order to protect yourselves and everyone else."

Her cheeks went faintly pink. "Yeah, well. Now she's gone."

The statement broke some kind of dam, because the ugly crying began for real.

"Crap," I said. I moved over and wrapped Lulu up. "Sorry for whatever I just prompted, but let it out if you need to."

"My mom got caught up with dark magic, but I think she was trying to do the right thing. And now she's gone."

"She's coming back," I said, fighting my own tears, because she *was* coming back, and I'd damn well see to it. "I swear to you on all that's good and holy, including my OK Kiddo stuff—which my mother nearly showed to Connor, by the way."

She perked up, wiped her eyes. "Wait, what? She did?"

"Yes, and it was mortifying, and that was the last time I saw my mom or my dad, and that will not be my last memory of them. It will *abso-fucking-lutely* not be. We're going to get them back," I said again, as if repeating the words could manifest the result.

I let her go and wiped my own eyes. "Why didn't you tell me? I wouldn't have cared one way or the other."

"Because it's better if you don't know. It's better for everyone if no one knows. Because that way, I can't be used against someone."

It took me a moment to fully understand what she meant. "You think someone would use you as a weapon." It was a total re-arranging of my world. Of everything I knew, had been told, about Lulu, her relationship to magic, and her relationship to her parents.

"No slip-ups," she said. "No mistakes."

"And the fairies?" I asked.

"I was wrong about Claudia. I was scared and I was angry."

"Downside of avoiding using your magic," I said. "You aren't trained to control it. At least, not as an adult."

"Yeah, well. Hard to tell your mother, a dark magic addict, that you want to learn how to get better at it."

"I imagine it would be, yeah."

A flush colored Lulu's cheeks.

"You've told someone else," I said. And someone she was faintly embarrassed about. "You told . . . Alexei."

She cleared her throat. "He was harassing me. I told him so he'd leave me alone."

"Or you told him because you needed someone to tell, and you trusted him." I said the words kindly, as I knew her telling him wasn't a slight against me. Connor, after all, knew about the monster. Ugly truths had to be carefully shared. "I don't like to ask, but—"

"You can tell Connor," she said. "And the Ombuds." She rubbed her eyes again. "If I'm going to help with the work, they'll all need to know."

I glanced back at the books. "Have you found anything so far?"

"Some," she said, "but most of it general. I've been researching the process of sealing a demon. The steps, the material, the magic."

"Good, that's good. We don't have anything yet about the actual mechanics of the process. So anything you can find would be great. That way, when we find her sigil, we'll be ready."

"Yeah," she said. "We'll be ready."

We sat for a few minutes in silence, adjusting to our new selves. "The magic you described," I began. "None of it sounded evil."

She pushed her hair behind her ears. "I mean, that's the complicated part. Dark magic isn't, like, inherently evil. It's just part of the universe of magic. It's old magic, and yeah, it can be used for very bad things. Evil things. That's where the problems arise."

"Slippery slope and addiction."

"Yep. Old magic is heavy. Powerful. Pricey. The trick is understanding the boundaries. And that requires a very careful hand."

"How'd you know all this?"

"Not at all because I snuck into the Cadogan House library during sleepovers."

"I know you did that," I said with a grin. "The Librarian told my mother. I just figured you were looking at the anatomy books."

"You weren't entirely wrong. I was curious! And Seth Tate told your mother about the old magic during my mother's Unfortunate Time. Your mother told mine eventually."

Seth Tate was Chicago's former playboy mayor and a Messenger, a kind of angel with a very complicated backstory. He and my mom had been friends of a type before he'd left politics for a life of religious service.

"We need a new name for 'dark' magic," I said. "I mean, aside from the gross Colonial racism nonsense, it's not accurate from a good-versus-evil standpoint, and it's meaningless since most Sups are nocturnal. When you think about it that way, it's *all* dark magic."

"You have a point. Blood magic?"

"Uh, no. That's my exclusive territory. And Hot Boy magic is Connor's."

"If we don't want to just say old magic, how about alt magic? Ur-magic. Wild magic. Ooh, eldritch magic. That's not bad. Kind of a mouthful, though."

"That's what she said."

I said it just for the laugh I knew it would get and was still thrilled when she responded. She hadn't laughed nearly enough lately. Which was when something hit me.

"It was the fairies, wasn't it?"

She blinked, looked at me. "What?"

"You've seemed unhappy lately. And it started around the time when the fairies started messing with the green land. We think that's what made the wards weak enough to let the demon through. Did it affect you, too?"

"If you're asking if the magic made me sad, no. It was uncomfortable, though. It made my awareness of magic . . . constant."

"Like when you suddenly realize you're breathing? Like, as an activity, and you wonder if you'll remember to breath if you don't think about it."

A corner of her mouth lifted. "I actually thought I was the only one who did that."

"Nope. So, what did make you sad?"

"Well, that whole thing with Riley." Riley was a shifter and ex-boyfriend who'd been framed by the fairies for murder. Clearing him of those charges had brought up some difficult feelings for her, including about the role of magic in her life.

"Also being past twenty," she continued, "and still not feeling authentic. Not feeling comfortable in my skin. Not feeling . . . like me."

"You're not alone there, either." But I didn't make my confession to her.

"Then let's figure out who we are," she said, and put her head on my shoulder. "So we can be us."

"In the meantime," I said, "I'll take anything you can give me about Rosantine."

"Working on it," she said with a yawn. "And what we have to do when we nail her. Let's make a pact not to be so weird in the future. To, maybe, admit who and what we are and deal with it. We've both been pretending for so long. Do you wonder what it'll be like to just be ourselves? To peel back the layers?"

The fact that I was still hiding something from her made my heart clench. "Is this a naked thing?"

She smiled, bumped my shoulder with hers. And for the first time in a long time, that smile looked real and unburdened. "I think we've spent enough time worrying about other people and hiding who we really are. Maybe we deserve to be ourselves."

She fell asleep with her head on my shoulder and my arms still wrapped around her as if I might protect her from herself, from her fears, from the magic that permeated our world and was looking for an opportunity to sink its claws into her.

And from those who'd try to use her—and her magic—against the rest of us.

EIGHTEEN

I found myself in an Auto after dusk, headed south. I needed to go to the office, but instead I was headed for Hyde Park. Headed for Cadogan House—or where Cadogan House had been.

I was tense when the Auto turned the last corner, gripping the edge of my seat as if I could will Cadogan House back to its location. I also hoped against hope that Rose would be there waiting, maybe searching for a Cornerstone, and my sword would be enough to bring her down, and this part of the nightmare would be over.

But there was nothing. Just . . . nothing. No scent of demon. No House.

I climbed out of the vehicle, walked down the sidewalk. There were no guards at the gate tonight, because what would have been the point?

I walked through the gate, stared at the empty spot, and felt nothing different than I had before. I closed my eyes and reached out, felt that faint pulse of magic again. But if my mother or Aunt Mallory had worked out how to return the House, they hadn't achieved it yet.

I wasn't the only one disappointed. I could feel monster straining toward the House, reaching out to it—to the sword—and feeling panicked by its absence. That didn't make me feel any better, especially since we were running out of time. I felt helpless. Useless. And pitiful for feeling those things when I was still here, still safe. I was entitled to my feelings, I knew. And maybe they were even understandable. But I didn't especially want them.

I gave myself a minute to settle, breathing in and out and letting that action become the focus of my awareness. After a minute, I opened my eyes again and looked around. Maybe I'd see something. Maybe I'd hear something. Maybe Rosantine, narcissist that she was, would come back to the site of her triumph.

I was an investigator. So I'd investigate.

I stepped onto the grass, began walking a perimeter around the House. I checked the ground, glanced among the trees. Not looking for anything in particular. Just . . . looking. I found nothing unusual on the side of the House, nothing in the back. And I was rounding the back corner toward the House's other side when I saw a glimmer of something on the ground.

I crouched down, swiped my fingers over the grass, and found them stained with something dark, gritty, and greasy.

I lifted my fingers, sniffed. The substance smelled of sulfur.

Was this a remnant of the not-fire that had seemingly consumed the House? Or the demon spell that had managed it? I hadn't seen any near the warehouse, but then Rose hadn't set anything on fire there, magical or otherwise.

I stood up again, shined a flashlight on the ground, hoping I'd find more traces of it in other places. I found a few more spots within a ten-foot square area, but nothing farther than that. The rain had probably washed most of it away.

I tried to take a few photos but knew it was too dark to do much good. But I still had the handkerchief Roger had given me—I'd planned to give it back to him tonight—so I swept it over one of the marks. I confirmed I'd picked up some of the grit, then folded it up and put it in my jacket pocket. Maybe Petra would have some ideas about what it was, or why.

I walked back around the House, found nothing else of interest. Until I reached the front sidewalk and found Connor standing there.

"Hi," he said.

"Hi. What are you doing here?"

"Looking for you. I was worried. You weren't at the loft, and Theo said you hadn't come into the office yet. Lulu thought you'd be here. What are you doing?"

"Looking for information. I found some kind of greasy grit on the grass, so I got a sample for Petra. I should get to the office so she can test it."

But Connor didn't move. "What if she'd come back? You shouldn't have come here alone. You can't stand here all night, and you can't will the House back into this world."

"I'm capable of taking care of myself, as you're well aware."

"Not against a demon."

I stepped up to him, my anger rising to replace the fear. "I held my own. Did you drive all the way out here to tell me I can't take care of myself?"

"Of course not," he said, the words tossed out.

I looked at him for a moment—really looked—and saw the emotions that mirrored mine riding on a wave of fatigue. And I thought of the pressure he was under, the weight he was carrying.

"If you want to fight," I said. "We can fight."

Connor's eyes widened. "What? Why would I want to fight you?"

"Because you need to fight someone, and I can handle you. Because you're scared and exhausted and furious."

He scoffed. "I am not scared of anything."

"You're scared for your parents. And you're scared for the Pack. And you're scared for your future."

He looked away, hands on his hips, and arrogance in every gorgeous inch of him.

"Fine. If that's how it has to be, so be it." And before he could object—or fight back—I grabbed his hand and pulled him through the yard and around Where-The-House-Had-Been.

"Let go," he protested, but didn't make much effort to pull away.

"No," I said simply, and led him into the back garden.

"Who's the bossy one now?" he asked.

"Me," I said, with unerring confidence in the word. "Right now, I'm the boss, because you need a minute to not be. You are burning up from the inside trying to solve the Pack's problems on your own."

He looked at me, and the shield fell, and I could see his exhaustion fully now. The urge to do the right thing for the Pack—and his uncertainty about what that was—were wearing him down.

"What do you see?" I asked.

He blinked. "What?"

"What do you see?"

He looked around. "Trees. Grass. Water."

"Vampires? Shifters?"

"No," he said. "Not now."

I nodded. "We have privacy. So start screaming."

He stared at me. "What?"

I turned to him, put my hand on his chest, just above his thudding heart. "You're afraid for your parents. You're angry at the demon. You're pissed at the interlopers. Let it out."

"And what will that fucking fix?"

"Well, you'll feel better, and I won't worry about you as much. And if you clear your head, you'll see better what you need to do next. You can even shift if you want to," I added with a grin. "I'll make sure no one calls animal control."

Connor watched me for a long time, then let out a breath that I bet he'd been holding for a very long time.

"I don't know what to do for them," he said. "I don't know

what to do about the challenge. The Pack doesn't like indecision; that's weakness. They'd rather see a bad choice than no choice at all. And my uncles . . ." He strode forward a few paces, stretching his arms, then turned back, hands on his hips. "They won't make a call either way. But they've made it pretty clear they think I should wait until Dad comes back . . . or doesn't. We've had the Pack for so long, and we've held the coronet for so long. I feel like it's slipping from my grasp, and under my watch."

I didn't argue. Didn't contradict or offer solutions, as he hadn't asked for any. I just let him say the things that were clawing at his heart.

"I'm pissed the Pack can't see through Cade's bullshit. I'm pissed he thinks he's entitled to rule the Pack. The fucking *arrogance* of it." His magic was bolder now, hotter, and seemed to push the chill from the air. "They sit around in Memphis, doing nothing for the Pack's survival but bitching about decisions made up here. Hard decisions. And they think they know better than the shifters who've worked their asses off, who've sacrificed, to hold the Pack together."

He linked his hands atop his head. "I'm pissed a demon thinks she can walk into my city—our city—and pour destruction over it. I'm pissed she hurt you and Theo and stole my parents. I hate wondering if I'll ever see them again. I hate battling an enemy I can't see."

His eyes glittered. "I hate Jonathan Black. He is a grifter and a liar, and he looks at you like you're a prize."

That one had me blinking. "Not a prize," I said. "A tool."

Connor cocked an eyebrow. "Is that better?"

"No. It just is."

Connor sighed, came to me, put his hands on my arms. "You aren't a prize or a tool. You're your own person. My person."

I lifted an eyebrow. "Is being owned better than being a tool?"

"When you're owned by the prince, yes."

The casual arrogance was back, which lifted my own spirits.

"Since you're feeling better, you want me to give you some scritches?"

He snorted, and that turned into a gale of laughter that echoed across the grounds. There was magic in that laughter, I thought. Joy and love and happiness in it, even if just for a moment. And it was just what we needed.

"No," he said. "But you should take a turn. Get it out, so you can clear the cache and get back to work." He sat on a bench behind us, crossed his arms, and stretched out his legs. "Go ahead."

I didn't need any more encouragement than that.

"If I'd stopped Rosantine at the gate, my parents would still be here. Your parents would still be here. I'm pissed a sociopath like her has magical powers. I'm pissed off she's screwing with Chicago. I'm furious that I can't even know whether my feelings are because of me or because of Rosantine."

Connor just watched me with that level stare that made my self-consciousness evaporate.

"I'm pissed off that people like Cade exist, spreading their bullshit around and expecting other people to bow down. I'm pissed there are people in the Pack who buy it. And I really want you to kick Cade's ass for putting you in this position when the entire Pack—*the entire Pack*—should be focused on getting your parents back. They should be supporting you. And instead they're partying."

"Not all of them," he said quietly. Not yet an Apex, but their advocate even still.

"I'm pissed my best friend fireballed me. I'm pissed I just found out last night that she's only able to do dark magic, and she's been able to do it since she was a kid, and she's been playing the 'my mother embarrasses me' part so no one would find out about her skills and use her for them. Or use them both."

Connor sat forward. "Seriously?"

I nodded. "She thought it would hurt her and her mother. I think, now that she's told me, she feels . . . relieved."

"Being vulnerable can do that," he said with a sly grin, then rose and came to me, wrapped his arms around me.

And then it just blurted out of me.

"You're going to die."

That hadn't been the subtle introduction to the topic I'd intended. He leaned back, his expression absolutely flat. "Are you going to take me out?"

"I'm serious," I said, my voice softer this time. "I'm immortal, Connor. And you . . . aren't."

He looked at me for a long, quiet moment. "And?"

I blinked. "And what?"

"And are you ending things with me?"

"I—what? No." That was literally the furthest thing from my mind.

"So you're trying to tell me that when I'm gone, you'll be devastated? You'll mourn every day for the rest of your immortal life? You'll constantly beat your breast and scream from the rooftops that no man could ever compare to me."

It was my turn to give him a flat look. "You aren't taking me seriously."

"I am," he said, and I saw in his eyes, which darkened with purpose, that he meant it. "I'm a shifter, Lis. We may live longer than humans, but we're still mortal. We understand that and do our best to enjoy life for as long as we've got it. Thus, the partying."

"Thus," I said. I took his hand, running a fingertip across knuckles scarred by god knew how many fights with shifters and battles with motorcycle carburetors. "So, it doesn't bother you that I'm immortal and, when you're gone, I'll have to take a series of really hot lovers?"

He flicked my ear. "Touch another man, and I'll haunt you forever."

"Can shifters become ghosts?"

"I . . . don't actually know. You want me to talk to Ariel and figure it out?"

"No. She'd séance you on purpose."

"I'm pretty sure she's moved on. Neither of us knows what the future will bring, Lis." A corner of his mouth lifted, probably because he'd seen the frustration in my eyes. "I know you prefer rules and deadlines. But we can't control the future, as much as we'd like to." He pulled me closer. "I plan on enjoying every moment that I have with you."

But that didn't loosen the fist around my heart.

He lifted our joined hands, pressed a kiss to my knuckles that lingered. "Shifters have a philosophy: You can't control the world. You can only control your reaction to it. Sometimes that means we have to accept things we don't like. So we drink and we grapple and we dance and we ride. And sometimes we fight." He tipped up my chin with a finger. "I'm fighting for you, for us. I fight the Pack way. You fight the vampire way. And I bet we come out right where we need to be."

For a moment, we stood together, united against the world.

But we'd taken long enough for ourselves. We'd gotten out what we needed out. And we had to get back to solving our problems.

"I haven't had a chance to tell you: Breonna came to see me last night."

His eyes went hot again. "She did what?"

"She came to the office. It was mostly blustering, but I think she was hoping she'd have a chance to make a play for you. Romantically."

His dubious snort had my spirits lifting higher. "As if."

"She's convinced dating a vampire is a liability."

Connor met my gaze again. "It isn't. You've proven yourself to the Pack more than enough times. But even if it was?" He put a finger beneath my chin, lifted it so our gazes aligned. "The Pack is important to me," he agreed. "You're more important. You rank higher, Elisa."

I stared at him. I hadn't needed that, and I was a little intimidated by what that meant. "Thank you," was the only thing I could think to say.

He wrapped his arms around me again. "I love you, brat."

"I love you, too, puppy. Let's go find a demon."

"Sorry I'm late," I said, hustling into the Ombuds' office with apology pastries. I put them on the side table, pulled the handkerchief from my pocket, offered it to Petra.

"Is that my handkerchief?" Roger asked.

"It is. But it's full of demon dust."

While Roger put his hands into the pockets of his dark gray slacks, Petra reached out her hand. Which summed them up pretty well, I thought.

"I went to Cadogan House," I said. "That's why I'm late. I needed to clear my head, and I walked around the lawn. There were spots in the side yard of whatever that is. Maybe ash or ground-up stone?" I pulled out my screen. "I took some photos, but they're probably too dark. I'm sending them now, just in case."

The images appeared almost instantaneously on Petra's screen. They looked, as expected, like darkness. And not much else.

"Here," Roger said, offering an open evidence bag. Petra dropped the handkerchief in. "I've got a meeting downtown, and I can drop this off at the lab."

"Is the lab run by a cousin of Petra's?" Theo asked with a grin.

"Har har," she said, and chewed the edge of a knobby apple fritter.

"Anything I've missed?" I asked.

"There's still no evidence of a Cornerstone near Cadogan

House," Petra said. "But if there had been—and the corresponding ward—surely it would have been triggered already." She leaned forward. "Is it true about the challenge?"

"It is," I said. "Connor hasn't decided what to do about it yet."

"He has a choice?" Theo asked, then held up his hands. "I'm not being sarcastic. I don't know much about Pack rules in that area."

"I think it's a gray area because his dad's . . . absent. It's not exactly Connor's challenge to accept."

Theo nodded. "Tough spot."

"Yeah, it is. And while I'm passing along news, Lulu will be helping us with some of the research and planning regarding demons."

They all looked at one another.

"Will she?" Roger asked, and I told them what she'd told me, or enough of it that they'd understand the situation.

Theo whistled. "That's a lot of burden for her to bear as a kid."

"Yeah, it was," I said. "I'm still mad she didn't come to me about it." However hypocritical that was, given my own secret. "But we need help and she's willing to offer it. So I'm happy giving her a chance. If anybody has issues with that, you can talk to me."

"I don't think we have any issues," Roger said, then looked at Petra. "Tell her about the visitor."

"Oh god," I said, taking my chair. "Was it Breonna again?"

"Correct letter, wrong name," Petra said, picking a bit of apple from the pastry. "Jonathan Black."

It only occurred to me then that I hadn't spoken to him since the warehouse fight. We weren't friends, maybe not even allies, but it seemed strange that he hadn't been in touch given that our lives had been on the line.

"And what did he have to say?"

"Null."

I tried to translate. "He said nothing?"

"He said the city had null spots. Places in Chicago where there's absolute-zero magic—the total absence of a magical signature."

I narrowed my eyes. "Okay. That's got to be relatively rare. We've got ley lines, vampire Houses, fairies. Magic is, like, sunk into the bones of this place."

"Rare," Petra agreed. "There's a lot of background magic in Chicago. But remember what we learned about the Cornerstones at Hugo's place?"

"The stones didn't give off any magic." I leaned forward. "Is he thinking we could find the Cornerstone locations by looking for null spots?"

"He didn't come out and say it," Petra said. "Because how would he know about the Cornerstones?"

I sat back again. How *would* he know about the Cornerstones? "Maybe his omniscient clients, whoever they are, told him. And that's an awfully big gift to drop into our lap." I narrowed my eyes. "What did he want in return?"

"To keep him posted about Rosantine," Petra said. "He said he was a little shell-shocked from the last fight and wanted to know when she was under wraps."

"Which is bullshit," Theo said.

"Oh, totally," I agreed.

"But he had a point about the null spots," Petra said. "So I got some time on a NASA satellite."

Roger choked on coffee. "Excuse me? Did you just say you bought satellite time from NASA?"

"No, just borrowed. The lead tech on one of its Earth-observing satellites is—"

"Your cousin?" Theo and I guessed simultaneously, then enjoyed a fist bump.

"Actually no," Petra said primly. "She's my second cousin."

"And what did the satellite info show you?" I asked. We could get the family story later.

"Wait," Theo said. "Back up. There's a satellite that can see magic?"

Petra's grin was slow and wide. "There wasn't before, but there is now. We had a talk about testing some spectrascope technology, and they're interested to add that capability to their search for extraterrestrial life." She swept her hair off her shoulders dramatically. "Anyway, Sheela agreed to test and run the specs, and voilà." She shifted her gaze to Roger and her smile was canny. "Leasing an Ombud-patented process to NASA should give us a nice cushion in the budget."

"Coyotes," Theo said. "In terms of additional funds. Just want to put that out there."

"So what did you find?" I asked Petra. We could discuss coyotes later, too.

"More null spots than Black seemed to suggest," she said. The overhead screen became a satellite image of Chicago with our ward map as an overlay. The wards, Cornerstones, and ley lines were visible, as were thousands of little black dots. It looked like a swarm of gnats.

"Nearly four thousand magical voids detected using this method," Petra said. "Those are spots in Chicago with an absolute-zero magical signature."

"Those can't all be Cornerstones," I said.

"Oh, definitely not. Like I said, Chicago has a lot of ambient magical energy floating around out there, so most spots in Chicago are going to register some kind of magic. And there could be lots of reasons for spots that show up as absolute zero. Bank vaults. Geological quirks. The remains of the Manhattan Project lab, which sounds fake, but is totally real."

"That's so many places," Theo said. "How does that help us?"

"Well," Petra said, "it's a finite number. A limited number of sites is better than all the sites, at least in my mind. But you're right. We can't search that many spots in person. So I did one more analysis."

Another map filled the screen. This time, the gnats had been replaced by a few dozen blue dots spread across town. She looked at us with the smile of a proud parent. "Anyone want to guess how I narrowed it down?"

"Leo's coffee locations?" I asked, natch.

"No."

"Starbucks?" Theo asked, and Petra rolled her eyes.

"It is not coffee-related, you addicts." She lifted her brows, waited. "Since there are no takers, I'll tell you." She glanced at me. "You said something at the warehouse that intrigued me."

I waved a genteel hand. "Carry on."

"You pointed out that the Cornerstones were voids. But the wards were not."

"Oooooh," Roger said, "I got it. These aren't just voids. They're voids beside powerful magic."

"Bingo," Petra said. "Of those few thousand voids, there are thirty-four that are next to something powerful." She flipped to another image. This one looked like a weather radar image—a splotch of green with a smaller splotch of red beside it. "Zero magic, high magic. I'm calling them 'hot spots.'"

"You're a freaking genius," Theo said.

"Feel free to pass that on to Dr. Anderson," Petra muttered.

"Thirty-four hot spots—while undeniably genius—is still a lot of ground to cover given our deadline," Roger said. "We've got two days. Can we narrow that down?"

"I'm going to check in with Armin about his algorithm and see if we can make some predictions about possible ward locations. Unfortunately, that's where we're stuck, unless the CPD wants to send folks out to every possible location."

"And have them literally digging in the dirt?" Roger asked. "Unlikely."

"I don't think we have to do that," I said, looking over the map. The pattern appeared random, at least based on geography or ley line location. But that didn't mean they weren't ascertainable. "In fact, I bet Rosantine's already done some of that for us."

Theo narrowed his gaze. "What do you mean?"

"Rosantine said she could 'tell' where the wards were."

Petra nodded. "I see where you're going—maybe she can sense the voids, too. Maybe that's how she figured out Cornerstones existed in the first place."

Roger sat forward, linked his hands together, and there was eagerness in his face. "And has been working through the hot spots systematically, looking for an unguarded ward."

Theo nodded. "So, if we can figure out the ones she's already eliminated, we can mark them off our list."

"She feeds off chaos," Petra said. "So maybe we search news stories for the last few days that suggest the kind of chaos chain reactions she can trigger. If it's near one of these thirty-four hot spots, we mark it off the list and don't need to check there."

Theo looked at me. "Because if she'd actually found a ward and Cornerstone, it would have signaled, and we'd already know about it."

"Exactly," Petra said.

"We need cops at the hot spots," Roger said. "Not to look for the Cornerstones—but to look for her."

Cousin Armin sent his algorithm, which was essentially based on the theory we'd worked out with sugar packets at the coffeehouse: Since the wards were triggered by proximity, perhaps the Guardians had divided Chicago into geographic regions, with a ward and Cornerstone for each region that triggered if Rose got close enough.

For example, the ghosts at South Gate would have been triggered to attack as long as Rose stepped within the ward's perimeter. If she'd been a few miles away from South Gate, the ghosts might have appeared at a farmhouse or even in the middle of a field. Of course, she'd gone directly for South Gate, because that's where the Cornerstone had been. We still didn't know how many wards there were, but we were getting closer.

We worked for hours, checking headlines for chaos chains and adding them to the map if they matched a void. We eliminated five more that way, in addition to three that didn't match the algorithm for likely ward spots.

I also learned there was a lot of deeply weird stuff going on in Chicago. I mean, as residents and Ombuds, we'd known there were things that went bump in the night, and that the city had systemic issues that drove crime and violence.

But when you started really looking for the chaos? Deeply weird stuff.

Women attacking spouses with chickens. Bar fights with pickled eggs and sports memorabilia pulled from the walls. River nymphs fighting over aesthetician appointments in the middle of Michigan Avenue. So many weird things, in fact, that it was hard to figure out which ones might have been demon-spawned versus the usual Chicago nonsense.

"Based on the timing," Roger said, head turning from the chronology we'd sketched of her movements to the map, "she's hit four spots in a row without finding anything." He looked back at us. "She's probably due for a win."

"So we stop her before she gets there," Theo said. "And that's that. And how do we do that?"

"We pick one of the hot spots," I said, "and Roger sends her a message telling her to meet us there."

The office went quiet.

"You want to try to trap her," Theo said.

"I'm completely open to alternatives. But I don't know of any, and my parents' lives are on the line here, and like Roger said, we're running out of time. I'm more than willing to take the risk."

"She'd be interested," Petra said. "It's one of the hot spots, so there's potentially a Cornerstone and a corresponding ward."

"There are risks," Roger said. "To you, to the neighborhood."

"Or she could make us hostages," Theo offered. "Or use us for bait, information, ransom money. The possibilities are boundless."

"I'm beginning to think you aren't into this quest," I said dryly.

His smile was mirthless. "Oh, I'm into it. I just don't see the point in hoping for the best where chaos demons are concerned."

I couldn't blame him.

"If you can't safely bring her in," Roger said, "you let her go. You don't risk yourselves, property, or other citizens."

"So that's a yes," Theo said, and Roger picked up his screen.

"I'll call Gwen and have CPD get ready. Give me twenty to get protections in place," he said, "and I'll send the message."

While he made the necessary calls, Theo and I tried to strategize. There wasn't much preparation we could do—not for a Sup whose calling card was the unpredictable. But we did what we could.

Petra put a map on-screen. Peony Park was a former stone quarry in the Bridgeport neighborhood and was now home to athletic fields, a pond, and a hilltop meadow.

"Ghosts?" Theo wondered. "I mean, if it is a ward?"

"I don't know," I said. "There's a pond, and they like variety. Maybe water monsters."

Theo cursed. "We go in armed. As many arms as we can carry. Octopus-level armament."

"And every bullet we send her way will probably ricochet into a person. Chaos," I noted.

He nodded, looked at Petra. "You can zap her if she needs it."

"Eager" was how I'd describe Petra's expression.

"Oh, sure. The sky is awesome tonight. There's a storm coming in, and it's brimming with energy." She held up her double espresso. "Ditto."

"How do we play her?" Theo asked.

"We'll have to see how it feels," I said. "I'll go in front and talk to her. You two stay behind me. Petra, be ready to blast her if she even thinks about wiggling her nose."

"What?" her stare was blank.

"Old witch joke," I said. "Never mind. Just have the lightning ready. Getting her unconscious may be the only way we get her out of there."

"And then what do we do with her?" Petra asked.

"We bring her back here," I said. "And put her in one of the concrete boxes."

A portion of the brick factory had been converted into a super-natural prison—a large room that held individual concrete cells for particularly dangerous supernaturals.

"I don't know if that will hold her," I said. "But it's the best option we've got."

NINETEEN

Officers would be stationed around the park's perimeter. I could have used a wolf or two—or at least some howls—but I didn't think this was the time to ask Connor for help. At least I had an extra dagger tucked into my boot, and Theo had charmed zip ties in the event we were able to bring her down. And monster, should it deign to help.

I felt its matter-of-fact *No, thank you*. It was a creature of bravado except, apparently, where demons were concerned. Or when the odds were against us.

"Fuel," Petra said from the passenger's seat, and handed me a bottle of blood. Theo got cold brew, and she got electrolytes. For presumably electrolytic reasons.

We parked three blocks away from the hill and climbed out of the car. She was near—the air was tinged with bitterness—but the park was quiet. I'd forgotten the meadow was dotted with large, blocky animal sculptures. They'd been created for a Gilded Age exhibition and had been saved for the park when the exhibition had been dismantled. They'd freaked me out as a child, so this wasn't a park we'd visited often.

"Be careful," I said, and we started forward.

The grass was soft beneath our feet, and lightning darted in the west from the new storm pressing toward us. The temperature had dropped a good ten degrees in the time it had taken us to cross town.

Rosantine stood, as promised, in the semicircle created by the sculptures, ground lights aimed at her like a diva at a concert. She wore head-to-toe black tonight—boots, skirt, long jacket.

As we got closer, my heart began to speed up. I wanted her in hand *now*. I wanted my parents back now. And I had to force myself to stay calm.

"Eglantine," I said. "Are you ready to surrender?"

Her expression, well lit as it was, stayed dry. "I don't surrender."

"Where are my parents?" I asked.

"Not here," she said.

"Why did you take the House?"

"Because I have work to do."

"Because the people in the House could stop you? Or because there are things in the House that scare you?"

Her eyes flared with anger. "I'm scared of nothing."

"Then bring back the House."

"All right," she said. "Tell me the location of the remaining Cornerstones."

Theo and I looked at each other, snorted.

"Can you believe?" Theo asked.

"I know, I know," I said. "Rosantine—can we call you Rosantine?" I asked, then didn't wait for her response. "First, she thinks we'd actually believe her promise to bring the House back. Second, if we knew the locations of the Cornerstones, would we be here right now?"

"The ones who exiled me made a plan," she said, with a tone that read of boredom at our antics.

"And we aren't privy to it," Theo said, gesturing toward the car. "Our schedule is full, so we'd really like to go ahead and arrest you."

Her fingers began twitching.

"Hand flick," I said.

We all looked around. For a moment, there was nothing, either of the improbable variety or of a corresponding ward. But I should have known that chaos doesn't operate on a schedule.

There was a tearing sound, a wrenching groan, and the earth shook.

"What is it?" Theo asked.

I watched Rosantine close her eyes, breathe in magic.

"It's not a ward," I said quietly, as if my voice alone might trigger one. "Just her."

"So why doesn't she leave?" Theo asked, hand on his weapon as his eyes scanned the park. "No ward means no Cornerstone. And that's what she wants."

"Because she's hungry," I said grimly. "Rose, Eglantine, whatever. Stop the magic immediately. You're surrounded by officers, and you're coming with us."

As expected, she ignored me.

"Petra!" I called out, keeping my eyes on the demon. "Do your thing."

I felt the charge in the air, the light turning a pale shade of blue as Petra charged herself somewhere behind me. And then a vacuum as power was sucked from the air, condensed.

A bolt of lightning flew from my left toward Rosantine, whose eyes snapped open with concern. She hadn't liked lightning the last time she'd met it. But the warehouse machine's magic must have been different than Petra's, as she batted the bolt aside like it was nothing more than an insect. It struck a tree at the edge of the park, which split with a *crack* of sound.

Rose closed her eyes again.

The scent of sulfur swirled in the air, and we watched, dumbfounded, as one of the white statues—something vaguely gorilla-like—hauled itself out of the ground with its curled marble knuckles. It opened its mouth to scream, showing enormous teeth, but made no sound other than the scrape of stone against stone.

"*Shit,*" I whispered as sweat trickled down my back despite the chill in the air.

"Is that . . ." Petra began.

"An animated sculpture of a very pissed-off gorilla?" I asked, pushing down the rush of childhood fear. "It really is."

It was nearly six feet tall, the lower half of its body stained with rings of green and brown from its decades in the dirt. And it moved with a lurching gate that had every hair on my body standing on end.

"How long for you to recharge?" I asked Petra amid another chorus of thunder.

"Another minute," she said.

Another rupturing sound; another moving sculpture. This one was elephantine but bulkier, stockier. And then the metaphorical gates were open. While Rosantine watched, fed on the fear and confusion, a dozen stone animals—all of them taller than us—began dragging themselves toward us.

"Dislike," Theo said. "Really, really dislike."

"Yeah," I said. This was a new variety of demon-fueled horror show. We were now surrounded by animals, and they were picking up speed as they moved, becoming more lifelike as they moved.

The gorilla screamed silently again, slammed its fist into the dirt. Dirt flew up from the crater it made, the concussion shaking the earth beneath us a few feet away.

We might have darted through the circle to the car, abandoning the field to them. But that would leave a dozen rock monsters headed for the park's boundaries and into Bridgeport.

Instead, we moved closer to one another.

"Thoughts?" I asked. "Suggestions? Teleportation possibilities?"

"Pants soiling," Theo said. "That's my only current thought."

"We can't break stone with our weapons," Petra said, and it sounded more a curiosity—an interesting dilemma—than a concern.

"Well, Theo and I can't," I said. "I'm not ruining my blade on those things, and I doubt a gun will do more than send shrapnel into the air." Which made me worry about Theo the most. He was the most human of us all. (Technically, he was the only human, but I loved a good *Star Trek* callback.)

"And they're getting faster," Theo said. "I would like a very specific plan to avoid becoming dead."

"Hold until they get close," I decided. "Hold, and when I give you the signal, run."

"Did you say hold?" Petra asked, shifting nervously from foot to foot.

"Yes. Let's see how well they maneuver."

"You're thinking they'll take out some of their own," Theo said. "That sounds much too easy."

"It won't be," I said. "She'll see to that."

A bull as boxy as the elephant paused a few yards away, pawed at the ground, anticipating—a fight? Dinner? Props from a demon?

"It's like a henge," Theo said. "If the henge stones became animate and tried to bash your brains in."

The circle tightened. A bear with wide shoulders shook its head as it moved forward, the motion lifting the *screech* of grinding rock into the air. Their bulk blotted out the ground lights beyond as they drew nearer like a noose, only small gaps between the animals now . . .

"Go!" I shouted, and we darted into the gaps, ran through the circle. Behind us, the crunch of stone animals striking one another echoed out. When I'd put fifty feet between us, I looked back.

Lightning lit the park, putting the animals in stark silhouette. It looked like an archeological ruin, the ground littered with the broken stones and pieces of sculpture. But only three or four animals had crumbled enough to stop moving.

And then the rest were giving chase again.

"Petra!" I called out, hoping she'd had time to recharge.

I kept my eyes on the monsters until she lit a spark—a bright blue flame that burned in her palm—and threw it at a charging rhinoceros that was a yard away from her. It jagged through the air on a strangely angular path before striking the rhino in the head.

With a tremendous *crack*, its head split from its body and dropped to the ground, its lifeless eyes staring up. Both pieces went still, frozen into stone again.

"Damn," Petra said after she'd walked over and looked down at the granite carnage. "That's more horrifying than I thought it would be."

"Yeah," I said, and tried not to think about the call the mayor was going to make about ruined sculptures.

"Duck!" she called out.

I did, heard the whoosh of air as something big and heavy swung over my head. I hit the ground and rolled just in time to avoid the gorilla's pounding fist. It had made no sound in its approach, and I hadn't even heard the grinding rock over the near-constant thunder.

The pounding left a foot-deep hole in the soil, right where my head had been.

I vaulted back to my feet, ducked again as it swung its other arm. As it shifted its weight, I pivoted close enough to smell its sulfurous stench, tried to shove it onto its side.

It didn't move an inch.

It flung back an arm, and then I was airborne. I hit the ground hard, was glad at least for rain-softened grass, but still needed a moment to unscramble my brain.

These things have to have a weakness, I thought, climbing to my feet again and immediately jumping to the side as it ran toward me. A path here rose to crest the central hill in a series of steps . . . and I realized the creatures' fundamental flaw.

Physics.

I jumped over the rail and began to climb the stairs, heard only the light swish of grass as the creature tracked me. We reached the top nearly at the same moment. I stood there, watching as it pivoted to face me, and opened its arms to take me down

I waited until I could hear the slide of stone against stone, until it was leaning toward me—and then I dropped back. With nothing but air to grab, it tripped down one step, and then gravity picked up the fight, pulling it down riser after riser until it moved like a boulder, rolling head over feet. It hit the pavement with a bright, tremendous *crack* and shattered into a shower of pieces.

I took one breath, turned back toward my companions just as Petra sent a bolt into a wild boar that shattered it right down the middle. But I didn't see Theo.

"Damn," I said, and ran to the lookout at the edge of the hill.

Relief swamped me when I saw Theo climbing toward me in the grass, the bear close on his heels. But the rain had slopped up the grass, and the animal couldn't get traction on the incline, which put a gap between them.

"Up here, Theo!" I called out, and went over the lookout rail to extend a hand; once he was up here, we'd lure the bear to the stairs and use that trick again.

But the bear regained its footing. And this time, it climbed faster.

"It's moving!" I called out. "Hurry!"

He picked up what speed he could on the hill, until his foot slipped, and he went down on his belly. The bear swiped, but Theo yanked his foot back just in time and instinctively swept out his casted arm. The bear had been reaching up again, and the cast, heavy and solid, caught it off balance and sent it staggering backward, then tumbling down the hill. It struck a boulder in the landscape, bounced into the air, and hit the sidewalk at the bottom. It shattered like a piñata.

Theo climbed over the rail, looked back. "That's just . . . terrible," he said, chest heaving as he caught his breath. "R-I-P, bear."

"It's kind of pitiful, right?"

"And the mayor's going to be pissed."

"She can blame the demon," I said, and we both jumped when lightning crashed within a few blocks, the thunder nearly instantaneous and just as terrible.

"Maybe let's get off this hill?" he suggested.

"During a lightning storm, good call."

We ran back to join Petra. "You okay?" I asked.

"Having a ball," she said, and looked like it. Her straight hair was a little frizzled now, as if the lightning had given her a different kind of buzz. There were still half a dozen animals milling in the open space, but Petra was doing a pretty effective job of making countertops and bathroom tile out of them.

And it took me a moment to realize who'd find that very, very disappointing.

I looked back at Rosantine. Her lip was curled, her shoulders tight, and there was a hungry look in her eyes.

"Demon magic incoming," I said.

She flicked out a hand again and . . . *wait.*

That wasn't just a flick—she was drawing something with her fingers, tracing a shape in the air. If a sigil was the key to her power, who wanted to bet she was drawing the same sigil in order to use that power?

Her movements were so fast, and over so quickly, that I wasn't able to "read" what she'd drawn. And the angle was too awkward for me to get a sense of its shape. But there were definitely intentional gestures there.

And I'd been staring long enough that I nearly missed the tricksy glance she gave to the flashing sky.

"Everybody down!" Petra said.

Theo cursed, grabbed my arm, and pulled me to my knees as the world flashed green and every hair on my body stood at attention.

"Shit," I said, heart pounding as I braced for the literal lightning strike. The odds of any one of us being struck by lightning were extremely limited. Unless you had a chaos demon doing the work. The epitome of the improbable becoming exceedingly fucking probable.

Lightning was having quite the week in Chicago.

Petra reached her hands to the sky—and took the full force of the lightning. The world flashed green once more, then twice, and the hard *clap* of sound was louder than anything I'd ever heard.

Her body shook and sparked and flashed once, then twice. She was still for a moment that lasted entirely too long, and I'd have sworn my heart skipped several beats. Then she shook her head, blinked.

"Phew," she said with a rather satisfied smile. "That was a good one."

"You're okay?" I asked, climbing to my feet.

"Well, sure. And fully charged." And then Petra looked back toward where Rosantine had stood—at least until she cursed like a sailor on a very good shore leave.

"She's gone," Theo said, hands on his hips. "She's fucking gone."

"At least the animals are down," I said. Without her beckoning magic, they'd frozen in place again. I closed my eyes, gave myself a moment to exhale, and then opened them again.

"We need to find video of Rosantine working her magic," I said.

"Why?" Theo asked.

"Because she's doing the sigil. That's the hand flick."

"Oh, my god," Petra said, and dropped her head back. "Of course it is. How did I miss that?"

"Well, *chaos*," Theo pointed out. "What are our video options?"

Petra whistled. "I can look into it, but I don't think we have any surveillance from the warehouse that's clear enough."

"What about Hugo's video from the warehouse?" I asked.

"There wasn't any," she said, "or at least not that was usable. Apparently the system hadn't been upgraded in a while."

Crap. We'd been close.

She must have seen the disappointment in my face. "I'll get the day-shift folks on it, and they can coordinate with the CPD. Maybe there's security footage from some of the other null spots we identified."

"Good thought," I said, and looked at Theo. "And speaking of Hugo, the CPD needs to put a guard on him. Not just the warehouse, not just the shed, but on him. She may not know who he is, but if she finds out, she might think he has knowledge about the Cornerstones." Just like she had with us.

Sirens and lights flashed as CPD cruisers rolled up to the park. Officers emerged, looked over the broken sculptures.

"Some demon shit again," one of them said.

I figured that summed it up pretty well.

I was soaked to the bone and went back to the town house to clean up. Connor, Alexei, and Lulu were all at the dining room table, poring over books she'd apparently brought from the loft. I was anticipating the day she brought Eleanor of Aquitaine with her so the cat (demon) could hate me in multiple locations.

Connor looked up, his smile fading to concern. "Why are you so wet?"

"Well," I said, pulling off my boots, "it's pouring outside. We tried to lure Rosantine into a trap, got attacked by the sculptures in Peony Park, and got rained on. And she got away."

Connor rose, and I could see the fight in his eyes—concern for my safety and frustration that he hadn't known I'd be taking the risk.

"Are you all right?" he asked, voice deadly serious.

"We're all fine. It was a last-minute plan, and I just came by to change and recharge. Let me do that, and I'll tell you everything."

I threw my hair into a very untidy topknot and changed clothes, then came back down for blood of the drinking variety. I'd had enough fighting for the night.

I took a seat at the table while I drank, pushing aside a book of old prints of demonic creatures, and told them the whole story.

In the chair beside me, Connor rubbed a hand over his face, then leaned over to put an arm around me, kiss my temple. "Sometimes I wonder about your job."

"Sometimes I wonder about it, too," I said. "But I'm okay."

"I can't believe you arranged to meet her," Lulu said.

"No other choice," I said. "We're running out of time. We managed to identify the hot spots, and we had to take a chance. We also had CPD backup and very shitty weather, which is very good weather where Petra is concerned. That had no effect on Rosantine. But we got a hand flick," I said, and told them what we'd figured out.

Lulu just stared. "It sounds really freaking obvious when you say it out loud—sure, they need to have a connection to their magical key in order to do the magic."

"But also counterintuitive," I said. "It's her weakness—her true name in symbolic form. Superman didn't wear kryptonite on a chain around his neck. Anyway," I said, moving on from superheroes before Connor tried to correct me about a story in issue something or other from this or that series, "we've got a video search underway. Hopefully, we'll find shots of her and can use that to sketch out the sigil."

"You're getting close," Connor said.

"Yeah." I checked the clock automatically. "I just wish we'd do it a little faster. What's been going on here?"

"Books," Alexei said. "Humans have very weird beliefs about supernaturals."

I smiled. "Yeah, they do."

"Per my assignment," Lulu said, gesturing to the books, "I've been trying on how to seal the demon once you find her sigil."

"Thank you again for helping," I said.

"Yeah, well." She pushed hair behind her ears, the movement almost bashful. "Sometimes you have to claw your way outside your comfort zone because a demon has sent your parents into another dimension."

"Put that on a motivational poster," Connor said, and she smiled a little.

"I thought I was helping protect me and my mom—and the city—by avoiding it altogether. But now there's a demon in Chicago, so I'm stepping up." She shifted in her seat. "Anyway, I reviewed the spells created to seal the seventy-two demons Solomon identified. Each demon has a different spell, but chunks of the spell are similar across all of them. Each chunk is correlated with a certain skill or attribute. So, for example, demons who can predict the future always have obsidian in the spellworking. Demons that are fast need laurel and certain chanted words."

"It's like a recipe book," I said.

Lulu nodded eagerly. "Kind of like that, yeah. Some cookies have white sugar. Some have brown sugar. You change the ingredient and the amount depending on the cookie you're trying to make. I think, if I keep looking at her attributes, we can figure out the magic we need to seal her again."

"And how are things at the Pack?" I asked, glancing between Connor and Alexei.

Alexei looked at Connor. Connor just growled.

"Uncles or interlopers?"

"Both," they said simultaneously.

"Uncles still have no opinion," Connor said, "and Cade threw a party in a bar downtown. Got half the Pack members in Chicago good and drunk."

"You mean more to them than booze," Lulu said, turning a page of her book. "But they aren't going to turn down free drinks."

Connor grunted, ran a hand through his hair. "Word is spreading. Other NAC members are coming into town because they think they'll get to witness a challenge. Other Packs are calling because there's business that needs to be done, and they need to know who's going to do it."

"What do you want to do?"

He looked at me. "What?"

"If you had to make a decision today, what do you want to do?"

He blinked. "I'd accept the challenge and send Cade running back to Memphis, tail between his legs. And that would put Dad in a hell of a spot."

"Sometimes it's okay not to decide." We all looked at Lulu, who lifted a shoulder. "I'm just saying. Running out the clock is a tried and true strategy."

"Smart girl," Alexei said, but Connor made no comment.

I rose, intending to head back to the office, but Connor met me before I reached the front door.

"Do me a favor," he said, taking my hand. He still wore boots, and I was in socked feet, which made him even taller than usual.

"Okay," I said, looking up at him. "What?"

He smiled. "Work here for the rest of the night."

I frowned at him. "Why?"

"Because she's going to be pissed, which makes the world a dangerous place. Have the team come over here if you want. But I'll feel better if you're here." He kissed me softly, just a brushing of lips. "If you're safe."

I made a show of sighing haggardly, even though I was fine with working in comfy pants and thick socks for the rest of the night. "Fine," I said. "But I want food."

I got Roger's okay to work remotely, a pepperoni pie and accompanying pan of brownies, and Theo's and Petra's declinations. They opted to stay at the office, as they thought they'd concentrate better in that environment.

By the time dawn was close, the dinner table was littered with blood and soda bottles, empty pizza boxes, and discarded crusts.

We ate while we worked. Lulu and Alexei searched her books, made notes, discussed quietly. I searched websites, news clips, anything that might show me a clear image of Rose's hand flick. Connor was a gamer and knew more about the underground web than me, so he searched those portals.

At fifteen minutes before dawn, with the house quiet, I'd gone down to get a drink when my screen buzzed. There was no caller identification.

"Elisa," I said, answering it.

"It's Miranda. We need to talk."

"About?"

"Connor and the assholes."

"Worst band name ever," I muttered, and slipped out of the kitchen. I walked into the conservatory at the back of the house, then into the cool night air. I needed a moment in the darkness. "You have five minutes," I said, lifting the screen up again. "We're on a little bit of a deadline here."

"I know," she said, with no trace of sarcasm. "It's about that. Connor has to agree to the challenge."

"Then you should tell him that."

"He won't listen to me. But he might listen to you." And it sounded like actual hurt in her voice at that admission.

"He understands the issues," I said. "We've talked about it. And he's trying to find an option that doesn't screw the family or the Pack."

She went quiet for a second. "He's not afraid to fight, is he?"

I didn't know what it cost a shifter—supernaturals known for their bravado and eagerness to rumble—to ask that question. It made me nervous, but I couldn't show that to her. If she was calling me, she needed something else. She needed bravado.

"Has he ever been afraid to fight?" I asked, voice flat.

There was gravity in the silence that followed. "He's an alpha and he's strong," Miranda said. "But I don't know this Cade, and I haven't been able to dig up much on him. It's just—would they have come all this way if they didn't think they could win?"

"Yeah," I said. "They're shifters. They think they can beat anyone."

"I don't mean that," she said. "I mean . . . it might not be a clean challenge."

It took me a moment to grasp her implication. "You think they're going to cheat?"

"I'm not accusing anyone of that," she said, as if it was the basest insult. "But I think you need to be careful. If you really care about him, and you really support him, then you have to have his back."

I heard the fear in her voice, and it scared me to my bones.

"I do and will," I said. "Tell anyone in the Pack who needs to hear it—they try to play dirty, and they meet my sword."

Connor slept fitfully, body occasionally shaking as if he were fighting some unseen attacker. He curled into me, and I banded my arms around him, holding him tight against the fear and fury, hoping he could find a way through.

TWENTY

And then there was only one more night. Tomorrow, the House, our parents, would be lost to us forever. So we were hustling.

Connor and Alexei were already gone when I left for the office that night. I still didn't know what Connor intended to do about the challenge, and I wondered if he'd use Lulu's strategy—wait and see if we could get the House back in time. And when his father was here, they could decide together.

Lulu was stationed at the table again with a smoothie that looked nearly as unsavory as Connor's. I kissed the top of her head as I headed for the door.

"We could use a little luck," I told her. "So if you've got any juju for that, feel free to use it."

"We'll get it done," Lulu said, giving me a look of confidence that had me almost believing it was possible. "I'm getting close."

So we didn't have a plan exactly, but we had a plan for a plan. And that was something. On the way out, I looked at Lulu, grinned fully. "I missed you. I mean—"

"I know what you mean," she interrupted with a grin. "I missed me, too. Let's toast this asshole."

Wind whipped at the windshield as I took an Auto to the office. I didn't feel especially good about the update I sent Micah and the other Houses on the way, but there was no point in hiding the truth: We were doing everything we could to find Rose and her sigil, and we wouldn't give up. But we were running out of time.

"Anything new?" I asked, taking off my jacket.

"We think there are eight wards and Cornerstones," Petra said.

I stopped. "What? You got that far?"

"Process of elimination," Petra said, "and one really bad game of darts."

Theo lifted a hand. "It wasn't bad for me, because I won, which means I got the last Mallocake in the vending machine."

"Man, my mother loved those," I murmured, then realized I'd used the past tense. "*Loves* them," I corrected. "She loves them, just interdimensionally right now."

"They're amazing," Theo said, and popped the map onto the screen. "The algorithm helped a lot, so thanks to Armin."

"Praise be to Armin," I murmured, and reviewed the colored blobs that now covered Chicago, each a different color, and each a different Cornerstone.

"Their zones of influence, let's say, are a guess," Petra said. "We don't really know their boundaries, but those are the best mathematical conclusions. And that assumes we're right about eight. I'm feeling eighty percent confidence on that."

"I've just sent Gwen the six new locations," Roger said. "She'll send out uniforms, who will let us know if Rose is spotted."

"It would make sense for me and Elisa to check them out," Theo said. "Maybe we'll get lucky."

"Anything on the video front?" Petra asked.

I shook my head. "I found no footage clear enough to tell what she's doing. I viewed everything the CPD had, every social media and news video I could find. None were ever clear or close enough to get details other than—" I spun my hand in the air.

Theo frowned at me. "I don't recall it looking quite like that."

"It seems you overplayed your hand," Roger said, offering the daddest of dad jokes.

"There's more video to review," Petra said. "So you can have at it."

I sighed, and tried to garner the enthusiasm for spending hours *not* finding what we needed.

She pulled out her buzzing screen, read it with hope. And then her shoulders slumped.

"What's wrong?" Theo asked.

"So," she said, frowning at her screen, "the ash from Cadogan's yard was a no-go. It's literally just ash. Charcoal, really."

"Damn."

But then she went very still. "Holy crap, you guys. Holy absolute crap."

There was elation in her voice, so I peeked over at her screen. She was looking at a black-and-white photo with a barely discernable circle in the center of it. "What is that?"

"Your picture of the Cadogan House lawn," she said.

"Wait—what? There was nothing on the Cadogan House lawn. I mean, certainly not a circle. Just a few dots of ash."

"I sent the pics to the lab along with the ash, just in case they could enhance. They ran some filters on it." She swiped to show a second photograph. The circle was clearer in this one, and there were fuzzy marks inside it.

My heart began to beat.

"Holy absolute crap," I said. "We got Rosantine's sigil."

What we had, really, was a *suggestion* of Rosantine's sigil. A whiff of it. A circle with some vague marks inside, which apparently described eighty percent of demon sigils, and didn't give us nearly enough to command her, much less to seal her.

But it was a place to start. We put the ward visits on hold for now and put the phantom sigil's outline, or what we could see of it, on-screen. Then we went back to the flicking videos to find the details.

Two hours later, I was frustrated and ready to scream. I'd found absolutely nothing, and wasted more time in the process. That we were so close to our goal—and our deadline—made the frustration worse.

My screen buzzed, and I was hoping against hope for a good old-fashioned demon confrontation. But it was Hugo's name that appeared—the warehouse Machinist. I was irritable, and for some reason assumed he wanted to talk to me about *Jakob's Quest*. Which was ridiculous.

I tried to shake off the attitude and answered. "Hey, Hugo. What's up?"

"I have your video."

"My video?"

"Of the demon outside the warehouse. I thought you might want to see it."

It took several seconds for my brain to catch up. I held up a hand to stop the general chatter in the room. "Wait," I said. "I thought that video didn't work."

"Well, it didn't at first. But I'm still feeling guilty about what happened—all that damage—so I played with it a while, did some research. My dad installed the security system, and the video used a very old codex. Once I found that, it played like a top. I'm going to upgrade the system—but you don't care about that right now." He smiled. "Anyway, I have the video now. It's not much, and it may not help, but I've got it."

Hope instantly deflated.

"Why don't you think it would help?" Because there was no point in wasting time to watch it if it wasn't going to help us get her.

"Mostly she just stands there and wiggles her fingers."

I went absolutely still. "Hugo, are you saying you got her hand movements on camera?"

"Well, yeah." He paused. "Is that good?"

"It's the best thing I've heard all week," I said. "You might have just saved Chicago."

"Down with Korkath!" he said. Which I assumed was a *JQ* rallying cry.

Hugo sent the video to me, and I sent the video to the team. Two minutes later, we identified the gestures. We conferenced in Lulu at the town house, and she sketched out the sigil as she watched Rosantine move. Then she played the video again, refined the sketch. Then again a third time.

"That's as good as it's going to get," Lulu announced, and put the image on screen.

She'd used a brush and ink, so the circle and series of marks inside it were dark and fluid against the white paper.

"Scanning," Petra said, then pulled up the photo from the Cadogan House lawn as a comparison. Lulu's drawing matched the general outlines in that one nearly exactly.

"Searching," Petra said, as she looked for a match to the images in the catalogs of supernatural and demon lore.

Two minutes later, Petra hooted. "I fucking found her," she said. "Her name is fucking Andaras."

I mean, it was "Andaras," not "fucking Andaras," but close enough. She wasn't one of Solomon's seventy-two demons, but Solomon's list of demons was hardly the only one out there. Medieval influencers loved their demon lists.

According to those guides, Andaras was a demon of "most wondrous chaos" and esteemed for her beauty and ability to "moveth the heavy things." Such as vampire Houses, one would assume.

We had the wards, which the CPD was monitoring. We had the sigil, which we could use to seal Rose when we understood the process for doing so.

Which meant I was heading back to the town house to help Lulu finalize the spell. I brought printed copies of the sigil, and while we plied Lulu with kale-and-lemon smoothies, I explained to Connor and Alexei how we'd managed to find its shape.

"It took a while, but we did it. Down with Korkath!"

Connor's grin was boyishly charming. "How do you know about Korkath?"

"Hugo Horner is a *JQ* fan. I'm sure you can find him online."

His brows lifted. "How do you know Hugo Horner?"

He said it like the name was common currency. "Wait—how do *you* know Hugo Horner?"

"He's famous in *JQ* circles. He's played for years. I watch his streams sometimes."

Connor had tried, once and unsuccessfully, to explain to me the point of watching someone else play a video game, but the concept eluded me.

"He's the Machinist," I said. "His family has guarded and repaired the warehouse machine since it was built."

"No shit." He put his hands on his hips. "I wondered if he had a day job. Maybe I'll invite him on a quest."

"Maybe after we nail the demon?"

"Afterward," he said with a nod.

There were more smoothies, some curses, and our often frustrated efforts to find weird ingredients in Chicago in the middle of the night. Anything we couldn't find required Lulu to retool the spell again.

And because demons were inherently untrustworthy, we had to ensure we had the House back—with everyone safe—before we sealed Rosantine away. That was going to require negotiating.

"We need a lawyer."

Lulu looked at me, surprise in her expression. "Why would we need a lawyer?"

"Because we need to get a supernatural to do something, and Sups are weird about contracts and agreements." I'd already learned that lesson once this week. "We need a lawyer who can draw up a contract Rose can't weasel her way out of. Maybe with a magical binding." If vampires could use a magical summons on me, I figured we could use a magical contract on a demon.

"You have someone in mind?"

"Surprising no one, my dad has several lawyers," I said. "I'll give the firm a call."

I did that, and let Lulu and the lawyer speak to each other about the necessary terms for a demonic contract. As you do.

I kept looking at the clock, as we were down to less than twenty-four hours. I knew I wasn't fighting alone, and that helped. That I had a group of amazing people to rely on, and they were actively working the problem. I could breathe. I could rest. Which was good—because I knew I'd need all my strength tomorrow.

Connor and I took a bottle of wine upstairs. We only had twenty minutes before dawn broke, but I needed the momentary distraction.

I poured while he lit the fire in the master bedroom's fireplace, then brought him a glass.

"You've made a decision," I said, watching him.

He nodded thoughtfully. "I just sent a message to have relayed to Cade."

"Damn," I said with a grin. "Not even telling him directly. That sends a message, too. And the message is?"

"I do not accept his challenge. I'm not the Apex of the North American Central Pack, so it shouldn't have been directed at me, anyway. And I certainly can't accept it on my dad's behalf."

There was something more there. "But?"

"But," he said, "tomorrow is another day entirely."

And he refused to tell me anything else.

TWENTY-ONE

"Get out of my house."

Lulu, still in pajamas twenty minutes after dusk, sat at the dining room table with paper and pens and glared at me.

"So that's a no on the waffles?" I asked.

"Get out of my house," she said again.

"Technically," Connor said, "it's my house. In that I own it, and you're all squatters."

"For right now, it's my house. We only have a few hours, and I'm ninety-eight percent done. I need quiet, and no magic, in order to finish the last bit. Could you all just scurry away to the office and maybe get everyone assembled?"

"You *are* close," I said.

She rubbed her tired eyes. "So close. Go. Please get out of my house."

"We're getting," I said, pushing the guys toward the door before Connor could get into the finer points of mortgages and property ownership.

Alexei stayed with Lulu, although he waited in the SUV outside, ready to transport her when the time came. Connor borrowed another Pack SUV and drove us to the Ombuds' office. I stared at the moon while en route, willing the nearly invisible sliver of shadow to hold, to remain in place for a little longer.

I sent messages to everyone, arranging for our rendezvous at the office and bugging them until I had confirmations. And when I got to the office, I paced the floor and checked the time until my screen beeped again.

I lifted it, found the message we'd been waiting for.

I'VE GOT IT, Lulu said. WE'RE ON OUR WAY.

Less than an hour later, we were assembled: me, Petra, Roger, Theo. Connor and Alexei. Lulu, Ariel, and Gwen.

We were the demon-catching dream team. Or so we hoped.

"Power Rangers," Lulu began, walking in front of us like a commander preparing to lead her troops into battle. Which wasn't far off.

She'd even dressed the part in black military-style boots (found on consignment), black leggings, and a black hooded vest over a black tee. Not the usual garb for an artist, but she was playing a different role tonight.

If she had any remaining qualms about using her magic, she wasn't showing it. Honestly, it seemed like I was the only one having trouble adjusting to how well she was adjusting. Maybe that's because she'd been holding her real self back for so long.

"Power Rangers," I repeated blankly. "The dudes with the colors?"

"Yeah. But in this case, it's chicks with magic." She pointed to each of us in turn. "Necromancer, aeromancer, vampire . . . and me. I think, if we work together, we have enough power to seal the demon."

Ariel tilted her head at Lulu. "I thought you decided not to do any more magic. Especially after fireballing Elisa."

Petra must have updated Ariel, as I hadn't had time to fill her in on Lulu's new, if possibly temporary, hobby.

"I had decided that," Lulu said. "Because my specialty—my skill—is working with dark magic."

"*Old* magic," I corrected.

"Old magic," she agreed. "Long story short, I had been thinking about magic as a dichotomy: white or black, good or bad."

"Colonial nonsense," Petra said.

"Truth," Lulu said. "And I don't want to think about it that way anymore." She looked at me. "You're a vampire from a millennia-old lineage, and your magic—your body—is fueled by blood." Then Petra. "You're an aeromancer—that's elemental magic." Then Ariel. "You can speak to the dead. That's a skill as old as life itself. Maybe the problem isn't the magic. Maybe the problem is people who use magic to hurt other people."

"So how do we all play into this?" Ariel asked.

"I work the spell. Petra provides juice." She looked at Ariel. "You ask the ghosts for help in keeping the demon contained until the seal is fully in place. Human, canine, whatever."

"And me?" I asked.

"You're the muscle," Lulu said with a grin, then looked at Connor and Alexei. "You, too. She doesn't like wolves, so we'll use that.

"We do this at Cadogan House," she continued, "because we need her to get the House back before we seal her fully. It's easiest to start that process at the House.

"This is going to be a multistage process," Lulu added, pointing to the drawings she'd prepared that morning. Her enormous sketchpad was poised on an old-school easel Roger had dug out of a closet.

"The overview," she said, "is we call the demon. Then we draw the sigil," she said, pointing to an illustration of the symbol. "Then we do the spell."

"How long will the spell take?" I asked.

"Not long," she said. "The spell gives the power direction. Candle, ingredients, mix, a little bit of hand-flicking, since that's the language Rosantine uses. Then Rosantine—the demon Andaras—should appear in the sigil, and she'll be at our command."

"And we tell her to bring back the House and reveal the truth about the Bermuda Triangle," Petra said.

"First part only," Lulu said. "When the House is back, we seal her. She gets sent back to hell, and we all enjoy that dinner at Cadogan House we'd been planning to have." There was a drawing of that, too, down to her mom's blue hair and her dad's resting scowl.

"That sounds simplistic," Roger said with an apologetic wince. "Not that I underestimate your skills, but . . ."

"But you've never seen my skills," Lulu said matter-of-factly. "And I'm not battle-tested. It's okay to say that, because it's true." She gave me a look full of meaning, and I nodded my understanding. "That's why we have the big guns. And, to be clear, it's not simple, and it won't be easy."

She flipped to the next drawing. It was the sigil, with names at four compass points. Her, me, Petra, Ariel. She pointed to the symbol's outer circle. "This is the 'do not pass' line. We're talking 'Balrog, do not pass.' If we don't keep the circle secure, she'll get out. And she'll be smart enough to leave—we'll never get the House back. And, to add sprinkles on the cake, we're working on the clock," she reminded. "Full moon is at two seventeen a.m. We don't get the House back by then, and we're in trouble."

And our parents would be trapped.

"How could this go wrong?" Gwen asked.

Everyone else in the room, from human to shifter, gave a sarcastic laugh.

"I mean, I understand Murphy's Law," she said with a sly smile. "And it's Chicago. But I mean specifically. The mayor wants to be prepared."

"Managing expectations," Roger told us.

"That depends on whether we manage to hold the circle," Lulu said. "Because we do not breach the circle. The circle is inviolate." She gave each of us a teacherly stare.

"Don't fudge the circle," Ariel said. "We got it."

"If we don't hold it," Lulu continued, "general chaos of the demon variety. Death, destruction. I can't be more specific than that, because part of her magic is related to improbability."

"And what if she refuses to return the House?" Roger asked.

"If she's properly commanded, she can't refuse. We'll be in djinn territory—you make the wish, they obey."

"If we can't command her," I said, "we negotiate. The House is the number one priority, because that has the time limit."

That put a grim cast over the room, but it couldn't be helped. Getting Cadogan back was life or death. Just like stopping Rosantine.

The sky was indigo, the moon just near full. The clouds were bright white shards—thin and jagged—against the sky. It was a nightmare sky, like an ominous background for a horror movie.

And we were preparing to call a demon.

"Look," Theo said, putting in the earbuds that would keep us all connected during the fight, "I'm not excluded from this because I'm a guy, right? Or because I have a cast?"

"Of course not," I said with a grin. "You're excluded because you're human."

"I'm . . . not sure how to take that."

"You could be glad the city's survival doesn't depend on your magical performance under severe pressure and time constraints."

After a moment, he nodded. "Yeah, that works."

"You are the clock," I reminded him. "That's a crucial job. Alarms and alerts ready."

Then he reached out with his casted hand, squeezed my fingers. "We're going to get them back."

"Thank you. And why is your hand so clammy?" I held it up to see it better in the (ever-growing) moonlight. I'd feared to see spectral ooze, but they looked like normal fingers.

"Demon wrangling makes me sweaty," he said, and wiped his fingers on his jeans. "Don't tell anyone."

I snorted. "Anyone who isn't a little sweaty hasn't been paying attention."

Petra walked toward us—stumbled, really, since her gaze was on the sky. "The sky is garbage. But I saved a little from the Peony Park lightning."

"Wait," I said. "You've been storing lightning *inside* yourself?"

She lifted a shoulder. "My sparkling—or should I say sparking—personality can take it."

"Obligatory sad trombone sound," Ariel said. "Because that was truly awful."

I looked at Lulu. "Do you have what you need?"

"I do." She blew out a breath. "And I'm nervous."

"Good," I said. "You should be." Pep talk time! "We should all be nervous, because we're about to do some big magic. But we're going to do it, and we're going to handle whatever comes at us, and we're going to get Cadogan House back. Let's rock and roll." Then I held up a hand. "Strike that last thing. I want a redo."

Petra snorted. "Too late, and all the good catchphrases are taken anyway. Let's just proceed with the mission," she said, and put a fist in the air.

"And how are we going to do that?" Lulu asked.

"We're going to hold the circle," we said simultaneously.

Because we made good little soldiers.

Lulu, Petra, Ariel, and I took positions in the yard, each of us at a compass point, twenty feet between us. Theo, Connor, Alexei, their friends, Gwen, and the CPD officers she'd enlisted stood near the gate, out of the line of fire. Or so I hoped.

We checked our comm system, and Lulu opened what looked like a paint can, dipped a brush in the glimmering gold liquid inside, wiped it against the edge to adjust the amount of paint.

"What is that, exactly?" Ariel asked.

"Salt. Water. Shavings from an ash tree. Amethyst dust. Cornstarch and gold dust to make it easier to see."

"So, just the basic recipe," Connor said, which made her smile, as he'd probably intended.

Lulu looked at me, Petra, Ariel. "You're my steering committee. I start any old-magic nonsense that's not supposed to happen, and you call me out."

Petra wiggled her fingers. "Done."

"Done," Ariel said. "You mess up, and I use my friends in low places."

"Done," I said. "I have sharp things."

Lulu nodded. "Then here goes nothing," she said, and began to draw.

Even in the darkness, even on grass, even under pressure, her motions were practiced, confident, and beautiful. A giant circle of gold shimmered to life in the moonlight, and she began the marks inside it. She painted liberally, her brush loaded and flinging the liquid with each stroke until her shoes were gilded, too.

"It looks like a dance." I didn't need to turn to know Alexei had said it. Not given the awe in his voice.

"Last bit," Lulu called out, and swung the brush above the ground so paint landed in a sweeping arc.

The earth began to rumble.

Lulu tossed the brush a few feet away, wiped her hands on her apron, then moved to a pile of materials that sat on a wooden tray at her point in the circle. She chanted—slow, steady, and quiet. Then she added something to a silver bowl, closed her eyes, put her palms together. Her wrists still touching, she began pivoting her hands and fingers in a pretty dance that was very different from the sharp motions Rosantine had made while signing her sigil.

"Petra," I said. "Your turn. Ariel, get ready."

Petra stepped forward, pulling off her gloves. She held out her hands, paused to concentrate. Pale blue flames popped into her palms.

I unsheathed my sword, moved a step closer to the sigil. The ground shuddered again.

Petra turned toward Lulu, blew across her palm. The flame became a spark that crackled, reached toward Lulu's silver bowl and ignited its contents so a pale blue flame covered the surface.

We all looked back toward the sigil. It was still wet paint on damp grass.

"Shit," I heard Lulu say, but didn't dare move.

"What's the problem?" I called out, and could all but hear the minutes ticking down.

"I don't know. Maybe the charm? Maybe it's the metal in the paint? I don't know. Shit."

"We're right there," I said. "And you got this. Plenty of time."

I crossed the fingers of my free hand.

"One more time," Lulu said. She and Petra reset, went through the steps again. Words—Lulu's voice shakier this time. Flame and spark—Petra's hands a little less steady.

And then . . . nothing.

Lulu sniffed, and I knew she was holding back tears of fear and frustration.

And then everything happened at once.

Another rumble, this one hard enough to trigger a car alarm down the block. The movement tipped over the table, sending paint and candle and bowl into the grass. The flame rushed toward the sigil, and the sigil began to burn, the lines of paint sizzling like fire along a fuse. The yellow-gray smoke that rose from it stank of sulfur. The wind picked up, sending streamers of smoke into the air, rustling fall-crisped leaves.

"Incoming," Petra said, but held her position. We all did, because we were the last defense against the demon in case the sigil didn't hold.

A crack of sound, and the air seemed to rupture. A face emerged from that breach above the sigil, screaming in anguished fury. Then the rest of it appeared, shoved bodily through the gap we'd created.

It was shaped like Rosantine but had no clothes or hair. Its skin undulated with alternating ash and flame, and its teeth were yellow and sharp. Its eyes were gleaming yellow, the pupils long and rectangular, more goat than human. They had me wishing for holy water and a crucifix—which wouldn't hurt me, contrary to folklore.

"You are commanded," Lulu said.

It raised its arms, screamed into the night with enough force to ripple the air above the sigil. But it didn't take a step out of it.

"You are commanded!" Lulu said again, this time a scream of anger that had her body bowing with the effort.

The demon closed its mouth.

The demon turned in a circle as if taking us all in, as if committing our faces to memory for later revenge.

"Release me," it said. The voice was hoarse, but undeniably Rosantine's.

"No," Lulu said. "You are commanded."

"Release me," she said, another burst of magic filled the air, hot and sour.

She chanted low in some hard and guttural tongue. The air around the sigil wavered, and a face, then two, then dozens emerged from the boundary around her. Bodies followed, their skin as fiery as hers.

"Legions," I heard Lulu say. "Solomon didn't mention this. What is happening?"

"Demonettes," Petra said, tossing a spark at one even as she held her link to the circle. "Strongly dislike."

Rosantine hadn't been loosed—she was still stuck within the sigil. But she was far from under our command. Had we done the spell wrong? Missed some crucial part of the sigil? The one we'd drawn had burned as it was supposed to, but the effect wasn't nearly strong enough, even with Petra's spark.

"Hold the circle!" I said as a dozen more of the fire creatures followed her out. "And loose the army!"

The howls came in a wave that crashed over us all—ghostly and living alike—as Ariel's army joined the party. I heard the living ones move behind me, two dozen shifters in wolf form, and saw real, actual terror in Rosantine's eyes.

And I reveled in it. I couldn't step out of the circle, but I'd damn well protect it from the . . . well, "demonettes" worked.

Have at it, I murmured to monster, and it stretched into my body instantly, gripping the sword around my fingers.

A demonette emerged near our feet, and we slashed through it, slicing it in half. It seemed to be boneless and dissolved into ash that was reabsorbed into the circle. And fueled another demonette that emerged a foot away.

We swung the sword, took that one out, then pivoted toward one that was stretching for us from behind. We struck its arm, then back again through its torso. Ash. Reabsorption.

Would there be an end to this?

Fire slashed at the back of my thigh, and I swung the sword behind me, nearly hitting the gray wolf that was chomping at the demonette's leg. It made a sound like the hissing of steam and dissolved. Connor coughed smoke.

"Sorry about that," I said. "You okay?"

He gave me an "as if" look and trotted to the next monster.

There were more of them now, and we spun in an arc, my blade going red-hot from contact with the creatures' fire. Slashing, plunging, striking seemed to make no difference. They dissolved easily but kept re-forming.

"Fifteen minutes," Theo called out. "We're down to fifteen minutes."

I had to push down panic, ignore the fear. They kept coming, a seemingly endless supply of monsters for us to kill. What had I missed?

I sliced through another, then another, my arms slick with sweat, and thought back to what Claudia had said. *You must feel your way.*

Crap. *Feel* your way? Had she meant that literally?

"Crap," I said, this time aloud. "I think I have to breach the circle."

TWENTY-TWO

"Elisa," came Lulu's stern voice. "What was the number one rule?"

"Don't breach the circle . . . unless you have a solid reason? I think we have to draw the sigil on the demon. I think that's the next step. Claudia said we had to 'feel' our way to command her successfully."

There was silence for a moment.

"Oh," she said, the sound heavy and grim. "I see."

"Am I right?"

Across the circle, she pushed hair behind her ears with a paint-smeared finger, her other hand still extended toward the sigil. "Maybe? But I don't know how to do it safely. Going into the circle would be . . . bad."

"What specific kind of bad?" I asked, slicing the arm from a demonette with particularly spindly fingers.

"It will hurt."

"On a scale of one to sunlight?"

"Sunlight in Key West."

"Shit."

"I could maybe work up a protection, but it would take time."

"Which we don't have." Heat flared on my back as a demonette tried to flank me, I turned, caught it through the middle, brushed away the flakes of ash, and looked around.

Lulu. Connor and his wolves. Ariel and her ghosts. Petra. Me. Black. Two dozen Sups weren't enough to command this woman, even locked into a sigil . . . and they were running out of time.

Desperate Sups called for desperate measures. It had to be done, and I was the best one to do it.

"I'll heal," I said. "When I give you the signal, keep her occupied. She's really vain. Use that. And then you have to keep her still long enough for me to draw it."

I heard her hesitation, knew she'd have preferred to do that part.

"You can't both do this and hold the sigil. I'm the best option." Even if it scared me to death.

"Nine minutes!" Theo called out.

I managed to tell Connor what I needed, saw the instinctive rejection of the idea in his eyes. But he rubbed his muzzle against my leg, gave a series of yips to communicate with the others. He and Alexei stayed near me to protect me from demonettes while I did what I had to do.

I prepared myself for what I knew was really going to suck.

"I meant to ask you about your dye job," Lulu called out, and had Rosantine whipping toward her. "Does the fake-ass color not bother you? I mean, I think it's super brave."

She had Rosantine's furious attention now and kept talking as I circled around, putting myself just behind Rosantine and out of her peripheral vision. I had to be fast. I just wasn't sure if I could be fast enough.

The other real wolves and all the ghostly army moved to her other side. She instinctively moved away from the howling . . . and closer to me.

I looked down at the sigil one last time, ensuring I'd committed the design to memory. And when Rosantine was close enough, distracted enough, I plunged my hand into the circle.

* * *

So far this week, I'd been thrown to the ground, fireballed, mauled by a panther, and clawed by a ghost. And that was just the highlight reel. But no pain I'd experienced before—and hopefully ever would again—was as bad as willfully breaching a demon circle.

The heat was unfathomable. The pain so instant and cruel that my legs nearly failed me, and I had to use half of my strength and will just to stay upright. It felt like every nerve was being simultaneously stabbed and pressed onto a hot stovetop. But this was only the first step.

I ignored the tears that welled and fell, tried to push the pain into a corner of my attention.

I punched farther through the magic, sweat joining the tears on my face, until I touched Rosantine and drew a quick circle on her shoulder with a fingertip. I hoped I wasn't supposed to see anything happen, because her skin stayed clear.

She jerked, snapped her head back to look at me. Gone now was any semblance of the pretty looks and soft voice. She tried to pull away, but Lulu held her firm.

Demonettes clawed around me, trying to get close enough to pull me off or break our connection. But Connor and Alexei swiped and generally pummeled so I could do my work.

Each line in the sigil took effort; I had to consciously force my assaulted nerves to respond, my fingers to move. My knees were wobbling now, my vision blurry. My mouth felt like sandpaper from the sheer heat of the circle, and my eyes burned from smoke and magic.

Rosantine screamed her fury, vibrated from the effort of trying to beat back Lulu's hold.

"Seven!" Theo called out over the roaring wind and the unending crackle of the sigil's flame.

"Last one," was all I managed to say, and in barely a hoarse whisper, as I drew the final mark.

There was a contraction, an expansion, and the pop of obligation settling into place. The fire dropped to a low blue shimmer on the ground, and Rosantine sank to her knees, looked back at me with banked fury.

"You," I managed before falling to my knees, "are commanded."

There was silence for a moment. I ventured a look at my hand, expecting to find horrifically charred skin—and was shocked to find it looked completely normal. That power, that heat, had been magic. Not fire.

"Lis?" Connor asked.

"I'm okay," I said, and could feel the weight of Rosantine's obligation under my skin. I might be able to command her, but I'd have to carry those chains until the order was carried out.

"Five minutes," Theo said. His voice was quieter now that the fire was no longer roaring.

Slowly, I climbed to my feet, adjusting to the weight, and looked at Rosantine.

"Return Cadogan House and its inhabitants. Immediately."

Rosantine grinned, and there was evil in it—actual malice—that had my blood running cold. "The moon turns. Even if I must do as you ask, I am strong enough to delay. I am strong enough to wait until it is too late. Until there is nothing but stone and glass."

Fury roared inside me, and I nearly lunged at her, until Lulu's voice, powerful and booming, called out.

"Andaras!" Lulu said, the word a demand. "You have been commanded. You will return Cadogan House and its inhabitants, alive and well, immediately."

"No."

Lulu clucked her tongue. "I don't think you understand. You have no choice—if you wish to live. You do as you are commanded, and you will live. But if the House and its inhabitants are not returned in time"—her voice was low, terrifying—"you will die by our hands. Those are your only choices."

She bared her teeth, but there was more desperation than anger in her eyes now. "You will seal me. To be sealed is death."

"Not literal death," Lulu said. "And that's your other option. Make your choice, or we will make it for you."

I pushed glamour into the chains that bound me and Rosantine, watched her fight back against us. Then gave her another push. She growled in frustration, but I saw the magic move over her eyes, urging her on.

"I will return your House."

"Great," I said, my heart beating with terrible, delicate hope. "We have a deal in principle. Here are the entire terms." I turned to the vampire who stood with Theo and the others; they'd agreed to meet us at the House to see this through. They handed me a screen. I looked it over, held it out to Rose.

"This is the contract which will bind you. You can read its terms, but basically, the House comes back in the same condition in which it left, as do the occupants, the furnishings, et cetera. It's all detailed in the fine print. In exchange, you will be sealed in the hell from which you came."

"I will sign no contract."

"Then you will die," I said, the ticking of seconds loud as the beat of my heart.

"Four," Theo said.

"I'll get out again," she said. "And when I do, I'm coming for you first."

I looked at Rosantine and the sigil that glowed against her demon skin. "Doubtful," I said, but gestured to the army of humans, ghosts, and Sups around us. "We'll all be here waiting for you, and we know your moves."

Her lips moved in a silent curse, but she nodded. "I agree to your terms."

The screen lit up in acknowledgment of the agreement, and the sigil that marked her turned from blood red to pale blue.

I took the screen again, handed it back to the attorney. "Appreciate your service," I told them. They gave me a wink, moved back into the crowd.

"Your time is ticking down," I told Rosantine. "Three minutes or you're toast."

She looked defeated, and I'd have called it pitiful if I didn't know how dangerous she was. But she reached out, put her hand on the sigil, and the fire rose again. She made the symbol with her other hand, as if uniting the two magics, and chanted words that had magic lifting in the air.

With a roar of sound and magic, flames erupted where the House had stood. But this time, they worked in reverse. As the flames descended to the ground again, the House appeared. The widow's walk, the dark turrets, the stone and windows, the portico, down to the foundation.

I stayed on my knees, knew tears tracked down my soot-stained face.

And I wasn't the only one relieved.

Monster's relief was palpable . . . and clarifying.

It wasn't lusting for violence or trying to convince me to use my mother's sword. It wasn't hypnotized by the lure of whatever power already was bound there.

It wanted to go *home*. It wanted to be reunited, rejoined, reconnected to the part of it still bound there.

Tears flowed now as a shard of guilt struck at my heart. I had misunderstood it for so, so long. And I had fought it that entire time.

I'm sorry, I told it. *I didn't understand. But I do now.*

*   *   *

The House was dark, and looked cold and lifeless. Anger began to build, mixed with a heady dose of fear at the possibility the vampires and people inside hadn't survived the exchange, or the portal magic had done more damage than we'd understood. That the contract, the deal, had all been in vain, and she'd killed everyone the night the House had disappeared.

She wouldn't survive the night, I thought, and felt the cold certainty that I'd take her life if she'd taken the lives of family.

"Oh!"

I heard someone in the crowd call out, and shifted my gaze from Rosantine back to the House.

And the light that had appeared in the front room. There was a flicker in an upper window, and then in the light above the portico, sending a cone of light across the front steps.

A horrendous squeak of wood against wood emerged from the front door, as if the House had settled poorly and just slightly askew, throwing the frame out of square. But none of that mattered, because vampires began to file out.

My mother came out first, sword in hand and watchful, in case the magic that had sent them away threatened them again. My father emerged behind her, gaze wary and searching for me.

My tears started falling immediately.

"Elisa, stay in the circle!" Lulu called out, but the words turned to a sob as her mother, her bright blue hair in a braid around her head, and her father followed behind. Then Uncle Malik, then Connor's parents behind him, and I felt the pulse of Connor's wildly joyful magic.

They walked cautiously down the steps to the sidewalk, gaze darting between the demon inside the sigil and the army who'd come to send her home.

"We have to hold the circle," I said. "The demon who entrapped you is inside it."

Every vampire on the lawn turned raging silver eyes on Rose.

"Meet the demon Andaras," I said.

"Lulu?" her mother asked cautiously.

"Hi, Mom. Just, you know, commanding a demon."

Aunt Mallory's gaze went vague as she looked over the demon, the sigil, as if seeing the magic behind and beneath. She started forward, hands rising as if to insert her own magic, but my mother put a hand around her wrist, stopped her.

Inside the circle, Rose seemed to curl within herself, as if that would save her from the rage of a terrified mother.

"Let them finish," my mom said. "They've come this far, and they deserve to finish it."

"We had a bargain," Rosantine called out. There was actual fear in her voice now; if she was ready and willing to be sent back to her realm, she must have thought that whatever Mallory had in store would be much, much worse.

But whatever the reason, she was right. It was time to close this chapter.

"Is everyone inside the House okay?" I asked.

"We're fine," Dad said.

I glanced at Lulu, nodded.

"You are commanded," Lulu said. "And you are sealed."

On cue, Petra lit the sigil directly with her blue flame. It spread quickly across the marks, the fire rising nearly a foot off the ground. Unlike demon fire, it smelled astringent and clean. Like a good facial mask.

"Andaras," Lulu said, "you have agreed to be committed back to your dimension and to be sealed therein until the death of the universe. Go to hell," she said, and slammed a hand on the shimmering sigil she'd painted, extinguishing it.

"Damn," I heard Petra murmur. "*That* was a good tagline."

Rosantine screamed as flames rose, engulfed her. She didn't burn, but as with the House, they swept her clean away.

There was a moment of silence as the flames guttered, leaving a crisp ring of singed grass.

And then the running started.

The four of us stepped away from the circle. My parents wrapped themselves around me. And with that, the fear, the worry, the guilt of the last week was ripped away. Even monster seemed to enjoy the embrace, its own relief—that its other component had returned—palpable.

We'll figure it out, I told it.

I looked over, found Connor with his parents. His mother looked up at him from her petite height, her hands on his face. Gabriel stood beside them, a hand on his son's shoulder. They'd have much to talk about, I thought. But now they had plenty of time to do it.

The reunion became a party. Word spread, and the displaced vampires returned, along with a few dozen from Washington House who'd come to celebrate their Master's return. A few of the Cadogan vampires had started a band, and they played outside in the cool fall air while sipping Blood4You offered by the local distributor at a heavy discount. He was relieved one of his biggest customers had returned to this plane of existence.

The Keenes didn't stay long; they had other business to handle, and their own reunion to take part in. Connor and I shared a quiet kiss before he left with them, holding his mother's hand as they moved down the sidewalk.

The Bells and Sullivans gathered on the House's back patio with Uncle Malik, Micah, the Ombuds, and a few of Washington House's vampires.

We explained the events of the last few days, from Cornerstones to Power Rangers.

"What did you experience?" I asked.

"Outside the House was darkness," Dad said. "There were no

scents, no sounds. Just emptiness. We were still alive and well in the House, and everything in the House worked as it would have if we'd still been in Hyde Park. But outside was ... nothing."

"We think it was a bubble universe," Mallory said, pushing a lock of blue hair behind her ears as she sat beside Lulu, an arm wrapped around her daughter. Catcher sat beside them, a few more grays peeking through his cropped dark hair, but his eyes hard and focused as they always were. "At least, that was Paige's guess."

Paige and the Librarian were sipping champagne in another part of the yard.

"We tried to come back from our end," Mallory said. "But couldn't break through the bubble. Then we tried to break through just long enough to send a message." She looked at us hopefully. "Did anything get through?"

Lulu shook her head. "But the magic in the air could have garbled the transmission."

"Did you find anything in the documents in the library?" I wondered. That had been bugging me for days.

"It was the journal of a sorceress who'd lived in Chicago—one of those who'd been exiled. It's the story of her time in Chicago," Mallory said. "We didn't find anything relating to the demon, unfortunately."

"Andaras should be stuck where she is for a good, long while," Lulu said. "It's possible—probably likely—that she'll try to escape again. But not anytime soon. And this time, we'll be ready."

"Can the wards be rebuilt?" my mother asked.

"Theoretically," Petra said. "As long as the Cornerstones are good, the defenses will be, too. We need to re-up the spells on the wards that were tripped. And it wouldn't be a bad idea to reconfigure the defenses on the other Cornerstones so they aren't worse than the demons themselves."

Lulu looked at her parents. "I can help with that."

"I like that," Mallory said, and kissed Lulu's forehead. "I like it a lot."

"I still can't get over that you're doing magic now," my mom said.

"I'm not sure yet how much I'm going to do or not," Lulu said. "I'm going to take it one step at a time." She looked at her mother. "But I didn't want to hide anymore. I didn't want to worry anymore. So I'm going to try to be out there, be who I am, and if we face enemies because of it—"

"We face them," her dad said. "Together."

"Together," my dad echoed as the band played, and the House stood strong and stoic in the darkness.

TWENTY-THREE

The Pack, including Connor, were called to NAC headquarters at dusk the next night.

Connor had gone with his parents to HQ after the rescue, and he hadn't come home since I'd awoken at dawn. He'd sent me a message asking me to join them, but that had been it. No indication of what his father intended to do . . . or what Connor intended to do about that.

I wanted to be prepared. And this seemed like the time to dress in full vampire apparel: black leather leggings, knee-high black leather boots, black crop top with corset-like ties, and the reddest lipstick I could find. I tucked a dagger in my boot, just in case. Katana belted at my side, just in case. I probably wouldn't need them, probably wouldn't use them. But like Miranda, I didn't think the interlopers were trustworthy.

I took an Auto to Pack HQ and found the place buzzing with anticipatory magic. I wasn't the only one who wasn't sure what to expect.

There were shifters everywhere—albeit not blocking traffic this time. On the sidewalk, in the open garage, in the Pack's business area. I went directly to the inner rooms, avoiding the bar, and knocked on the door.

Connor's uncle Eli opened it, looking down at me from height.

He took in the leather, nodded approvingly, then moved aside to let me in.

Connor's dad sat at the worn table, an infant on his lap. A niece, I thought, and probably the daughter of Fallon, the only Keene sister, and Jeff Christopher, a former Ombud and Fallon's husband. She'd given up her spot in the line of succession for Jeff, who was a Pack shifter but a different animal. And given the way they beamed at each other and their daughter, they both looked excessively happy about their situation.

Connor stood in front of the table in jeans and a Pack T-shirt. His expression was steady, and his gaze was on me.

I gave him the slightest nod, wished I understood what was about to happen.

"Since we're all here," Gabriel said, lifting his gaze to me with a smile, "I think we'd better get started." He rose, handed the baby back to Fallon, gave the tiny girl a final kiss on the forehead. "They're assembled?" he asked no one in particular.

From the volume of magic, I assumed "they" was the Pack, possibly including the interlopers. If they hadn't already been kicked out of the city.

"They're in the bar," Eli confirmed.

Gabriel looked at Connor. "You need a minute?"

Connor nodded. At Gabriel's gesture, all the shifters filed out. Some going through the door that led to the bar, others through one that led farther into the family's area. Fallon handed Jeff the baby, and she went into the bar. Jeff gave me a wink across the room and took the baby into the back.

And then we were alone.

Connor strode toward me, every movement confident, relaxed.

"Hey," he said, looking down, that curl of dark hair over his forehead.

"Hey," I said, and brushed it back. "Everything okay?"

"It is." He looked toward the door. "Or will be."

"And are you going to tell me what's about to happen?"

His grin widened. "I'm not yet sure what's going to happen."

But I saw the spark in his eye—and the hunger.

I put a hand on his face, rubbed a thumb across his lips, then leaned up and kissed him, nipping at his lip. "Go kick his ass."

He brushed his fingers against mine. "We fight for each other," he whispered, and walked into the bar.

Connor joined his family at the front. I took a spot with Alexei and Dan on the side.

"Any predictions?" I asked.

"Not a lick," Alexei said, and squeezed my hand. "But it should be entertaining."

The interlopers were at the back of the room, standing shoulder to shoulder. Joe had no expression. Breonna's bravado was fading, and she looked slightly sick. Cade looked defiant.

Gabriel stepped forward. "I've returned from the dead," he said, voice booming across the bar, which erupted in cheers. "And since I've heard some bullshit was spreading while I was gone, my disappearance had nothing to do with vampires, and everything to do with a demon. That demon was captured by the work of many, including vampires and my son, and Cadogan House returned to Chicago. Anyone who tells you otherwise is a filthy liar."

That had the crowd looking around for the interlopers, whose expressions didn't change.

"I learned a few things in those days I was gone. I learned not to fuck with demons."

The crowd chuckled nervously.

"I was reminded vampires don't give up." He gave a smile to me. "And I was reminded that there are those who want to lift the Pack up and those who want to bring it down. Cade Drummond," he said, the name a command that echoed magically through the room, "attempted to issue a challenge while I was gone. He had some grievances—shit he didn't take to his local leaders, shit he didn't offer to help correct—and instead decided the best way to address them was to get the Pack arrested for public intox."

He settled his gaze on Cade. "I'm sure I heard that wrong, Drummond."

A line of shifters opened in the crowd between the Apex and the interloper, but Cade made no response.

"I guess not," Gabriel said. "And when Cadogan House disappeared—and with it allies to our Pack—instead of joining those who were fighting to get us back, he tried to dethrone me."

The rumblings of the Pack grew louder now, harsher.

"I think it takes a particular kind of coward to issue a challenge like that. What do you think, Cade? Are you a particular kind of coward?"

Cade's lip curled. But he didn't move. I wasn't sure if that was stubbornness or the power of his Apex's magic.

"Connor didn't accept that challenge—how could he? He wasn't Apex. I sure as hell hadn't given up the throne, and I don't think the Pack convened to make changes. So what could he do?"

Gabriel's gaze grew hotter and angrier, searing Cade from across the room. "You tried to hurt the Pack in order to boost yourself up. Fucking reprehensible is what that is. But here's the thing, Cade Drummond." He hit each consonant like a drum. "Being in that House, in that nothingness, for several days reminded me of something. I like sitting back with a beer and my family, with my brothers and sister and nieces and nephews, with my son and his girl. And it's time I spend a little more time doing that."

"Oh, shit," Dan said, magic building in the room at the Apex's pronouncement.

"I'm not saying I'm retiring today. But it's time to begin the end." He looked at Connor. "And pass the throne."

The magic was buzzing now—with surprise, concern, excitement.

"Because of that, I'm inclined to give Connor the choice you didn't. Con," his dad said, "what do you think we should do with this miserable excuse for Pack?"

Connor stepped to his father, and they embraced each other. And something Connor whispered had Gabriel's smile widening.

"Yeah," he said. "I'd do the same."

And then he stepped aside, and Connor stepped into his father's spotlight. He looked at his mother, then at me, and then that gaze—ever so slowly—moved to Cade Drummond. And there was danger in it.

"Cade Drummond," Connor said, his voice and magic booming across the room. "I formally accept your challenge."

Chairs and tables were moved to the edges of the room, and Connor and Cade stepped into the empty space.

"I have one condition," Connor said.

Cade snorted. "I guess your vampire girlfriend has made you paranoid about rules."

"If you're asking if I've learned anything from her, yes. But mostly I just think you're a lazy cheat." That had appreciative snickers running through the crowd.

Cade's eyes flashed. "What's your condition?"

"You lose, and all three of you go back to Memphis, and spend some time volunteering with our family services organization down there."

Cade's jaw went hard. I knew he wanted to tell Connor to go fuck himself, but that wouldn't be a very Apex thing to say to that particular condition.

"I have a condition, too." Cade said. "We fight as humans."

That had Connor's brows lifting. "You surprise me, Cade. I figured you for a tuck-tail-and-run kind of fighter." He glanced at his father, who nodded his agreement.

"Agreed," Connor said.

"Then let's get this done," Cade said, and the two of them stripped down to gym shorts.

It was easy to see why Cade wanted to fight in human form; he was big and bulky and had obviously spent a lot of time in the weight room. He was probably heavier than Connor pound for pound, but gym fit and fighting fit were two very different things.

Music started, hard and loud.

"Now we'll see if Connor has Apex in him," Dan whispered.

I turned to look at him. "What does that mean?"

"Just watch," he said.

Cade didn't waste time but came forward, spinning into a roundhouse kick that caught Connor on the shoulder—and sent the crowd into a frenzy. He was more agile than I'd thought.

But he turned his back on Connor, and Connor took the opportunity with a kick to the lower back that sent Cade forward. Cade righted himself, turned around, then came in swinging. He wanted to win fast, probably thought his best chance against Connor was one shot after another until he got Connor down.

Connor blocked a high punch, a low kick. Then he pivoted into a crescent kick that put Cade on the floor—but he was on his feet again in seconds. Connor tried a right hook, but Cade spun away.

They reset, met again in the middle, fast strikes and blocks at supernatural speed. Connor managed another right hook that caught Cade's chin, but Cade landed a punch on Connor's shoulder that had pain flashing across his face.

I focused all my attention on Connor, as if I could pour my own strength into him. Even monster seemed to lean forward, to urge him on.

Cade tried a spinning kick. Connor hit the ground, rolled to avoid the shot. And when Cade tried to kick Connor on the ground, Connor grabbed his foot, twisted, sending him off balance and to the floor. He hit with a hard *thud*, then rolled and came up again.

Connor dodged a blow, then another.

"Quit fucking around," Cade gritted out, and this time aimed lower, hitting Connor in the hip. But Connor spun away in time, so the blow was glancing. He came back with a round kick that had Cade's head spinning back, then dropped down to avoid a clumsy jab.

"Just toying with him," Alexei murmured. "Tiring him out."

"What?"

"Oh, yeah," Dan said, with cool amusement. "They're both alpha, but Cade's got nothing special. Not on Connor." He put two fingers in his mouth, whistled. "Fuck him up, Connor!" he shouted, then glanced at me apologetically.

"Sorry."

"No worries," I said, but watched more closely now, trying to see what they did. There was a blooming bruise on Connor's right cheekbone, and one of Cade's eyes was cut and bleeding, adding that particular peppery magic to the air. But with each shot, Cade's fist seemed to grow heavier.

And then Cade swept Connor's legs and sent Connor to the floor.

"Wanna ask your girlfriend to help you up?" Cade asked, body slicked with perspiration.

"Don't need help," Connor said, flipping himself to his feet again. He was sweaty, too. He flung damp curls from his eyes, grinned back at Cade. "Want me to ask *your* girlfriend?"

Cade cursed and barreled toward Connor, picking him up at the waist and sending them both careering into the opposite wall. Shifters scattered to avoid the shot and the plaster that flew from the divot they'd made. Then they hit the floor, grappling and trying to gain purchase on sweat-soaked bodies.

"Get up!" someone called out, and they were hauled to their feet again and pushed back to the center of the room. Both were breathing heavy now. And Cade, who'd managed to hold out this long, was getting cocky.

"You know what's going to happen to vampires when I'm head of the Pack? Stakes," Cade said. "It's the best they deserve."

I think he was trying to upset Connor, to put him off his focus. Unfortunately for Cade, it had the opposite effect.

In a strike so fast the motion was blurred, Connor punched him in the face, then again, and again. Cade wobbled, hit the ground on his butt.

Connor leaned down. "Say that again, asshole."

Cade licked blood from his upper lip. "Stakes," he said, drawing out the word slowly. And climbed to his feet.

And then I felt something click into place. Magic, seating itself home. And it was coming from Connor.

He closed his eyes as magic—new magic—spread through the room. It was strong and bright and clean. I'd have said it felt like sunlight, if sunlight was something I could easily feel.

Connor had come into his power. And Connor had the power of an Apex.

"I fucking knew it," Dan said with no little pride.

The rest of the crowd had gone silent.

Desperation glowed on Cade's face. He knew he had no options now, so he stood up and roared his anger. He ran forward, apparently intending to tackle Connor to the floor. But Connor rotated, kicked Cade in the stomach, which had him hitting the floor hard enough to bounce. He groaned, and Connor fell on top of him, put a knee in his lower back, then grabbed Cade's right leg, and twisted to put pressure on his knee.

Cade wheezed in pain, hands grasping at the floor.

"We done?" Connor asked.

It was five long seconds before he gritted his teeth, pounded a fist on the floor.

There was utter silence.

Slowly, Connor climbed to his feet, pushed his hair from his eyes. "You lost, asshole. Get the fuck out of our bar."

I saw the flash of silver behind Connor. Fucking Breonna. She was fast, and she came at him with the speed of desperation.

I pushed forward and put my body between theirs, then executed a low kick that had her sprawling to the floor. The knife popped out of her fingers, reflecting light and magic. I caught it neatly with one hand.

"Never pull a blade on a shifter," I said, and felt Connor's body close behind mine. I held out the knife, and he plucked it from my fingers.

"Thanks for the assist," he whispered, his voice low and full of magic and power, and it sent a delicious shiver down my spine.

"Anytime," I said, working to maintain my own control.

"Haul all three of them out," Gabriel said, stepping forward on the dais again. "I want them out of the city within the hour."

"On it," Dan said, and he and a couple more shifters moved to their new charges. "Let's go, assholes. You get to ride in the back of a van for a while."

Connor could have shifted to heal the injuries instantly. But he hadn't. At least not yet. Maybe because he wanted the Pack to see what he'd taken on, and what he could withstand. Or maybe he just wasn't feeling the pain yet; power was a hell of an anesthetic.

"This won't be the last challenge," Gabriel said when we'd assembled in the family room again. "But you held your own, and you will again. An Apex must be strong to hold the Pack together." Then he shifted his gaze to me. "An Apex's mate must be equally strong. For they help hold the Apex together." He grinned. "And nice kick."

"Thank you. I was trained by the best."

Gabriel snorted. "Of course you were, kiddo. Sullivans fight for what they care for. That includes you." He turned away to talk to his brothers, and I looked at Connor, found him grinning hungrily at me.

"What?" I asked.

"Let's get married."

I watched him for a second, rolled my eyes. "You're drunk on power."

"Yeah," he agreed, with the sexiest grin I'd ever seen. "And it feels so good. But that's not why I asked you."

I looked at him again, and his eyes seemed clear. "Are you serious?"

He considered that for a moment. "Yeah, I am. Marry me, Elisa."

There were gasps and silences around the room as aunts and uncles realized their nephew, the heir to the North American Central Pack, and an Apex who'd just come into his power and beaten his first challenger, had proposed.

To a vampire.

And I didn't really care what they thought. Because I knew who he was and who we were together. "Okay," I said. "Let's get married."

Connor squeezed me into a hug, and the room erupted into (mostly) cheers, and left me breathless. "I'll spend the rest of my life," he whispered, "proving that this is the best decision you've ever made."

I leaned back, grinned at those brilliantly blue eyes. "Is that a dare?"

"It's a promise," he said with utter confidence.

EPILOGUE

For as long as he could remember, he'd been a survivor. Ignored by his father. Placed by his mother with the human who would raise him as one of her own, but always knowing he was something different. Something more. So he watched, listened, read.

And he waited.

Now he wore a yellow vest bright enough to singe the eyes and jeans that were worn and dirty at the knees. It was the boots that gave him away, or would have if anyone had been watching. They were new. Expensive. Unmarred by work and better suited to an urban hike than tossing dirt from the trench he stood in.

But no one looked. The vest bore the name of a Chicago construction company, a gift from a client, and the steel and plastic barriers around the hole he'd dug looked real enough. The trench was already six feet deep, and the shovel pinged when he hit something solid.

He crouched in the hole, brilliantly lit by the noon sun, and brushed dirt from the stone at his feet, then from the carvings that marked it.

He rose, dusted his hands, then flipped the shovel upside down, lifted his arms, and muttered in a language not spoken in a thousand years. With all the strength he could muster, supernatural and otherwise, he slammed metal against stone, sending chips into the air. Another murmur of sacred words, another strike.

"Third time's the charm," he said, sweat now dotting his brow, and made his final incantation.

The shovel's blunt end became a metaphorical spear, making a jagged crack through the center of the rock. It broke apart with a deep and seemingly devastated *thrum* that sent a shockwave through the earth as magic was released, dissipated. He could feel the ward burning away, like old wicks consumed by fire.

What had been a Cornerstone was now rubble. And it was fucking exhilarating.

A definite flaw in the system, he thought, that taking out a Cornerstone could dismantle the entire thing. But they were called "Cornerstones" for a reason.

He dropped the shovel atop the now dead stone, then climbed from the hole. He pulled off the vest and tossed it in, too, then ran a hand through hair tousled by the release of magic. He shook it off, the dregs of that old spell, and felt his bones settle comfortably again, relieved of the itch of the city's defenses.

Then he looked at the western horizon. The wave would travel, and they would know this wall was gone. They would know he had opened the door for them just a bit more.

Jonathan Black smiled as the sun passed overhead and the world moved one degree closer to dusk.

"Come in," he murmured in that long-dead language to anyone who might hear. "I've prepared the way."

A thousand miles away, a hundred miles away, they began their march toward Chicago—the city where demons were welcome once again.

Chloe Neill is the *New York Times* and *USA Today* bestselling author of the Captain Kit Brightling, Heirs of Chicagoland, Chicagoland Vampires, Devil's Isle, and Dark Elite novels. She was born and raised in the South but now makes her home in the Midwest, where she lives with her gamer husband and their bosses/dogs, Baxter and Scout. Chloe is a voracious reader and obsessive Maker of Things; the crafting rotation currently involves baking and quilting. She believes she is exceedingly witty; her husband has been known to disagree.

CONNECT ONLINE

ChloeNeill.com
 AuthorChloeNeill
🐦 ChloeNeill